Incandescent

RIVER SAVAGE

Incandescent

First edition: August 2014

Edited by Becky Johnson, Hot Tree Editing
Cover design ©: Louisa Maggio at LM Creations
Image: stockphoto.com
Formatting by Max Henry at Max Effect
Information address: riversavageauthor@gmail.com

Prologue

THE RUMBLE OF A MOTORCYCLE WAKES ME FROM MY sleep, stirring the once peaceful night. Reaching out to Zane, my hand finds the coolness of the empty sheets.

"Zane?" I whisper into the darkness. Looking toward the red light of his alarm clock illuminating the otherwise pitch-black room, the clock numbers blink incessantly.

A shiver of alarm runs through me as though ice just replaced my spine. My heart beats double time, the rhythm now matching the rapid blinking of the clock. Something doesn't feel right.

Grabbing my robe from the end of the bed, I wrap it around myself and creep out of the bedroom in search of my fiancé.

"Zane," I whisper again as I walk down the long darkened hall.

The burning stench hits me first, its strength potent enough to overpower my taste buds. A wave of heat blankets me as it takes a moment to register the dangerous flames dancing before my eyes. The front of my four-bedroom home burns rapidly, engulfing everything in sight.

I stand fixed, mesmerized by the bright orange cinder, as if the seductive blaze calls to me.

The house shudders; the explosion knocks me off balance, forcing me down to the shaky ground. Dazed, I drop to my hands and begin to crawl my way to the back door, the hallway now swallowed by the blackened smoke. The open flames lick out as I force myself to the only available exit.

Reaching the door, my fingers close around the brass handle. The metal singes my skin but doesn't stop me in my escape. Panic stirs when the handle doesn't turn. Frantically, I pull harder, wrestling with the lock.

Inky darkness fogs my view as I struggle to fill my lungs. My breathing labors, my fight slowing.

I don't want to die.

1

Kadence

three years later

SITTING AT MY DESK, I HOLD IN MY FRUSTRATION. THIS
meeting is not how I wanted to end my workday. I look
across at the angry brown eyes of one very upset father. Mr.
Hill leans forward, just as irritated at the wait.

His son, Tommy, sits by his side, the black eye he earned
in class today is almost swollen shut.

Zayden Knight sits on the opposite side of the room
waiting quietly for his mother to arrive. His dark, overgrown
hair hangs over his forehead, covering one eye. Zayden is the
last person I'd expect to deliver the punch. If I hadn't had
seen him with my own eyes, I wouldn't have believed it.

I requested both parents meet me at three; it's now quarter

past the hour. The classroom clock ticks over, another minute that she's late. Mr. Hill clears his throat and I look up, about to apologize again for the delay, when the door pushes open.

My eyes do a quick sweep of the tall man as he walks forward, but the sound of his motorcycle boots squeaking on the vinyl floor draws my attention. The fact that a man just walked into my classroom unannounced doesn't register to me; instead, the leather riding boots hold me captive, sending me back to the night that I don't ever want to relive. I force my eyes up, the leather of his cut pushing me deeper into the memory, and for a split second, I think he's someone else.

Anger slowly creeps its way up my spine. My eyes frantically sweep his chest; the patch sewn on the left side of his vest comes into view reading Knights Rebels MC. Exhaling a breath I didn't know I was holding, I will my erratic heart to calm. *It's not them.*

Everyone in Rushford knows who the Knights Rebels are. Years ago, our small town feared them; known to run on the wrong side of the law, people kept their distance. The Rebels ran this town the way they saw fit. Guns, drugs and women, they went above and beyond the law. I'm not sure what happened, but a few years back, they started cleaning their act up and they now hold the respect of most of the town. Charity runs keep them active in the community; their crazy parties keep them popular with the women, but most importantly, keeping the drugs out of town earns them that respect.

I keep my distance. Associating with them is something I've never done, even if they have cleaned up their act. After what happened with Zane, my asshole ex, I avoid people like them. I know all too well what they're capable of, the reminder branded on my skin.

Pulling my thoughts from the past, I look up at the man who just barged into my classroom.

"Hello, can I help you?" I address him, standing from my chair and walking around the front of the desk. He ignores me and goes straight to where Zayden sits.

"Hey, buddy, how you doin'?" he squats down to Zayden's level.

"Hey, Dad." Zayden carefully looks up, a glum expression on his face. He lowers his head, and I wonder how much trouble he will find himself in tonight.

I had no idea Zayden's dad was a part of the MC. The name Knight clicks in my head and it all falls into place. *Shit, he's not just part of the MC. His family is the MC.*

The man eventually looks up at me, finally giving me his attention. His watchful gaze follows the length of me before he stands to full height. His dark hair is a sexy mess, as if he just ran his hand through it. The five o'clock shadow over his tense jaw shows signs of graying; not in an old man kind of way, but that of a sexy, hot, older guy. His piercing green eyes, the color of jade, make me look twice.

Smiling at me, the man takes a large step toward me, his presence overpowering at the sheer height of him. I falter, a little shaky on my heels and look up at him. I feel short on the best of days, wearing heels to keep my head above most people's chins, but standing in front of him with his at least six-foot frame towering over me, I feel like a small child again. Extending my hand toward him, he takes it in his as I greet him. "Hello, I'm Miss Turner, Zayden's teacher. I was expecting Mrs. Knight," I rush out like a fumbling schoolgirl. *Oh, my God, kill me now.*

He stares down at me, his green eyes never leaving mine nor saying anything; his large calloused hand still firmly grips mine.

"Yeah, sorry about that," he finally responds, breaking our weird moment. "Z's mom only just called me about the meeting; she's been held up." He clears his throat, like it's a lie, but continues, "I came when I got the call."

He finally releases his awkward hold on me and takes a step back. With the loss of his grip, I have to move my hand to the front of my desk to support my unease. For some reason, other than stupidity, I have no idea what he said so I just nod my head. He grins, noticing my reaction, and I smile back, lost in his.

Jesus, Kadence, get it together, you've met good-looking men before.

I take a deep breath, shaking off the stupid look I'm sure I'm wearing. I'm surprised and appalled by my attraction. I've never reacted to someone like this before.

"Well, in that case, let's get started shall we?" I ask, hoping my voice doesn't give away his effect on me. *Yeah, 'cause the stupid grin you just had on your face didn't?*

Walking back around my desk, I take a large breath, hoping it calms my beating heart before sitting. I watch as he folds himself into the small grade-school chair, and I hold back a smile at how ridiculous he looks. I address Zayden's dad first, not certain if his wife relayed what I told her over the phone.

"I'm not sure what your wife has told you, Mr. Knight."

"Ex-wife," he interrupts me, his tone telling me that I need to remember that.

"Right, okay," I continue, ignoring the pleasure I get from

hearing he isn't married.

"Well, as I was telling your ex-wife, Zayden was involved in an altercation with another student today," I tell him, looking over at Mr. Hill and his son. "Ending with Tommy's black eye."

"This true, Z?" Hot biker dad turns, looking at his son.

In my head, hot biker shouldn't be in my vocabulary, but with his long legs outstretched in front of my desk, the sexy-as-sin riding boots crossed over at the ankle, and the way I hear the leather move when he turns to look at Z, I can't help call him anything but.

"Yeah, Dad," Zayden replies, his eyes lowered.

"Your son is a menace just like your club, Knight, and I won't allow him to bully my kid in class. I want something done about it!" Mr. Hill yells, standing from his seat.

I'm not surprised by Mr. Hill's outburst; he's been sitting on the edge of his seat, ready to chew someone's head off for the last twenty minutes. Yeah, I value my time too, but that's not Mr. Knight's fault; he came when he found out. I don't know why I'm siding with him. I should be more concerned for Mr. Hill's wellbeing when Mr. Knight stands from his own seat and takes a rather large step toward him.

"Excuse me, I was talkin' to my boy. I'll address you when he explains to me why he saw fit to put his hands on your son," Mr. Knight pushes out with gritted teeth. Fuck, he even speaks sexy biker. *What the hell is sexy biker? Get it together, Kadence.*

Sensing the situation could get out of hand, I stand. "Mr. Knight, Mr. Hill, please sit down," I demand, hoping the slight tremor I feel doesn't show.

Mr. Hill sits first, obviously realizing he is in over his head with the fuming badass.

"You wanna give me a moment to talk with my boy?" Mr. Knight asks, looking over at me. I don't know why I do it, but I nod my head and sit back in my chair. I watch him spare one more look at Mr. Hill, a silent warning to keep his mouth shut.

Jesus, how can he be the one in control right now?

"Now, you wanna tell me why you put your hands on someone, Z?" He squats down in front of his son's chair, arms stretched out to keep him steady, his muscled arms bulging under the strain of their position. I can make out the large Knights Rebels tattoo and I wonder what else he has hidden under his clothes.

"Tommy was pulling Sarah's hair, told her she was a whore like her mom. I told him to quit it but he started on me. You always said if someone puts their hands on me, I'm allowed to stand up for myself," he responds quietly, calmly, given that the two hundred-pound man is squatting in front of him, scowling something fierce. I look at Tommy and see his face is ashen at Zayden's confession.

"Is this true?" Mr. Hill turns to look at Tommy, who sinks further into his chair.

"I was only saying what you told me," he answers back.

Mr. Hill looks up at me; a small amount of embarrassment fills his cheeks as I raise my eyebrows.

Sarah's mom works over at Bare Assets, our local strip club in town. I have no problem with the place. Holly, my best friend, likes to drag me along sometimes for ladies' night. It's a well-respected establishment, and as far as I know, Sarah's mom works the bar, not a pole. *What an asshole.*

Awkward silence fills the room as I look between the two fathers. Mr. Hill looks down at his hands while Mr. Knight holds my gaze. His eyes show anger, no doubt at Mr. Hill, but I'm drawn to the intensity of it, like a fond memory pulling me in. I drag my eyes away, needing to break the connection, not prepared to let those feelings back in.

"Okay, well, regardless of the reasons, we still have a policy here that fighting is not allowed. Because both boys engaged in the fighting, they will both be given afterschool detention for five days."

Considering both boys have never been in trouble for fighting, I thought I would give them a chance to sort it out here before taking it to Principal Wilson. That guy is a real schmuck, no doubt suspending them on their first offense. Yes, Z was defending himself, but Tommy is the one with a swollen eye. Sending them home for three days off won't fix the problem.

Mr. Knight scoffs and then shakes his head, clearly not happy with the punishment. He looks over to his son, giving him a wink before turning back to me. His blatant disregard for the rules don't surprise me, and I can't help but call him on it.

"I hope from that wink, Mr. Knight, you're not condoning this behavior?" I challenge, cutting him off before he can begin to argue my decision.

"Listen, Mrs. —"

"Miss Turner," I correct him the same way he did me.

"Miss Turner." His deep, gravelly voice exaggerates the Miss and I hold back the need to roll my eyes at his insinuation.

"No, I don't condone violence. I will, however, be proud of my son if he stands up for someone who can't stand up for themselves."

"He gave another student a black eye," I shoot back. "Not to mention disrupted my class."

Pulling two eleven-year-old boys apart in the middle of the classroom is harder than most would think. For one, they're almost the same size as me. My five-foot-two frame is no match for two angry boys when they nearly put me on my ass.

"So? He was defending the girl and defending himself. I would have done the same," Mr. Knight continues to disagree with me. His anger confuses me a little. What does he expect me to say? Sure, it's fine your son clocked another student and left him with a swollen eye?

"Yes, I don't doubt that. However, the school board doesn't see it that way. Using violence against each other gets us nowhere." I stop myself from saying our school rules are probably different to the rules he follows.

I stand from my chair, trying to end the conversation before I come to blows with him. Something inside of me wants to argue with him, my quick temper often getting me in trouble, but this is more. The thought of pushing him sends a tingle down my spine. I need to stop this. I force myself not to engage with him anymore; the rules are simple, there's no point arguing. He obviously lives by his own set of rules. Unfortunately for his son, he must abide by the school's.

"My son has a right to defend himself. Where were you when all this was happening?" He stands, clearly not done with this battle, now questioning me.

"I was dealing with another student." I find myself on the defensive. "These boys are eleven years old, Mr. Knight. Old enough to be trusted and know violence is no way to handle things. Using your fists does not make you a man. He should have walked away and come and told me," I tell him, feeling small again under his height and gaze.

He laughs out loud, his eyes flashing with annoyance, evidently not agreeing with me. "Lady, you got no idea what makes a man. Someone puts his hands on me, I sure as hell will respond the same way."

Knowing I'm not going to get anywhere with this infuriating man, I straighten out my hand to shake his, ready to be out of his presence. My behavior is irrational I know. I've gone from feeling a spark to wanting to slap him for arguing with me.

"My decision is final, Mr. Knight. The boys will start their detention tomorrow. I hope I don't have to take this further next time," I say, hoping I don't have to see him again. Something about him gets me riled up. Sure he's hot, but his arrogant attitude is starting to annoy me. He stands quietly for a moment, not moving, not speaking, his eyes silently assessing me. The tension in the air is electrifying around us. I begin to feel a little uncomfortable with my hand outstretched before he takes it, the heat of his grip wrapping around mine.

"Well, Mrs. —"

"Miss," I snap at him this time and wince at my tone.

"Yes, of course." He smiles, like he wanted to hear it again. I try to pull my hand back but he tightens, pulling me forward, my free hand going to my desk as his thumb strokes the inside of my palm. The intimate move is not lost on me. *Oh, God, I'm bipolar, now I want to keep my hand here.*

"Thank you for your time, Miss Turner." He leans in close, the warmth of his breath just skimming the side of my ear before he lets go and moves back. I steady myself, unbalanced by the loss. *What the hell was that?*

Reaching out, he clicks his fingers to get Zayden's

attention. "Come on, Z," he says, waiting for him to stand. He then follows him out the door without a backward glance.

Following Mr. Knight's lead, Mr. Hill stands, his expression now somber. For a moment I forgot he was still here, lost in the impulse that was that man.

"Thank you for your time, Miss Turner. I'll have a word with Tommy about what he thinks he heard." He nods, not giving me his eyes. At least he has the good sense to look embarrassed.

Grabbing Tommy's bag, he wishes me a good evening and then turns and leaves, Tommy following close behind.

Falling back into my chair, I let out a shaky breath, glad that it's over. I can't believe I let Zayden's dad get to me like that. No man has ever instilled lust and anger just by looking at me. His presence screams confidence and testosterone, right down to the way he ran his eyes over me. I know he probably acts like that toward all women, yet the thought that he felt it too excites me.

It takes me a few minutes to calm my breathing and stop all lustful thoughts of Mr. Knight before I can even begin to pack up and gather my belongings. Shutting down the lights for the day, I lock up the room and walk down the hall to the teachers' lounge. I'm stopped in my tracks when I look up ahead. Standing by the lockers, I observe Mr. Knight kneeling in front of Z. His hand outstretched, around his neck, their heads leaning into each other, talking quietly. Zayden nods and smiles before his dad leans in further and kisses the top of his hair. The sight of this man being fatherly stirs something in me, more than his touch did. He exudes this type of power over people with his presence, but watching him talk with his son makes him vulnerable. I have no right thinking of him like that. The man is off limits, not to mention a walking smartass, but standing there at a distance, I can see how much he loves his son. The affection in his eyes leaves me with a sense of longing. *I want that.*

Shaking off the thought I turn into the teachers' lounge, impatient to get home to a glass of wine, thus cutting all thoughts of one Mr. Knight, aka arrogant ass, aka sexy hot biker.

2

Nix

PULLING UP TO THE TOWN SQUARE, I CUT THE ROAR OF my engine and wait for the rest of the boys to pull up. The yearly fair in Rushford is in full swing and I'm regretting signing us up to hold a stall. Brooks' old lady, Kelly, is on the town's organizing committee and suggested we get more involved in the community. I don't know how much more involved we can be; the club's by-laws allow us to do a few charity runs a year that we already use to give back to the town. This new idea they've come up with should pull in enough dough to help pay for the new town library opening in a few weeks.

Beau, the club's VP, pulls up beside me, shutting down his

bike. The women organizing this gig stand around checking us out. It always happens at these types of events, something about the leather and bikes have the women falling over themselves to get a ride.

Beau already has eyes for a pretty blonde standing to the right and I don't doubt he'll have her in his bed tonight. He always has women crawling all over him, carrying on about how much they love his long hair. Fucked if I know what they see in it, but who the hell knows when it comes to women. As President of Knights Rebels, my title alone has most of the women fighting with each other to get me off. I tend to stay away from easy. Easy pussy is just that. Easy. I love the chase. My thoughts go straight to last week when Z's teacher had my cock twitching; now that woman ain't like the ones lining up today.

Just thinking about her has the blood rushing to my cock. That smart little mouth on her, the way she stood up to me had me itching to hike up that pencil skirt she was wearing and bend her over the desk, bury myself deep in her and make her call out my name as I smacked her pert ass. *Fuck, I've got to stop thinking about her.*

Since I left the school, I haven't been able to get her off my mind. Her long, dark hair pulled away from her face just begged me to tug on it and take her mouth. Her legs were surprisingly long for someone so short and those fuck-me shoes she wore, don't even get me started. I had no idea that Z's teacher was sexy as fuck. Even her fiery temper had me squirming in the small fucking chair I sat in. There's nothing better than a woman who can give just as good as she gets, and pushing her last week proved she's that type of woman. The fire in her eyes, the way she had held her own, my cock was practically begging me to fuck her. I know I shouldn't have pushed her. Hell, I agreed with her to some point. Z's behavior lately is concerning me, but sitting in that room, with the little fucker and his dad throwing off his attitude just pissed me off. The MC has been through a lot the last few years getting the club clean, and while the majority of the town respect what we've accomplished, there are still a few who think we're no better than the men who started the club.

Miss Turner was different. I saw a flash of something in her eyes when I caught her watching me come in but she hid it as soon as I started to push. I know thinking of her is a waste of my time; sweet pussy like hers doesn't go for a man like me, and while I like a game of cat and mouse, a woman like her? That's one game I'll never win.

Getting off my bike, I watch as the rest of the Knights Rebels pull in next to us, backing their Harleys in a perfect straight line. Our club has been running since 1969 when my dad, Red Knight, founded the Originals with Beau's dad as his VP. He would tell the tale of how he grew up with the dream of having his own place to call home. He craved the brotherhood of a club, the camaraderie with like-minded people and the principle of freedom.

For me growing up in the clubhouse, the brothers were more like fathers, everyone looking out for each other as their own. Over the years, my pops lost his way and the club's beliefs changed. Power and greed became the driving force behind them turning outlaw.

These days, the club runs in a different direction, trying to keep our noses clean. Sometimes we find ourselves cleaning up other people's messes, but the day-to-day running, we stay legit.

It was one of the first things I did when I stepped up as Prez. It was never my intention to patch in and take over from Dad. I loved the club, love the brothers, but for a long time I didn't know if that life was what I wanted. Earning a living the way they did never sat well with me. I was torn; enlisting to serve my country was something I could see myself doing, running drugs was not.

My decision was made easy when a few weeks before my eighteenth birthday, life changed. Shit went down with a rival club, my mom becoming a victim in their war.

I never thought I would say it, but I hated my father for what his club brought to our family. The pain of losing a wife was too much for the old man. He was in a bad way, worse than me, and the club suffered for it. I stayed, wanting to seek revenge on those who destroyed our life. I was reckless, too far-gone. All I saw was blood. I wanted to make those fuckers pay.

Nothing was the same after that. After going down the path of anger and seeking revenge, I soon realized it wasn't who I was. The club retaliated and we got our vengeance, but it didn't take away the hurt or the pain that I was left with. Everything that I was searching for was for nothing. Losing my mom was for nothing. Patching-in and choosing this path didn't bring her back.

When I finally accepted that I had chosen this path, I slowly started to put my life back together. Too much blood had been spilled and most of the brothers felt the same way. The idea of changing and creating something strong encouraged me to step up, to embrace something that my father originally started. I did my time and worked my way up, doing a lot of shit I wish I didn't have to, but I pushed through, earning my position so when the time came, I could step in and take the club back to where it belonged. Cleaning up the mess wasn't something that happened overnight; that shit took time. A lot of allegiances were tested, leaving us vulnerable and open to attacks. Times were tough but we pushed through, coming out better on the other side.

"Dad!" Z calls out as he makes his way over to me. I watch his mom trailing behind in barely-there shorts and a tank that shows she isn't wearing a bra. Lately she's been dressing more like the young teenager I met, rather than the thirty-seven-year-old mother she is. I have to wonder why she feels the need to dress like trash.

"Hey, bud, how you doin'?" I ask as he climbs up on my bike.

"Good, I've got my tickets ready to go on some rides," he says excitedly.

"Hey, Nix." Addison smiles her fake smile, pushing up against me. Taking a step back from her, I ignore her attention and speak to Z.

"Go help Kelly set up with Beau and Brooks and I'll give you a few dollars for some extra rides," I tell him, scruffing his hair.

"Awesome!" he shouts, getting off the bike to follow Beau to the stall.

"You talk to Z about his weeklong detention?" I look back over at my ex-wife. Addison and I do the joint custody thing. Z stays with his mom four nights then back at mine for four nights. I hate not having him with me all the time, but I know kids need to have their moms in their lives. Even if she isn't the best.

Addison pouts her lips, pissed I'm not giving her the

18

attention she wants. I don't know why she pulls this act; it sure as shit isn't going to work on me after the fucked-up bullshit she pulled on me last week. Ringing me ten minutes after the scheduled meeting with the school and telling me she was tied up getting her nails done. Luckily I was in town and made the five-minute drive. Now I'm left annoyed at my encounter with Z's teacher and the unwanted thoughts of the sexy woman.

Addison shrugs, letting me know she didn't talk to him. I have to refrain from shaking some sense into her. She never used to be this way, only showing her true colors when I finally decided to end things. I was never in love with the woman. I thought I could make it work for the sake of Z, but in the end, it wasn't worth it. If she doesn't start acting like a good mother, and get her life sorted, we're going to have problems. One being Z will be living with me full time. I have no problem taking her to court.

Walking away from her before I lose it in front of the whole town, I get a look at the sweetest ass to grace my sight. The blue jeans are pulled tight, and hug every inch of the fine ass. Her small waist, the curve of her hips and her dark hair that hangs half way down her back makes her even more appealing. Now that's a woman I wouldn't mind banging. Adjusting myself in my jeans, I move forward, eager to get acquainted with the dark-haired beauty. I'm stopped dead in my tracks when I see the sexy body belongs to none other than Miss Turner. *Well, fuck me.*

If I didn't want to fuck her damn sexy ass in that tight skirt and fuck-me heels she was wearing last time I saw her, I'd be falling over backwards to pull off the jeans that look painted on today. She looks up, her eyes catching mine and her stance wavers for just one second, like she did when I shook her hand. Holy fuck, Miss Prim and Proper just might like herself some biker.

Walking toward her, I notice her take a deep breath, whether to calm her nerves or to gain patience I don't know, but I'm willing to rattle her cage a little more.

"Why, hello there, Miss Turner." I drag out the Miss just to piss her off, and also letting her know I'm particularly interested that there is no Mr. Turner.

She squares her shoulders and greets me back. "Hello, Mr. Knight." She sounds disinterested, but I know better. After the way our meeting ended and the tension now rolling off her, I doubt her disinterest.

"Nix," I say, wanting to hear my name come from her lips.

"Sorry?" she asks, looking more flustered every second I stand in front of her.

"My name is Nix." I repeat it even though I know she heard me the first time. Damn women and their games; she doesn't realize it makes me want her more. She smiles but doesn't offer me her name.

"Are you signing up for a ride?" I ask, moving the conversation forward. If I play it smart, I can have her willing and pissed in less than two minutes.

"No." She nervously laughs, "Not me. I wouldn't be caught dead on the back of one of those." She moves her head to indicate the row of bikes neatly lined up. The sight of her on the back of my bike flashes wickedly in my mind. What I would do to see that.

"Shame, I'd have grown hard seeing you in those fuck-me heels, straddling the back of my bike." I give her a grin and quickly turn my back to her, walking back to our stall before she can respond. I'd love to see the stunned look on her face as I walked off, but I'm hoping to see her again later to rattle her some more. If I have it my way, she'll be on the back of my bike in no time.

3

Kadence

"NEED SOME HELP, MISS TURNER?" NIX'S VOICE CALLS behind me as I try to pack the remaining boxes into my car. *Shit.*

After sauntering off with his dig about my heels and his bike, I've tried to avoid him at all costs. Being on the school committee board, I couldn't leave considering all proceeds of the fair would be going to the new library we petitioned for, but I did my best to not be alone with him.

"No, thank you. I'm good," I rush out, hoping he moves on. He gets me all flustered; I can't stand to even look at him.

"Here let me." He moves forward taking the box from my hands.

"I'm beginning to think that you don't listen to anyone," I remark, trying to keep my eyes off his ass as he bends at the waist to push the boxes into the trunk. After watching him all day, I've come to the realization that I want him. The way he is with Z just seals my opinion of him. The persona of a cocky, arrogant biker might be what he puts off, but under that he seems so different.

"You have no idea." He turns back around, catching me checking him out.

"Sorry?" I ask, trying to hide my embarrassment at being caught. Damn it.

"I said, you have no idea," he smirks, knowing he's got me fumbling.

"Well, maybe you should work on that. Women don't like it when men don't listen," I recover and smile at him.

"Is that what you need? A man who listens, Miss Turner?" He takes a step toward me but I hold my ground.

"I don't need anything, Mr. Knight, especially a man." I close the trunk, lock the car and start walking to the local diner to meet Missy and Sam for dinner.

"Where you runnin' off to?" He grabs my hand as I walk away.

"Dinner, I'm late," I explain as I pull out of his grasp.

"Well, have fun." He smirks as I nod and walk to where Sam is waiting for me at the front of Happy Chef. I don't look back. More than anything I need to get away from him before I do something stupid.

"Hey, who is that?" Sam asks as we walk in to find Missy.

"A student's parent." I brush it off as nothing. I don't need the girls knowing I'm lusting after him. I need to stop thinking about him and the words he said to me before I get myself into trouble.

My reprieve of Nix is short-lived when he walks in thirty minutes later, with two guys wearing the same cut as him. *How convenient.* He waves over as they sit opposite from us across the diner.

"Wow, you know the Knights Rebels?" Missy's grin spreads across her face and I can see the wheels ticking in her head from across the table. Great.

"No, one of them is a student's parent," I explain, annoyed that he followed me in. I need to stay away from him. It's like he's constantly been in my thoughts, and now he's continually in my presence. I need to get away from him and not have him in my space, making me want him more.

"They keep looking over here," Sam giggles.

"Just ignore them," I tell them, trying not to make eye contact. Where's the check? I need to get out of here fast.

"Mind if we join you?" Nix's rough voice asks, now standing at the table, his two friends on either side.

"Sure." Missy smiles, looking like all her Christmases came at once. The guys pull up chairs as Nix sits down next to me.

"Real smooth," I whisper to him, annoyed that my friends have now been pulled into conversations, leaving me stuck with Nix.

"So, Miss Turner, have you got a first name?" He leans in, trapping us in our own invisible bubble. His green eyes sparkle playfully, waiting for a reaction.

"Nope, it's just Miss Turner to you." I pull back, breaking his spell.

"That's okay, baby. I don't need to know your name, just need to know how hard you like it." His words go straight to my stomach, the sensation awakening a part of me that I thought was lost.

"You won't ever know how hard I like it, Mr. Knight," I snap, afraid he can see how much he affects me. He just smiles and shakes his head. The man is crass, but for the life of me, I can't seem to hate him for it. I try to engage in conversation with the rest of the table, but with Nix next me, it's making it hard to concentrate.

"How's Z?" I finally cave to him, but try to steer the conversation away from anything he could turn sexual or make me want to rip my clothes off and demand he take me with his dirty mouth.

"I don't know what's gotten into him. He's going through some stuff."

I nod in agreement. Z's behavior has been way off the last couple of weeks. The fight in class is the worst of it, but since detention started, his attitude hasn't changed. I bite my tongue to keep myself from saying anything; it's clearly time to call a meeting with both parents to discuss my concerns.

"Hey, Kadence, did you sign up for the charity ride?" Missy asks me from across the table, pulling me away from thinking how fun that meeting would go. I shake my head, remembering Nix asking me the same question earlier. The thought of sitting close to him, our bodies touching, is too much of a temptation.

"Kadence, huh? I like it even better than Miss Turner." He leans in close, too close for comfort, and I know if I turn my head, our noses would touch. He says my name again, trying it out on his lips, and as much as I hate myself for it, the sound coming from his mouth sends a jolt through my system.

"And Nix is your full name?" I ask, wondering if his mother called him that.

"No, Nix is short for Phoenix. Nix is just what everyone calls me."

As much as I like it, Nix suits him more, but being the smartass I am I decide to call him Phoenix from then on. I smile and nod, trying my hardest to keep myself in check. The thought of pushing him for a reaction gets me excited. We continue to play nice, until Nix decides to push again.

"So Kadence, what's the rule with teachers and parents dating?"

I have to laugh at that one. He's so sure of himself. I'm sure I wouldn't lose my job, but I don't want him to know that. Yes, he is attractive, and sparring with him is fun, more fun than I've had in a while, but I'm not sure crossing that line is wise.

"Not going to happen, Phoenix," I reply, loving that I get to call him by his name.

"So you're stubborn and sassy. I love a good chase," he responds, not one bit deterred.

"It would be a pretty boring chase, like a dog chasing his tail." I smile sweetly at him. The thrill of going back at him sends a swarm of butterflies through my stomach.

"Jesus, you're like my dream woman. Smart mouth, sexy clothes, perfect body," he laughs, shaking his head. "I'm not giving up on you, Kadence," he quietly promises before his cell rings from his pocket. Standing from the table, he takes the call over near the restrooms.

I'd be lying if I said those words did nothing to me, but I have to remember it would be a huge mistake to get involved with him. Okay, not huge, but a mistake nonetheless.

I have to give him credit though. He is persistent and it's working. Each one of his jabs tears at my resolve to keep my distance. My resolve that I don't find him utterly drool-worthy is being tested. The truth is he is hot as sin. One night with him would make any woman happy I have no doubt, but could I possibly do one night with a man who reminds me of something that was taken from me?

I have to leave. The tension between us is too much. My choice is leave immediately or crack under the pressure of his bad-boy charm. I say my goodbyes to the table while Nix is on the phone, and quickly leave out the front, annoyed that I'd let my guard down for a minute.

"You running off?" Nix startles me from behind as I reach for my door.

"Oh, God, Nix." I spin around and smack at his chest, annoyed that he snuck up behind me like a stealthy ninja. He grabs my wrist and before I can object, his mouth claims mine.

The light taste of beer on his lips and the warmth of his tongue demanding entry have me losing myself. Sliding his hands into my hair, he tugs back hard for better access, the sensation pulling me further into his assault. My stomach drops as our tongues collide, the throbbing between my legs beating to its own rhythm.

The kiss isn't sweet or sensual. It's hard and fast, just like him, and before I know it, my hands have taken over. Fisting his leather cut I pull his body to mine. His denim-covered cock presses into my stomach, making my knees weak. My brain stops functioning, my body controlling its need. I know what we're doing is wrong, but the taste of his lips and the hardness of his arousal are telling me different. I want this man. Want everything he is doing to me and then more. His hips push further, his thickness growing against me as I lean back against the car. Knowing I caused this reaction in him sets me on fire.

"Prez," someone calls out into the dark parking lot, breaking our connection.

"Fuck," he whispers, bringing his forehead to mine; his breathing is as erratic as mine. "Give me five," he yells back.

"Shit, that was a mistake," I mutter as my fingers soothe my swollen lips.

"Like hell it was," he hisses, taking a step back, watching me.

"I'm not interested in you," I lie. My hands shake in front of me, the rush of adrenaline that shot through me at his touch now leaves me feeling exposed. "In fact, I have a date tomorrow night, so if you'll excuse me." I turn and open my door, desperate to get away. His hand comes to the door, stopping me from closing it.

"If you kiss like that when you're not into it, I'd love to see how you kiss when you are," he challenges with an arrogance that seems to affect me. He smirks then lets go of my door.

"I don't intend for you to find out," I reply before slamming my door, starting the car and driving off. I have to force myself not to look back.

★★★

Sitting in a booth the following night at Fireside Bar, I think back to Nix's challenge. "If you kiss like that when you're not into it, I'd love to see how you kiss when you are."

The bastard is playing with me; I know it and now I can't get him out of my head. I've known the man for all of five minutes and I can honestly say he infuriates me. Infuriates me and makes me think of things I shouldn't be thinking about, especially about a student's dad. Taking a sip of my cocktail, I push all thoughts of Nix Knight and his amazing kissing abilities aside and attempt to enjoy my night.

After tossing and turning all night and thinking about that kiss, I woke this morning and vowed to not think of him again. Yeah, I was failing miserably. I wasn't lying when I told Nix I had a date tonight. My best friend Holly dragged me out tonight for a double date. She's been seeing some guy named Ben and they thought it would be a good idea to set me up with his roommate, Braydon.

So far things haven't progressed well, and I'm starting to regret agreeing to come along, something that I always seem to do around Holly.

Braydon is not my usual type, but he looks good, so that's a win at least. However, everything else is lacking. I like my men to be a little manlier, a man's man if you will. Someone who takes charge of the situation, but not someone who bosses me around, 'cause I sure as hell won't put up with that. I spent too many years with my ex-fiancé, letting him dictate to me. I was weak back then. Now I'm not afraid to stand up for myself.

Shaking my head of thoughts that won't change the past, I realize Braydon and Ben are still talking about the latest football game playing on the overhead screens. Great.

Looking over at Holly, I watch as she scans the club checking out the talent for the night. That's Holly, on a date and still scoping her options. I'm about to tell her to quit when she kicks me under the table.

"What?" I whisper-yell to her as I lean forward and rub the shin where she just planted her stiletto.

"Check out the hot piece of ass that keeps looking over

here," she whisper-yells back, and I turn my head to see the man who's been the center of my thoughts since the first day I met him, Nix Knight. Jesus, the man looks better each time I see him. I groan out loud when my eyes connect to his, and he gives me a wink. *What an ass.*

"Who the hell is that?" she questions, and I motion her to the ladies' room to talk.

Having escaped our table without even a glance from our dates, we push through the bathroom door when Holly starts firing out questions on who the sexy guy in leather is.

I've known Holly since college, meeting during first-day orientation. We realized we had a few classes together and so our friendship began. Her crazy personality brings out the fun in me, and she's been my best friend for over ten years; not a day goes by I'm not thankful for her. When I lost my house, she welcomed me in with open arms. I survived and fought my way through recovery with her help. She came to every appointment with me, sat with me after every surgery and setback. If it wasn't for Holly, her upbeat attitude and her crazy out-there moments, I don't know where I'd be. Three years later, we still live together and haven't killed each other, *yet.*

Pounding at the door startles me mid-way through my explanation about the badass biker who I met in my classroom last week, and the sexy, smartass man I kissed last night. The door pushes open, revealing none other than Mr. Sex On Legs himself. My best friend, or should I say ex-best friend, looks to me, her smile in place as she wiggles her eyebrows.

"I'll just wait outside." She looks to Nix, then back to me, mouthing, HOT, before leaving me alone with the insufferable man. *Traitor.*

Facing Nix, I prepare to give him a piece of my mind when he steps into my space, close enough for me to smell his cologne. *Shit, don't be swayed by the amazing smelling man, Kadence.*

"What the hell do you think you're doing?" I manage to get out while fighting the pull of his subtle cedar smell.

"I've come to ask you the same question, Kadence." I ignore the fact he uses my first name. One kiss and he thinks he knows me? No, it's more like he's gloating that he learned it last night and now won't stop calling me it. "What are you doing with the stick out there?" He moves closer as I step back into the counter.

"Who I date is none of your business, Mr. Knight." I use his last name, trying to put an air of professionalism between us. Even though his assessment of Braydon is correct, I don't need him to know my date is a bust.

"Well, you see, Kadence," again with my name, but this time the sound comes smoothly off his tongue and sends a shiver down my spine. Hell, every single thing he says to me pulls me further into his spell. I want to slap my own face to snap me out of it. "That's the problem, 'cause I'm gonna make it my business. After that kiss last night, I've decided I need more." His cocky attitude pulls me out of my stupidity and just pisses me off more.

"Step back," I hiss, ignoring his line about me being his business. This guy is smooth. I'll give him that, but I don't fall for cheesy lines. Nix just shakes his head. "Mr. Knight, step the fuck back now," I say again a little louder. His eyes flash with something that is unreadable, as he leans in closer.

"Oh, Miss Turner," he rasps like he's in pain. "My name and fuck coming out of those beautiful lips makes my cock rock hard." The filthy words coming from his mouth should disgust me, should make me feel dirty that I find him unbelievably sexy as hell, but they don't. *Jesus, what is wrong with me?*

Yes, there is some fierce electricity between us, and yes, I kissed him, but nothing can happen. I should be offended, but I'm not. Instead, it sends a thrill straight through me and I fight the urge to clench my thighs to soothe the ache he has created.

"Do those lines work on all the girls, Nix?" I say his name this time, his lips dangerously close to mine. If he leaned in and kissed me, I wonder if it would be like last night's: fierce and full of desperation.

His eyes narrow and a grin forms on his lips, lips that I know have the ability to make me come undone. "Tell me, Kadence, if I stuck my hand down these tight-as-sin jeans," his finger trails along the tops of my pants, "and touched your pussy, would you be wet for me?" he purrs, and my body responds before my brain can catch up; the shudder runs through me. He doesn't miss it, pushing further into me. Chest to chest. Nose to nose.

What the actual fuck is wrong with me? There are warning bells screaming at me to stay clear, but his words make me weak. I have never, ever, been so turned on in my life. Wetness pools in my lace panties and I can't even deny he is wrong. This pull he has over me is terrifying. If he told me to drop to my knees and take him in my mouth, I'm not sure I could refuse him.

The thought appalls me, yet at the same time, I become even wetter. Shaking my head out of the lust-induced fog he puts me under, I gather some much-needed strength and push the hard muscles of his chest. "Step back," I demand, and again he ignores me. Instead, he moves his mouth to my ear.

"Babe, I'm all for the struggle. Keep going. You're just making me harder." His breath caresses my skin.

My knee comes up connecting with his balls, and I cringe at the force I use. Stepping back and cupping himself, his face is a picture of agony. For a brief moment, I feel awful, hitting him where it hurts, but then I remember how much he provoked me, and subsequently, I don't feel so sorry.

"Fuckin' hell, woman," he gasps, the pain knocking him breathless.

"I told you to step back," I explain, fixing my top and ignoring the wetness between my legs. He has no right to keep teasing me with his dirty words that make me wet. Walking past him, I ignore his grunts of pain and push through the door, leaving him standing there as I make my way back to the table.

I find Holly sitting at the now empty table, a smirk on her face, but I just roll my eyes. If she only knew.

"Where are Ben and Braydon?" I ask, looking around the bar.

"Oh, your hot biker dude scared them off," she replies on a shrug. I turn to watch Nix slowly walk back to his table. Cheers and laughter fill the air as he looks over to give me one of his fucking winks again.

"That bastard," I grind out. I don't know what it is about him, but he knows how to get to me.

"I need to up my game," I say to myself more than to Holly. She laughs and declares I should just fuck him. *Maybe I should just sleep with him.* It wouldn't be a hardship, that's for sure. I'm not shy when it comes to sex, but a one-night stand with Nix? God, the thought alone leaves me craving it but I don't know if that would be a smart move. What I do know is that I'm ready to tell him what a shitty move it was getting rid of my date. Hit a man while he's down I say. Standing, shoulders squared, I decide I'm ready for round two. Thinking about round one, I shudder and realize I'll need a second pair of panties.

Nix

RESTING THE COLD BEER BETWEEN MY LEGS TO soothe the ache, the boys give me shit for striking out. I feel the same way: the woman is a tough nut to crack.

"You ready for round two, Prez?" Beau smirks behind his beer. Turning my head, I watch as Kadence storms over. I groan as my broken dick comes to life, apparently not caught up with the news that she doesn't like him. She stands at the end of the table, arms crossed over her chest, unaware that her position puts her sexy tits up on display.

Fuck, this woman is a tease.

"Hey, sweetheart," I say before taking a sip of my beer.

"Don't sweetheart me. What did you say to my date?" she

snaps, anger clear on her face, and I've never seen a more beautiful look on her. Her eyes blaze with fire and the need to push her more fills me. I can't wait to have her under me.

"Oh, the stiff?" I ask nonchalantly. "Just told him to run along; he didn't have what it takes to play with the big boys," I say as some of the brothers laugh into their drinks.

I've never pushed a woman this far before; chasing her and teasing her feels so damn good. Something about her pushes my buttons and leaves me wanting more. Most women fall at my feet begging to get in, but Kadence? No, this woman makes me want to do the begging. I've never wanted to fuck a woman so hard while spanking her ass at the same time. The way she reacts to me makes my dick hard and God help me, getting her riled up is a sight to see. I can see it in her eyes; she's fighting it. She wants me and I intend to give the lady what she wants.

"What do you want, Phoenix?" she demands, uncrossing her arms and assuming a relaxed position, but I'm not stupid. The woman is crazy mad and I've got a throbbing dick to prove it.

"What do I want?" I repeat her question, pausing to take another pull on my beer. "Well, after your little stunt in the bathroom, I wanna pull you down on this table and spank your ass," I tell her calmly. Even though my balls are aching, my cock is pulsing.

"You disgust me," she hisses and turns to walk away. I grab onto her hand, turning her my way. She tries to pull out of my grasp, but my hold on her is strong.

"You don't mean that. I've seen the way your eyes flash. You would love for me to spank that sexy ass right here for everyone to see. Wouldn't you?" Embarrassment floods her cheeks, and for a beat, I think I might have pushed her too far.

"Come on, Prez. Give the girl a break," Brooks says, smiling up at her. Brooks is the only bastard here married, and it doesn't surprise me that he'd be feeling like a schmuck having to listen to my shit. Kadence looks around the table, realizing our conversation has an audience. Recognition flashes when her eyes land on Jesse.

"You know Jesse?" I ask. My question comes out fast and harsh.

She nods, and then mumbles, "Hi Jesse."

What the fuck?

"Hey, sweetheart," he replies, and I look over at him, shooting daggers. Fuck me, the little bastard's calling her sweetheart? Hell the fuck no!

Kadence pulls back, breaking our connection, her expression guarded. "Well, I can't say it's been fun, Mr. Knight, but you chased my date away so I'm heading home." She turns, retreating from her spot. Her fight abandoned as she heads back to her blonde friend.

Turing my attention to Jesse, I pin him with my don't-fuck-with-me stare. The boys go quiet, and Jesse holds up his hands in mock surrender. "Calm down, boss man."

"How do you know her?" I ignore his comment, hoping he hasn't fucked her. I wouldn't put it past him. Jesse has fucked a hell of a lot of women.

"Whoa, nothing like that, Prez. I met Kadence a few years ago back in the burns center," he replies, looking back down at his beer.

Before Jesse patched in, he was a firefighter. After 9/11 and following in his father's footsteps, he enlisted and served his country. After two tours and an injury that required four surgeries over two years, he was medically discharged. With a messed up foot, his firefighting career was over. Unable to work, he came back to his hometown. It wasn't long after that he patched in. He came in when shit turned good, his uncle one of the originals, one of the men who helped me pull us clean. I can't imagine the goofy kid ever being okay with the fucked-up shit we used to be involved with. Not being able to have the career he's always wanted, he was in a bad place for a long time, but with the help of the club and seeing what we were about, he finally got his head straight. Volunteering his time at the local burn unit was one of the things that pulled him out of it.

Nodding my head, I take in the information. With my mind going crazy and wanting to know the details, I push further, "Well, what happened?"

"Kadence had an accident a few years back," he explains, looking uncomfortable with revealing what went down. Looking over I see Kadence and her friend getting ready to move.

"How bad of an accident?" I push, still watching her closely.

"Yeah, not going there, Nix," Jesse replies, shaking his head no. Fuck, I could push him for it, but I don't have the time. Nodding my head, I stand and drop a Benjamin on the table leaving them to follow Kadence out.

I don't know what I'm doing, but she is just too much of a temptation, one I can't let go.

"Hey, Kadence," I call out as I make my way out the front door. She stops and spins on her heel.

"Jesus, what now?" she snaps back. My cock stirs to life at

her attitude. Fuck, I'm a goner.

"Listen, I'm sorry. I don't know what it is about you. Shit," I exhale, feeling like this shit is way over my head. "I swear I don't usually act this way. You push all my buttons." I run my hand through my hair, frustrated I'm responding this way.

"It's fine, Nix. I was inappropriate in there too. I don't know what it is either, but you make it easy to fight with," she confesses, letting out a shaky breath in defeat, and I smile, knowing I have the same effect on her. "But nothing can happen between us. Z is one of my students, and it's frowned upon to date student's parents," she continues, letting me off the hook. Only I don't want to be let off.

"Why not? If you're feelin' anything like I'm feelin', then why not?" I question. "We're both grown-ass adults. We can do what we want."

"I don't date," she replies a little too quickly.

"Bullshit, I just ran your date off fifteen minutes ago," I say smugly. The pansy prick high-tailed it out of there as soon as he got the hint.

"Yes, how could I forget?" Her eyes narrow, still pissed off at me.

"Let me take you out," I blurt. What the fuck is wrong with me? She just told me she didn't date. When she kneed me in the balls, she must have made me lose some of my manhood because I don't ask women out on dates. Sure, I love the chase, but that's just to fuck, not what I'm asking of her now.

"Come on, baby. Don't leave me hangin'. The one time I ask a woman out, she knocks me back," I admit, prepared to begin begging. Fuck, this woman has me turned inside out.

"I find it very difficult to believe you haven't asked a

woman out?" If I didn't know me, I would be skeptical too.

"It's true. I don't normally have to." I give her a smirk and she scoffs at me.

"You're a dick," she snaps, turning her back to me.

"Come on, Kadence, one date," I call out.

"Phoenix, you and I, it's not going to work," she informs me over her shoulder. I move closer to close the distance between us. Her friend hangs back, enjoying the show, but I've only got eyes for Kadence.

"See, that's where you're wrong." I argue back, grasping her hand and turning her around. "I can see you fuckin' want me just as much as I want you. Tell me you haven't responded like this to someone before," I push, hoping I'm right, and not alone feeling these things. "Just one date," I repeat. I see her resolve starting to slip, her mind fighting her body. I can see the moment I have her.

"One date, then you'll leave me alone?" she questions.

I smile at her, nodding my head. One date is all I need to get my fill.

"One date," I repeat. Though deep down, something is telling me this will be more than one date. Women like her can break men like me. I'm already acting like a fool, begging for a date.

"Fine," she agrees, nodding her head. She doesn't look fine with it; her eyes flash with trepidation as she processes what she just agreed to, but I'm not about to give her time to think about it.

"Great, let's go," I say, grabbing her hand, pulling her to my side.

Pulling back slightly panicked, she yells, "What?"

"The date you just agreed to," I say, making it simple for

her, "it starts now."

For all I know, she'll try to blow me off next week, giving me some lame–ass excuse. If I'm getting a chance, I'm taking it now.

"Now?" Disbelief fills her voice.

"Yes, Kadence, now." I pull her along as she fights me to stay.

"But Holly." She looks back to her friend, no doubt pleading with her. The blonde just squeals in delight.

"Have a good night, Kadence. Text me." She waves her goodbye.

"Hold on. Where exactly are we going?" she questions, turning back when she knows she isn't being saved. Walking up to my bike, I motion her forward.

"We're going for a ride," I tell her, handing her the helmet.

"No, there is no way I'm getting on that bike," she rushes out, shaking her head, her long dark hair flying out around her.

"Well, it's our only form of transportation, baby." I inform her, trying to hide my excitement of getting her on my bike.

"Stop calling me baby," she snaps.

"Kadence, get your ass on the bike," I tell her again with a touch more authority.

"Nix," she sighs, using the name I prefer; however, after hearing her call me Phoenix, I think I'm beginning to like it more. "You can't just call me baby, boss me around and demand me to get on your bike."

"Yes, I can," I say, walking up to her. I take the helmet out of her hands and plant it on her head.

"Nix," she says as my fingers work on tightening the chinstrap. "I've never been on a bike before."

"Trust me, Kadence; I won't let anything happen to you." She steps back shaking her head under the black helmet, and I hold back my frustration. She's gonna make me work harder for it. *Pain-in-the-ass woman.*

"Last chance, Kadence, get your sweet ass on my bike or I'll put you on it," I insist, done with the damn fight. It's getting late and I'd much rather be doing something else than argue.

"Can't you just tell me where we're going and I'll meet you there in my car?" Walking forward, I ignore her question and place my hands to her hips.

"Nix," she screams as I lift her small frame up, turn and plant her on the back of my bike. *Done, problem solved.*

"This date is going great already," she sasses, sitting further back as I climb on my ride. I laugh on the inside. I don't know about her, but for me, a woman who gives just as good as she gets is what I call the start of a good date. However, I still feel obliged to let her know how I roll.

"Let me give you fair warning, Kadence. I tell you to get on my bike, you get on the bike. You give me sass, I'm gonna do what I told you I'd do. In this case, I planted your ass on my bike. Now, quit your bitchin' and slide down, or your sweet ass will hit the asphalt when I take off."

Letting out a breath in defeat, she slides forward, her short legs hugging my side. As much as I'd love to get her on the back with one of those tight skirts she wears, the tight jeans she's wearing are enough to make this ride uncomfortable.

She doesn't move close enough so I reach back, grab her hands and bring them around me. She gets the hint, her front now plastered to my back. Flicking the key over, I start my bike and let it come to life. The roar of my Harley's engine growls low. The muffler builds louder, the sound filling the still night. Kadence's grip tightens as I release the throttle, veering to the left. I take off steadily and ready to take Miss Turner on one hell of a ride.

5

Kadence

THE WIND RUSHES PAST US, COOL AIR BITES AT MY SKIN and the ends of my long hair stream behind me. We've been riding for what seems like twenty minutes, and I've regretted every second of it.

Okay, not really, I freaking love it.

Nix's body heat is keeping me warm, my front pressed into his back. It's the only reason I'm plastered up behind him. If the wind wasn't so damn cold, I'd be able to relax back a bit. Who am I kidding? His body feels amazing underneath my hands.

I am slightly concerned, however, that I've let this man push my buttons, kiss me senseless, speak to me dirty, demand a date and manhandle me all in the space of two nights. I know getting caught up with him could end badly. I've seen what men like him, and their clubs, are capable of doing. So if I know these things, know that one date with not only a biker but a parent will only end badly, then what the hell am I doing on the back of his bike, driving to who knows where, to do who knows what? *I've lost my damn mind.*

I think it's the way he talks to me. No one has ever spoken to me the way he does, and I can't control the reaction my body has to it. It's not even about the bossy side of him. Zane used to be bossy but in a different kind of way, a way that left no room for argument. With Nix, it's like his demands ignite the dirty part of me, the part that's hidden but still leaves room to argue back. Maybe it's not so hidden if he can ignite it with just one comment or one look. I sigh at the predicament I find myself in as I lean further into him. His hand comes down on my thigh, squeezing me, and I feel it go straight between my legs.

When he asked for a date, my first instinct was to blurt out yes. I nearly did. Holly would have loved that. I had to fight my body's instinctive reaction to jump him right there in front of the bar, begging him to spank me just like he promised. Then I remembered I was trying to hate him and thought that would go against everything I've been saying to him every time he pushes me.

I don't know why I agreed. I was so close to escaping, but deep down, I knew this was coming. He said something that made me realize he was right. I feel the same pull he feels too. I know it with every touch, every look. He's right. I've never responded this way to anyone before, and giving in to that pull is something my body has been craving so much. The decision was made, and for once, I'm going to give in to temptation. I didn't know tonight would be the night, but following the saying of just let go, I did just that. I let go.

So now I'm sitting on the back of his bike, his broad chest feeling amazing under my hands. I copped a little feel earlier when we went sharp around a corner, but after five minutes, I relaxed into him, my body automatically holding on to his ripped front, memorizing it before I see what is under his leather cut.

One date. I'll give myself one date. One night of letting go and then tomorrow, I can analyze everything I've done. I'm delusional to think he will want anything more. Men like him live the hard lifestyle. Women come and go; they get their fill and move on to the next one. He even said himself one date, so whatever happens, I'm going to put it down to the undeniable tension that's between us, and for once, act on it.

Nix slows his bike, turning the corner of a suburban street, easing into the drive of a modest two-story house. He pulls up alongside a black jacked-up Chevy. The porch light has been left on giving off a soft glow against the darkened night, making it feel warm and inviting. Shutting his bike down, Nix climbs off and leaves me sitting here wondering how the hell I'm going to get off.

"How was your first time on a bike?" He smirks, knowing I enjoyed it more than a lot.

"About as enjoyable as anyone feels being placed on the back of a bike for the first time, asshole." He shakes his head laughing, and then reaches out to help me off.

"I like that I'm your first." He pulls me to him. I ignore his comment, and the reaction I get from it, and step back, needing space.

"Where are we?" I look up at the house, unbuckling the chinstrap to remove the heavy black helmet. My hair gets caught as I lift it up. Nix comes forward, helping me untangle the mess.

"My place," he explains, taking the helmet and placing it in the side bag of the bike.

"I thought we were going out for a date?" I correct him, cocking my eyebrow at his forwardness. I shouldn't be surprised; the man has been nothing but forward.

"I didn't say where we were goin'. I'm gonna feed you, seein' that your date left before you ate, get to know you a little better, and then I'll take you home whenever you want," he informs me as we walk along the front path to his front porch.

He unlocks and opens the door and gestures me to walk through. I should say no, shouldn't even walk through his door, but my vagina is making all the decisions.

Making my way through the front entry, I'm silently amazed at the tidiness of his home. The large open-plan living area greets us as we make our way into the room. A large kitchen to the left, opens up to the dining area, and then extends further out into the living area. Two long black leather couches look inviting, sitting in front of a huge flat screen hanging on the wall. Looking around the room, I eye all the fine details to get a glimpse of him in his element. Nix opens up a large, paneled glass door out to the backyard. Flicking the light to give me more of a view, I walk forward and look out to the decking, blown away by the size of it.

"Wow," I breathe out, walking up to the doors. Nix walks out onto the decking and starts up the built in grill. I follow, heading to the railing that looks out to his large backyard. The in-ground pool sits to the left and a large expansive grassed area is to the right. The yard is lit up as the spotlights from the house shine over the pool area. It's huge and amazing. I feel a slight pang of jealousy at his home, a real family home.

Turning back around, I follow his movements. Closing the outside fridge, two beers in his hand, he passes me one after popping the top.

"Thanks." Taking a sip, I look around one more time. "Nice house." I motion around me.

"Thanks," he says, turning back to the grill. I take a seat, feeling a little out of my element in his house.

"So," I begin, trying to fill the silence between us. If we aren't fighting or being smartasses to each other, it seems we don't have much to say.

"Just relax, Kadence. I'm not gonna rip your clothes off just yet." *And we're back.*

"Yeah, yeah, Casanova, keep it in your pants. You aren't getting into mine." I watch as he looks at me, before walking forward like a predator stalking his prey. He stops short of getting in my space, but his tall frame standing over me communicates his formidable power.

"Kadence, don't lie. You and I both know that what's in those pants is aching for my cock." The ache was gone, but with one sentence, his deep gravelly voice has me building an itch I know he could scratch.

"You're good, you know that?"

"Kadence, I'm more than good." I roll my eyes at him. Seriously, the man has it bad for himself.

"Tell me honestly, does it work?" I ask, genuinely concerned. I'm hoping I'm not the only fool falling for his dirty words. *'Cause then I really would need to talk to my vagina.*

48

"I don't know, Kadence. Are your panties wet?" he responds, and this time I laugh out loud. He seriously must have taken classes or something.

"Geez, Phoenix, cut the bullshit, would you? Your dirty mouth might make some girls wet between the legs, but it's not the key to getting between mine. You need to work harder than that," I lie, standing from my chair and taking one step into his space. The truth is his dirty words are wearing me down, and if he keeps talking about wet pussies, I'm going to pull my pants down and demand he show mine some attention.

What am I saying? Am I really considering having sex with this man? This crass, dirty, sexy man who pushes my buttons, who irritates me while at the same time manages to turn me on? Of course I am. Why else would I get on his bike? I've had one-night stands before, before my accident that is. Could I let him in, possibly exposing that side of me without explaining? A part of me knows if he sees it, sees the ugliness, he will be disgusted by it or at least want an explanation.

I don't like to allow my past to define me, or let me shy away from people, but when ten percent of your body holds second-degree burns, it's hard to let someone see it. Granting permission for anyone to see the ugliness underneath can also be deeply empowering. I have the ability to control a part of it, so it doesn't restrict me. I've worked so hard to move past my insecurities of it all.

I made the decision a long time ago to own it and embrace the marks of my past, yet Nix's presence has me faltering, second-guessing that I'm strong enough to move past it. If I'm being honest, my insecurities are coming from the strange and intense connection I have with this demanding pigheaded man. It's like no other. His presence alone makes me feel less worthy, but at the same time, my strength keeps me holding on. I know I can't walk away from it even if I tried. The truth in that statement is that I sit here about to have dinner with him, knowing we will only end up naked. I've come this far; I want this just as much as he does.

Gathering more courage, I continue to tease him, "How about if you can last all through dinner, without your filthy mouth talking about my pussy, I might give you a taste of it." I wink and walk past him, hoping he doesn't see through the fake bravado I'm feeling right now.

He follows me, coming up behind me, his heat at my back. "Game on, Kadence," he breathes into my ear. His hot breath prickles my skin. I'm not sure if betting against the man is wise; I wouldn't put it past him to play dirty.

Turning around, I smile, hiding the intense rush his words leave me feeling. Yep, I'm going to do it.

Leaning in, I whisper into his ear. "I bet you don't last twenty minutes thinking about how wet I am between my legs." He groans and a look of anguish washes over his face as he reaches down to adjust himself.

"You play dirty, pretty girl, but you don't know who you're playing with."

He's right. I have no idea what I'm doing, but for one night, I'm up for finding out.

6

Nix

AFTER FINISHING DINNER, WE MAKE OUR WAY INSIDE
to tidy up the dishes. I've been on my best behavior, and I'm
satisfied that Kadence is surprised to learn that I'm not some
deadbeat asshole who earns money dealing in women or
drugs. Most people in town don't know the struggle the club
went through to get clean. The path my dad took was a lot
different to the one I now walk down. After we lost my mom,
the years that followed were what I had always said I didn't
want to live. I became a man I had vowed never to be. I didn't
want my children growing up and watching their father instill
fear into a town, living a life of crime and then watch them go
through life the same. After working our asses off for five

years, we now successfully run two bars, a new club downtown and a new ink joint we just opened up last week. The boys are happy; the club is free from any of that old bullshit, and I wouldn't want anything else. Except, maybe a sexy, hot teacher to warm my bed.

Our dinner conversation flowed easily, having a few jabs at each other along the way, her vexing me, me teasing her back. We didn't talk about my ex, and I was glad not to touch on the subject; last thing I wanted to speak about with a woman is my pain-in-the-ass ex. We avoided the whole classroom scene from last week. She clearly has an issue with me being a parent to one of her students, so I steered clear of anything that could have her back-pedaling.

I don't know what it is about this connection we have. Even in the last two hours, I feel more comfortable than I have ever before. Having a woman in my space, talking about club life is something that I would never normally do, but for the life of me, I can't seem to find a way to make myself stop. After I kissed her last night, I came home and fucking dreamt of her, of her hot mouth around my cock. Waking from the worst sleep ever, I vowed I would stop hassling her, only to have my plan ruined when she was out on a fucking date in one of my bars. I knew the moment I had seen her sitting there, looking bored out of her brain, that the guy would never be good enough for her. With a little push in the right direction, the asshole left without even a backward glance. I'm gonna cop it from the guys tomorrow, with me chasing some tail like some lovesick fool. The fuckers couldn't make that shit up.

Telling Kadence to go sit down, I make my way back to grab one more beer. If things don't go to plan tonight, I'll still need to be able to drive her home. If I have my way, she'll be in my bed tonight, and I can worry about that little detail tomorrow. I'm not getting my hopes up; with the way things sit between us, who knows how the night will end? The woman runs hot and cold. One minute, I think I've got her; the next, she's playing hard to get.

Sitting down on the sofa next to her, I hand her the beer, and watch her lips closely as she takes a drink. She's kicked her heels off in front of her. Her toes are painted a sexy pink. Seeing them naked in my home does something to my gut. I wouldn't usually bring a woman back here, but I didn't want to take her to the clubhouse. Saturday nights can get fucking crazy, and last thing I want her to see is the shit that can go down there.

"Are you going to be able to drive me home?" she asks, nodding at my drink. Putting my beer down beside me, I reach down and bring her right foot up to my lap. She turns her body and allows me to work my fingers, massaging the balls of her feet.

"Wasn't planning on drivin' you home tonight." I smirk when her eyes flash with panic for a second.

"Is that right?" she asks as she tries to pull her foot back.

"Relax," I say, keeping her foot there. "I'll take you home when you're ready," I add, waiting for her to tell me she's ready to go. It's like I'm hanging on, waiting for her to put an end to this. Fuck, I've never worked so hard for something before.

She relaxes into a comfortable position, leaning back into the arm of the sofa. My fingers work a little harder, and she sighs her approval, the sound going straight to my dick. She must feel me growing hard under her foot; as when she looks up at me, lust flashes through her eyes. I recognize the desire flowing between us.

Without hesitation, I lean forward and press my mouth to hers. Her soft, warm lips part slowly, granting me access. The tip of her wet tongue comes out first, surprising me and spurring me on. I greet her with my own, our tongues fighting in combat, like our personalities. Taking over the kiss, my mouth captures her moans, her submission to the pleasure. The taste of her on my mouth fills me with a need to devour more of her. All of her.

Bringing her hands up into my hair, she lightly pulls at it as I bite down on her bottom lip, tugging it between my teeth. Breaking our connection, I reposition myself, bringing my knee between the juncture of her legs; I lean forward, taking her mouth again, this time a little slower. Fisting a handful of her long dark hair, I tug hard, exposing her delicate neck. Latching on, I make it my mission to mark her.

All reason has left me.

The fact that I want to leave my mark on her should have me pulling back, but the thought of her seeing them tomorrow has me sucking harder. I know she'll be pissed, but that just makes it even better.

"Don't you fucking leave a mark," she pants, still fisting my hair. She pulls at it harder, the sting making me suck more.

Her heavy breathing fills the quiet room as she grinds herself up against my leg seeking the friction she needs. My greedy hands work to pull down her top, exposing her perfect tits in a fancy lace bra that makes my dick even harder. Her small erect nipples outlined by the black lace, beg for my attention. Squeezing one tightly between my thumb and finger, I roll over the fabric. She whimpers at the pressure, rubbing faster against my leg. Abandoning her neck, I take the erect nipple in my mouth, biting over her lace. Her hand reaches for my pants flicking the button open. Anticipation flows through me, begging for her soft touch. Fumbling with our position, I take over, jerking the zip down.

Kadence's hand slides in, her tight grip squeezes me firmly. The soft pad of her thumb runs along the head of my cock gathering the drop of pre-cum. Pulling her hand free, I sit back, fascinated, yet knowing what she's about to do. Her pink tongue slowly comes out, the teasing in her gaze has me anxiously waiting for it, and in one slow sweep, she tastes me.

Fuck that was hot.

My mouth smashes to hers, fighting access past her lips like a starved man dying of thirst for his first drink. Her hand finds its way back in my pants. Her touch is like an instant vault straight to my gut. I pull back, making work of her jeans, but her fingers stop me.

"Now, don't go all shy on me," I say, waiting to taste her. Fuck, I need to taste her on my lips as much as I need to breathe.

"Let's take it to the bedroom," she pants, pulling her legs out from under me and quickly standing. I force my breathing to calm before I follow her up taking her hand in mine, directing her up to the carpeted stairs to the master bedroom. With thoughts of taking her on the stairs, I push her up against the wall. Her hands wrap around my neck, pulling me down to her level. I drop one foot down to the stair below, her height so much shorter than my six-foot-two frame. My tongue intertwines with hers and I open my eyes to see hers closed shut. The tip of my cock sticks out from the tops of my jeans, begging me for attention. My head is in a craze, I don't know what I want to do with her.

"Bed," she pants, sounding just as crazy as I feel.

Pulling back, I drag her the rest of the way up to my bedroom, our bodies fumbling in the frantic need to get to the top. Flicking the light on, I walk her backwards into the room, stopping when her legs meet the side of my California King. I push her back in one fast movement and watch her fall as I pull my shirt up over my head. She comes up onto her elbows; her long hair hangs behind her. Her pert tits, still exposed from the top of her shirt, make my dick throb harder. Fuck, I need to see her. I follow her eyes as they scan over my chest, then my arms as she takes in the ink.

"Like what you see?" I smirk, knowing she does. I sure as fuck like what I'm seeing.

"You look okay." She smiles and I know she's playing, but the inner beast in me has me wanting to fuck her hard, and then get her to admit she's lying.

"Can you get the light?" she requests as I continue to get my fill of her on my bed.

"What?" I look down, admiring her laying there, her lips swollen from my kiss, her glazed eyes filled with appreciation. It's a sight I plan to burn into my memory and call on constantly.

"The light, can you get it?" she repeats, now looking unsure.

Planting my knee to the bed, I move up, my body covering hers. "Woman, if I'm getting a taste of this," I run my finger between her tits, down her stomach and between her legs, "I wanna see every inch of it." She shudders at my touch but doesn't say anything. I don't know what kind of dickheads she's been with before, but fucking her in the dark is not what

I had in mind. A body like hers needs to be worshiped, not fucking hidden.

"Take this off." I show her what I want, running my finger along the swell of her breasts. I can see she's struggling with something, but with what I don't know. She takes a large breath, like she's preparing herself, and then nods with unease.

I pull back waiting for her to tell me she changed her mind or that I've blown it. Instead, she sits up and reaches down to grab the hem of her shirt. Lifting it above her head, she tosses it to the side. Following her movements, I watch her release her pert tits from her bra, exposing her sweetly curved mounds. My hands find them immediately, the creamy flesh fitting just right in my hold. Capturing a rose-tipped nipple with my finger and thumb, I look back up at her. "Lose the pants, Kadence."

She pushes me back. My hold is lost as she stands in front of me. Our positions switched, I sit back and get ready for the show. Her movements are slow; her body turned slightly as I watch her pull them straight down her legs leaving her panties in place. Turning somewhat back to me, she cocks her eyebrow, waiting for me to get my fill.

"Jesus." I hold back a sigh. Nothing could have prepared me for the sight. I knew she was beautiful, but standing there in front of me? Fuck. Her soft porcelain skin shines against the glow of the ceiling light and her long, dark hair hangs over her breasts. There's this air of innocence about her, but at the same time, I know this woman could destroy me.

Her black lace panties hold all of my attention, the lace showing a little of the milky skin underneath. I'm anxious to see what's under there, to taste her on my tongue.

"Come here," I demand, ready for more. She turns her

body face on, and then takes one slow step to me, my eyes fixed on hers. Taking another step toward me, I reach forward, putting my hands to her waist, ready to pull her the rest of the way when I feel something under my fingers.

Moving my hand away, I take a closer look. She stops frozen as I run my eyes over the damaged skin. "Turn." My tone surprises me, the demand not meant to come out harsh as my eyes follow the path of the nasty scar. She does as she's told, turning to her side without argument, revealing her marred left side. Her flawless porcelain skin is scarred red and raw from the side of her waist to the high thigh. "Kadence?" My eyes search hers, waiting for an answer to my unasked question. I now know that Jesse was talking about this.

Looking back down, I can't take my gaze away from the angry, rigid skin. Her waist bears the worst. She pulls her leg away, turning her body to hide herself from me. My eyes look up and lock onto hers again not sure how to proceed. Pain, anger and determination stare back at me, waiting for my reaction. I feel tightness pull in my stomach as I look at her standing there vulnerable, but I don't react. The recognition that she survived something violent bothers me; I want to protect her from whatever nightmare she lived.

"What happened?" I ask, keeping my voice leveled so she doesn't pull back.

"I was in a fire," she answers with no emotion, no explanation. Her hands go to cover herself, but I reach forward to stop her. I want her to tell me every fucking detail, how it happened, why it happened, but I know she wouldn't feel comfortable enough to share, the look in her eyes telling me it's a no-go zone.

I stand, let her hands go, and move into her space. Leaning

down, I kiss her soft lips, letting her know she doesn't have to talk about it with me. She stands rigid, our brief moment still hanging between us. We're both quiet for a moment, staring back at each other. Unasked questions stir between us, both of us fighting our own battles. My hand goes to her heat, impatient to continue past the strange feelings flowing through me. Moving the lace material aside, I slide a finger down her bare center, and find her wet and hot.

She closes her eyes, becoming lost in the feeling. When she reopens them, desire replaces her apprehension. Lust replaces the anger. Spreading her open, I insert one finger into her tightness and lose myself in her snug heat. I pull out slowly, and then enter her again with a second finger.

"I can't wait to taste this sweet pussy, Kadence," I tease her. Her breathing labors as I work her over. Her hips come forward, rolling in a desperate effort seeking pleasure.

"Get on the bed," I order, removing my fingers and stepping back. Mumbling her annoyance, she walks to the bed, crawling to the center. The sight of her on her knees has me following her close behind. She turns and lays flat, her knees coming up, bent and closed together. I pull back and press my hands to her knees, spreading her wide. Moving down her body, the overpowering urge to taste her has my head between her legs. I calm my breathing; I don't need to blow my load before taking her. Reaching up, I pull her panties straight down, not slowly or delicately, but roughly. She looks down her body to me, her cheeks flushed with arousal as I inhale her sweet musky scent. Running my nose along her seam, I lightly touch her center, tormenting her with feather-like touches. God, she tastes amazing.

"Quit teasing me," she breathes out. I ignore her request

even though the sound of her bossy, sexed-up voice goes straight to my cock. Instead, I run my tongue along all the places that won't take her over the edge, teasing and savoring her taste. If I only have one night, I'm gonna fucking enjoy it. Her hand comes down, ready to reach the spot herself, but I grab her around the wrist, capturing it before she makes contact.

"Hands above your head," I demand. As much as I would love to watch her play with herself, I just don't think I'll be able to keep myself in check right now.

"Fuck off, Nix. Just give me your mouth," she spits out, her impatience coming through. I have to admit, I'm beginning to like every side to Kadence, but her feisty side? Fuck, it could undo me.

"Kadence, I'm not going to tell you again, put your fuckin' hands over your head, or you ain't getting my tongue." She huffs out her frustration as I blow my warm breath to her center.

"Fucking asshole," she hisses between clenched teeth, but I only smile at her frustration. She's just where I want her.

"I already told you, babe; I love it when you talk dirty to me." I add more pressure, and she calls out. Her hand comes down again and grabs my hair, the slight sting going straight to my throbbing cock.

"Hands, Kadence," I warn again directly into her sweet pussy, and she immediately obeys. Grinning into her dark haven, I award her with more pressure. Her hips reply, pushing into my face as I run the flat of my tongue up her middle.

"Fuck, honey." Her voice is hoarse as she nears her release. My tongue flicks harder, faster as I insert a finger, hooking it to find her G-spot. Her legs seize up, locking around my ears, and I know I've found the right spot. I feel her body tense, her orgasm closing in. As much as I want to take her over this very second, I want to feel her tighten around me, hugging me when I first make her come. I slow my movements, pulling my finger out from inside her.

"What the hell?" she pants, confused that I just stopped. "You rotten asshole!" She kicks at me as I stand to drop my pants. My neglected cock springs free, glad to be let out and begging to be deep inside of her.

"Kadence, I wanna bury myself deep in that tight little pussy the first time you come," I tell her, as I lean over and pull out a condom from the bedside drawer. Ripping it open with my teeth, I take my cock in my hand and stroke it a few times to soothe the ache. Her eyes shine in appreciation at each rough caress. Watching Kadence watch me, I roll the condom on and climb back between her legs. Lining myself up at the apex of her thighs, I lazily rub the head through her wetness.

"You're an asshole," she complains when I keep teasing her. I'm not trying to tease her; I'm trying to calm my raging thoughts of fucking her within an inch of her life.

"I don't know how long I'm gonna last, Kadence. You've got me so wound up," I admit. The taste of her covering my tongue and the sight of her laying underneath has me hanging on by a thread.

"Just fuck me, would you?" She hooks her feet behind me, greedy for me to fill her.

"Kadence," I growl as I ease myself inside of her. Jesus, I feel like I just found home. I try to switch my mind off and not surrender to the need of losing control and planting myself balls deep.

I draw out, and then inch my way in further, building momentum each time I slide into her heat. Her knees move up to accommodate me.

"Harder." Her breath comes out raw, her eyes burning with need. My speed picks up. I'm more than happy to meet her demands as I begin to pound into her. I feel my restraint slowly slipping as she comes up to meet each thrust. The sound of our bodies colliding, the soft whimpers leaving her mouth, all drive me forward, spiraling me into my sexual nirvana.

"Harder, Nix," she complains and my body responds as my movements become harsh, taking her the way I want to take her. "Yes," she cries out, receiving all that I give her while still begging for more. Fuck, I'm starting to suspect I've met my match.

Reaching down between us, I find her clit and flick it hard, worrying that I'm not gonna get her there before I blow my load. "Fuck, so tight," I grunt out with each thrust. "I could fuckin' live in here." I grind my hips harder into her. Her body responds to my dirty words like I knew she would.

"See how good you feel?" I urge as she arches to meet each powerful thrust. She gasps when I pound my hips harder into her.

"Fuck, my cock is never gonna get enough," I admit, the words leaving my mouth before I can sensor it. It's the truth. The feelings of never having her again make my body hum in frustration.

Her snugness is too much for my worked up state. Her soft cries of pleasure come out louder, letting me know she's close. I try to think of something, anything other than the tightness of her pussy milking me.

"Fuck, I can't hold it." Her deep confession is all I need.

"Come," I demand as she tightens around me. My eyes follow her hands as she grabs her tits, squeezing the tight little nipples between her fingers and screaming out her release, thrashing below me. A red flush floats across her neck and chest, her orgasm evident on her skin. The sight of it takes me over. Letting go, I feel my balls tense up, and a sensation run through me as I continue to pound into her, thrusting once, twice, and then a third time before exploding inside of her with a deep groan.

"Fuck me," I get out, between breaths.

"I just did," she jokes and I look down, leaning my forehead to hers. A light sheen of sweat over hers mixes with mine.

"Fuck," I say again. It seems like I've lost some brain cells or she just fucked them out of me. My breathing takes a while to come back to normal, so I stay buried inside of her.

She lays quietly, watching me closely, a comfortable silence between us. Her neck and chest still show signs of the red rash that I watched spread across her chest. I thought watching her get fired up was beautiful. Boy was I wrong. Her lying under me, her eyes softened after an intense orgasm, there isn't anything more beautiful. I run my fingers along the blush. "Fuck, you lit right up for me," I say and watch a new blush cover her cheeks.

"Don't go shy on me. It was so fuckin' hot. I wanna see it again," I tell her as I slowly pull out of her warmth, my body fighting the urge to stay planted. Leaning down, I take Kadence's mouth one more time, the kiss gentle but still hungry. Taking care of business, I take myself to the bathroom, telling her to stay where she is. If our first time is anything to go by, there is no way I'm letting her out of my sight.

Washing my hands, I grab a clean washcloth and wet it down. Never in my life have I taken care of a woman like this, but the impulse to look after her is too much to neglect. Walking back out, I see her sitting up on the side of the bed, her panties in place as she reaches for her jeans and straightens them out.

"What are you doing?" I ask, confused, considering I just told her to stay put. I am nowhere near ready for her to be gone, and if she thinks she's leaving, she has another thing coming.

"I should get going," she explains, picking up her denim jeans. Walking back over to the bed, I snatch them from her hands and throw them across the room.

"Nix!"

"No way in hell am I finished with you, woman," I smirk, pushing her back to the bed. She yelps as I land on top of her, her face loses the uncertainty, and her legs come around me, hugging me closer.

"You think you've got it in you to go again?" she challenges in her sassy tone.

"Kadence, that was just a starter."

"Well, if that's the starter, I can't wait for dessert." She smiles her fucking beautiful smile.

Yep, no fucking way I'm finished with her.

Z

Kadence

WHY DID I HAVE SEX WITH HIM? I SIT HERE WANTING to curl up and die. *Because you listened to your vagina.*

Five days after the most amazing sex of my life, I regret every second of it. *Okay maybe not the orgasms; those I would never regret.* Why for the life of me I thought things would be fine I have no idea, but now, I'm about to endure the most uncomfortable situation known to mankind and I only have myself to blame. *Stupid woman, Kadence.*

A knock at my door brings me from my thoughts, and I stand ready to come face to face with Z's mother, Addison Knight, and her ex-husband. The same man, who only five nights ago, was bringing me to the most intense orgasm I've ever experienced.

Fucking kill me now.

"Hello, Ms. Knight," I say, coming around from the desk, hoping I don't break out in a panic attack. "I'm Miss Turner." Her bright blue eyes size me up, and in one second, I feel reduced in her gaze. Her curvy figure, long legs and straight blonde hair are the complete and total opposite to me. I'm not a self-conscious person, other than my scar. I know I'm not ugly, but standing next to this tall, beautiful woman, it's like she just handed me a cup of self-doubt and forced me to drink from it.

She nods briefly, barely giving me her attention, looking around the room before taking a seat.

"My husband will be here in a moment," she states only to remind me of my mistake again. Oh, God, did she just say what I think she did? I try not to let the panic that's building on the inside show at hearing her call him her husband. What if they're not even divorced? How could I be so stupid? I can't even think about that right now. I need to keep myself composed and ready to see him again. Shaking it off, so I don't have a meltdown, I nod and walk back around my desk, wanting to have some space between myself and the soon-to-be-present Mr. Knight. I knew he was coming tonight. When I sent home a note for the meeting, Z returned it saying both his parents would be attending. I've had the whole day to process the situation and how I got myself into it. Asking myself over a thousand times why I would do such a foolish thing, for the life of me I can't give myself a perfectly honest answer. *Except that I wanted him. I still do. Shit.*

The sound of his motorcycle boots on the vinyl floor again warns me of his presence, the tap on the door verifying he's here

"Hey, baby," Ms. Knight calls to him as he walks straight past her and sits down in front of my desk. He flat out ignores her and only has eyes for me. Bright green eyes, full of anger and questions. *Oh, shit, he's pissed that I left.*

"Hello, Mr. Knight." I smile at him like the professional I am.

I can do this; just don't think about his head between your legs, Kadence.

His eyes narrow more and his tongue comes out to swipe his lower lip, reminding me how well he knows how to use it. Fuck, how am I not supposed to think about how many times that tongue made me come? I swallow past the uneasiness I feel having him in front of me.

"Miss Turner," he drawls, and if I didn't know he was angry, I would now with the way he speaks my name.

Steeling myself to talk, I focus my attention to Zayden's mom. She's oblivious of the tension between Nix and me, too busy looking at her phone. "Thank you both for seeing me tonight." I smile, wishing it to be over with already. "I called you both here to discuss my concern regarding Z's behavior."

"Zayden." Ms. Knight's head snaps up, her voice lashing out like a pissed-off momma.

"Sorry?" I look at her confused, wondering why she just barked his name back at me.

"His name is Zayden, not Z," she spits out. I didn't even realize I called him Z. Most of the kids in class call him Z, and after spending the night with Nix, I can't help but call him that.

"Don't fuckin' start, Addison," Nix speaks, his voice tightly controlled with anger. Still not looking her way, his eyes are firmly on me, silently claiming whatever it is he has to say. No doubt I'll be hearing it soon.

"His name is Zayden, Nix. Only his family calls him Z," she states, and I have to give it to her. She is a bitch, and I don't say that lightly. Jesus Christ.

"No, that's fine," I reply, dismissing her drama. Nix's brows furrow more, and for a brief moment, I think he must have a headache. *No, forget it. You know he's pissed at you, Kadence..*

I'm not going to lie; our night together was intense, more than intense. It was fierce and passionate, and most alarming of all, it felt right. I've had lovers who I would say were great, but Nix? He consumed me and exceeded my expectations, and then ruined me.

After the first time, Nix made sure he looked after me repeatedly. We both cut the bullshit bickering. Even though that part of our attraction is fun, it was as if we had finally found a level ground. I finally started to relax and we opened up to each other more. Since my accident, I have always kept myself covered, especially when being intimate. The one other person I've been with since the accident never argued with my request to turn the lights out or keep my clothes on. Even alone in the safety of my own bed, I've kept myself shielded. Until Nix. I knew he would push the issue. I saw it in his eyes when I asked him to turn the light off. He's not the type of man to back down. So instead of pushing him away and hiding myself, I sucked it up and exposed the one piece of myself I don't like people to see.

For one night, I allowed him to see my scarred body. I laid bare the ugliness that I keep hidden, the disfigured part of me that no matter what I say, no matter what I do, will always stare back at me, reminding me that I'll never be the same woman I was.

Creeping my way out in the early hours of the morning was low; I'm not going to deny it, but the whole night was a whirlwind of contradictions. After our second round, I was becoming too comfortable in his home, laying naked in his bed. I knew I was in way over my head and Nix was showing no signs of brushing me off. We connected, and as much as that sounds clichéd or even pathetic, we both felt it. It terrified me. It made me feel things that I had no business feeling, so I did the only thing I thought I could do. I ran. I ran so I wouldn't have to face him and try to explain why we shouldn't see each other again. Only now, it's so much worse.

Remembering I'm sitting in front of the very person I tried to avoid, I force my mind to forget Nix and our night together, and focus on the reasons why we are here.

"Zayden's —" I say, looking directly at Ms. Knight, making sure I use his full name. I watch her roll her eyes but I continue, "— recent behavior in class concerns me. This last week alone, I've had to pull him out of class every day for his rude behavior to not only the other students but also to me. He's not concentrating. I've found it hard to engage with him and now he's just completely withdrawn. In the span of few weeks, I've seen him go from easygoing to downright angry." I take a breath hoping I don't mess this up. I'm trying to keep it together, but the way Nix keeps looking at me, I'm about to fall into a mess on the floor.

Nix's gaze softens. He nods his head, agreeing with my assessment, while Z's mom just stares straight at me, no emotion to the facts of what I'm telling them. "I'm not sure if something has happened that you know of, something that could be making him lash out, or if it's something in the playground or the classroom, but I'm concerned. I have tried to talk with him, pulled him aside to see if I could help, but I don't feel like I'm getting through. At this stage, I would suggest the school counselor, someone neutral he can speak with, without any judgment. I can schedule that for him but I thought it was best to bring it to your attention first, offer you a chance to see if you want to address the issue yourselves," I say, treading carefully. I'd hate to think that something at home could be causing it, but nine times out of ten, these sorts of things are.

"Well, I can assure you it's nothing at home. Isn't that right, babe?" Addison looks over at Nix.

"Jesus, woman, will you cut the fuckin' act?" Nix bellows out. I'm startled for a moment. The intensity of his voice after being so quiet echoes in the empty classroom. His fist comes down on the desk in front of him, frightening me at the loud bang.

"Addi." He turns to face her, his large frame in a smaller chair looking every bit uncomfortable. His nickname for her does something to me that I have no idea how to process. "You and I both know something is going on with Z. I told you last week to talk to him. You failed to do it. Now, for once in his goddamn life, will you be the fucking mother I know you can be." He runs his hands over his face in frustration.

"Nix, he is fine," she responds, shaking her head like this whole thing is a waste of her time. "This is ridiculous. You know our son; it's just hormones. Let him be a boy."

I suddenly feel like I shouldn't be in this conversation. For one, I do not agree with her. Yes, Z is a boy, probably about to hit puberty, but he has gone from top of my class to detention every day; something is not adding up.

"Like fuck it's hormones. I've seen him pull back, and if you were a good mother, you would have seen it too. I fuckin' knew this shit was comin'," Nix argues, shaking his head.

Looking over at Addison, I see her face fall and I feel a little sorry for her. If my husband, ex or not, spoke to me in front of someone like that, I too would feel embarrassed.

"Maybe I can suggest—" I begin to say before Addison cuts me off.

"No, that's quite all right. You've done enough. Thanks for letting us know. We will deal with this at home, as a family," she responds coolly, rising from her chair. She looks down at Nix. "Will you walk me out, Nix?"

"Sit your ass down, now," he instructs her, still looking at me, not buying into her dramatics. She stands for a moment longer, not sure what to do, until she finally sits.

"Is there anythin' else?" His anger is evident, but I can feel his concern. I don't know what to say. I want to encourage them to seek some help, advise that ignoring it will only make it worse, but after Addison's outburst, I'm afraid I'll just argue with her. The woman apparently doesn't give a shit, but I do, and if I were his mother, I would be doing everything to find out what was happening.

"Z's not a bad kid," I say, knowing I just used the name Z, but my eyes are now firmly on Nix because he seems to be the only one concerned for his son. "But I am certain something is or has happened. Giving him detention every day for his behavior isn't going to stop him. He has proven that each time when he pushes further. I think if we can work together, then we can help him sort through this," I finish. Nix looks worried as he takes in my advice. Addison just looks bored.

"I don't believe my concerns are unwarranted," I add before Addison starts to whine again. "You know yourselves something is not right. At the very least, I would suggest talking to him, encouraging him to open up, but if that's something that you don't think he will talk to either of you about, then the school counselor is going to be your best outcome."

"Book it in," he agrees.

"Nix," Addison whines beside him.

"Shut it, Addison. I told you to talk to him last week. I've tried talkin' to him but he won't open up to me. Far as I know, it could be somethin' I'm doin'." He looks to me again. "Book it in."

I nod, agreeing with his decision.

"Nix, we can sort this out as a family."

"Family?" He looks to her like the idea of it offends him. "We stopped being a fuckin' family when you stopped caring."

"Nix."

"Save it, Addison. Let's go," he orders, rising from his chair.

She huffs out a breath standing, and then storms herself out of the room.

"Thanks' for lettin' us know. Appreciate it," Nix mutters, still not looking at me.

"No problem. I hope we can sort it out," I reply, still waiting for him to look at me. Now that his eyes have left mine, I feel a sense of loss. He nods and then, without a backward glance, he follows Addison out, leaving me alone.

Releasing a shaky breath, I lean forward over my desk and

try to get my racing heart under control. I congratulate myself on getting through my first encounter with him. Granted, he was pissed we didn't talk, but obviously something is going on with Z and that's our main concern right now. I just hope we can sort it out and get him to open up before his behavior escalates. I'm glad that I got through the meeting. I just pray next time I see him, he will be over his anger, and we can carry on as if nothing has happened. I hope I can say the same for myself. Falling for a sexy hot biker is one thing, a parent to one of my students is another.

5

Nix

WALKING BACK INTO HER CLASSROOM, I SLAM THE door shut. The loud bang vibrates the walls in the empty room. My anger is barely controllable. Between her and Addison, I need to calm myself, but I don't know how. Her head comes up fast from her paperwork, and confusion washes over her face.

"What?" she begins to say before I hold my hand up, cutting her off. I have no time for her fucking bullshit excuses. I've come back in order to say what I need to say.

"You got two options here, Kadence. Shut it and let me talk, or have me bend you over the table and spank your ass for the shit you pulled the other night." Her mouth closes fast, and my eyes are drawn to her throat, watching the movement of her swallowing. *Great, I have her fucking attention.*

Once I walked Addison out, I gave her another wake-up call: either start helping me parent our child or I take sole custody. She left in a huff, annoyed that I was siding with Kadence. It's not about taking sides. Something is going on with our son and I don't know how to get through to him. Kadence is right; we need to get a handle on this. I hung back trying to calm myself before getting on my bike pissed. Between the piss-poor excuse Addison just showed as a mother and the uneasiness I'm feeling knowing Z is dealing with some shit, there was no way I would have been able to ride. Something is going on with my boy and knowing that he won't talk to me guts me.

When I first got the notice that Kadence called a meeting, a small part of me thought that she was playing her games again, a test of some kind. That theory went out the window when I saw her sitting there, uncomfortable beyond anything, while at the same time trying not to respond to me. Waiting five minutes did nothing to calm me, so I decide I needed to confront her. I needed to know why she ran.

After checking the halls to make sure no one was hanging around, I discovered we were the last ones here for the day, making this the perfect time to have it out with her. Waking up alone in bed on Sunday, I was pissed, beyond pissed, and for the last five days, I've been stewing on it.

"What the fuck, Kadence?"

"What?" she stammers, and my hand comes up, silencing her again as I walk closer. She instantly quiets, and I can't hide my smile at the way she responds to my demands. Her eyes narrow at my smugness, but I don't give her chance to throw attitude. I'm already on the edge; her smartass mouth might just push me over.

"Push it, cause I'm itching to spank your ass, woman," I say, hoping that's how we will end here tonight. "Why'd you leave?" I ask the question that's been going around my head all week. She looks at me not saying anything, the silence deafening in the small room. "Are you going to answer me?" I demand after a moment of her just watching me.

"Oh, I can talk now, can I?" she retorts, folding her arms over her chest.

Running my hands over my face, I let out a frustrated sigh. "Fuck me. You always this difficult?"

"Only when men think they can boss me around," she responds, rising from her chair. "Go home, Nix. We're done. We agreed to one night. No need to get worked up about it," she says, walking around to the front of her desk. She's wearing another one of those fucking tight skirts again, and it just pisses me off more.

"Bullshit. You and I were both there that night. Don't act like you didn't feel it," I say, revealing more than I wanted.

She had snuck out sometime in the early morning and I didn't even notice. Sure, we agreed it was a one-night thing, but it still pissed me off that she didn't say goodbye, or didn't give me a chance to let her know I wanted to see her again. If I'm being honest, it was more than that. I thought we had made a connection. Yeah, she was my kid's teacher, but it's not like we couldn't work past that. The night turned from intense sex to something more, something I wanted to explore. Fuck, I sound like I grew a pussy overnight. I never acted like this. Fuck knows why I'm starting now.

"Phoenix, I had a great night, but this thing between us,"

she motions her hand in front of her, "it won't work." I move closer, now standing in front of her.

"Bullshit, Kadence," I argue. "You and I both know that's not true. The three times I had you proved that we would work." A slight blush strokes her cheek.

"Just because we had good sex doesn't mean anything, Nix," she fights back, thinking that's all this was. Fuck no.

"It was more than good sex, Kadence. It was fuckin' phenomenal. You know it. I know it." She rolls her eyes, but not before I get a glimpse of her agreement.

"Turn around and put your hands on the desk," I demand, wanting to remind her just how good it was. My control slips each time she informs me we won't work. I'll fucking show her just how much we work.

"No," she fires back, but I can see the fight in her body.

Leaning in closer, I reach out and grab her from behind the neck. Her body shivers at the contact and I smirk knowing how much I affect her.

"Turn around and put your hands on the goddamn desk," I grit out the demand again, knowing that she's fighting an internal battle. She holds her ground, not giving in. I'm not surprised though; she's more bullheaded than me.

"Come on, Miss Turner. Let me soothe that ache I know you got buildin'," I murmur into her ear. I don't miss the tremor that runs through her body, before she slowly turns, bends forward and places both hands on the desk. Fuck, yes. Her submission stirs my cock to life.

"Shit," she hisses, like her body didn't listen to her. "We could get caught," she says, shaking her head at what she's doing.

"We're here alone and I locked the door," I tell her as my

hand goes to her skirt. Lifting the material, I nearly blow my load seeing the sexy as fuck getup she's got going on underneath.

"Oh, baby, you wear this for me?" My finger trails the lace of the top of her stockings. The white lace thong she's wearing shows off the globes of her cheeks. Slapping my hand down on her skin, she lets out a deep groan at my contact. "Fuck, you like that?" I smile, leaning into her. It was one thing we didn't do the other night. One thing I'm going to rectify right now.

She doesn't answer me, so I pull back, bringing my hand down again harder. She cries out as I rub the red area. "Answer me, Kadence. You like bein' spanked?" I bite out as I run my finger along the seam of her thong. I can feel her heat over the lace, and I order my body to take it slow before I rip the offending item off and bury myself home.

"Yes," she cries, no shame in her admission.

"Good girl. Now tell me, did you wear this sexy outfit for someone else?" I ask again, bringing my hand down on her ass, hoping she doesn't say yes.

"No." She gasps as I press my body against hers, my hard cock letting her know what she does to it.

"Then who did you wear it for?" I question, pulling back and running my finger down her crack.

"Me," she replies, but I don't believe her. We both know she wore this for me; probably took her time finding something to tease me with.

Hooking my finger under the string, I pull back the elastic and slide my pointer down her bare center.

"Are you soakin' for me, Kadence?" I already know the answer when my fingers find her arousal.

"God, yes," she squeaks as my finger enters her in one forceful movement. Her wetness makes it a smooth entry, and I pull out, adding a second finger. Her hips jerk forward as I begin pumping her harder. Fuck, she is responsive; even the other night she caved to my every command. She might have fought me, but when push came to shove, she fucking caved.

"You like my cock the other night?" My fingers fuck her harder after every question.

"Yes, God, yes," she pants out, riding my fingers.

"You want my cock now, Kadence?" I ask, feeling her tighten around my fingers. Yeah, she wants my cock, fucking greedy pussy.

"Yes, fuck me, Nix." Her voice takes on a new tone as I build her up to the brink

"You sure you want my cock?" I ask as my thumb finds her clit.

"Yes!"

"Keep your hands on the desk and don't let go, okay?" I say, stepping back from her. My cock is straining in my jeans, and I'm sure she's gonna fucking hate me for it but I have to do it. I have to fucking teach her a lesson.

"Sorry, babe, I gotta go," I say, watching her head come up, turning to look over her shoulder.

"Don't fuck with me, Nix," she sneers, standing and turning to face me. Her eyes are inflamed with passion. Her hair's slightly tussled in her pony. Her skirt's hiked up, exposing her pussy, and the lace tops of her stockings are making my dick twitch harder, yelling out to not be an asshole and bury myself in her.

I lick my fingers clean, rolling my eyes at her sweet taste, I'm a fucking idiot; her taste has me questioning my sanity.

"Why did you leave?" I ask one last time, her eyes watching my fingers. I need to know I'm not the only one feeling like it was a little more. She has to feel it too.

"Phoenix, get out," she fumes, pulling her skirt down, pissed I played her. As much as I want to argue with her, demand that she tells me why, then make her beg me to fuck her, I don't. I'm already on edge and probably shouldn't have come back in, but seeing her again stirred the want in me and I knew I couldn't fight it. I watch her, wondering if I have lost my fucking mind. *Was I the only one to feel it?* She takes a shaky breath, her eyes ablaze with irritation, but I see the need in them. I know she's lying, but what can I do?

Her eyebrows rise, waiting for what I don't know. For me to argue some more? I don't. Tonight has pushed me too far. Instead, I turn and walk out of her classroom. I'm pissed that she's just too damn stubborn, and hope like fuck next time I see her, she has her head out of her ass and is ready to admit the truth: that I'm not the only one feeling this fucking connection.

9

Kadence

I WAKE TO THE SOUND OF HOLLY BANGING AROUND IN the kitchen. Fuck, kill me now; the woman wouldn't know a sleep in if it hit her in the face.

It's Saturday morning. Ten days since Nix spanked me and then left me laid bare on my desk, begging him to fuck me.

I have no idea what I was thinking letting him get to me.

Since our classroom meeting last week, I haven't seen or heard from him. It's not like I'd try to contact him. Sleeping with him the first time was a mistake. Bending over while he finger fucked me, well, that was something else. It's like I can't control the effect he has on me. Getting in my space and demanding to take me on my school desk was one of the hottest things I have ever done. Leaving me standing there horny and pissed off was not. The anger that flowed through me after realizing he played me has kept me grounded in my belief that I can't stand the man, and I'm more of an idiot for thinking it would be an easy one-night deal.

Groaning into my pillow, I force myself not to think about the asshole today, just like every other morning this last week, but every goddamn day, I fail miserably.

My door suddenly swings open, connecting with the wall behind.

"You still sulking over your sexy biker daddy?" Holly walks in, throwing herself right onto my king-size bed.

"No," I lie a little too quickly, moving over to let her lay down.

"I call bullshit."

"You can call it whatever you want. Like I've told you every time you asked, it was a mistake."

Holly pounced on me the moment I walked through the door Sunday morning. After giving her all the details, she then continued to pick apart everything that we did and chewed me out for leaving him. I promised I would think about calling him, but I was more concerned how she dealt with Ben after he ditched us at the bar. I knew she was going to dump his ass for leaving us. I felt a little bad that it was because of what Nix did but she didn't seem to mind, claiming he was lousy in bed anyway.

I've kept my sulking on the down low or at least in the confines of my room, but you don't get too much past Holly. I'm glad I managed to keep my second mistake with him from her. I already feel like a royal idiot. I don't need anyone else knowing. Besides, she will probably encourage me to see him again, even going as far as inviting him over for a home-cooked meal, and that's the last thing I ever want.

Lies. Yep, I've turned into the biggest liar.

If he walked in right now, I'd probably let him have his way, probably wouldn't even care if Holly watched.

Getting to know him the other night, I realize I was such a judgmental bitch. He's got great things going on with the club, a successful business owner, and he's a great dad, not to mention he's amazing in bed. His reaction to me leaving shouldn't have surprised me. I knew it was coming, could see it in his stare. The air of electricity around him while I sat there had me on alert. I wasn't expecting the disappointment in his eyes when he asked me for the truth and I lied. But Z is my student, and I should have never crossed that line. *I can't believe I let him get to me; I caved so easily.*

Holly watches me carefully, but doesn't say anything else; she simply shakes her head.

"So what're your plans for the weekend?" She changes the subject, knowing she won't get anything out of me. I sit up, reaching for my Kindle laying next to my bed.

"The second book in the erotic series I've been reading went live this week. I'm planning to stay in and read." I smile, excited for the kinky fuckery coming my way. I look up and watch Holly fake yawn.

"Blah, jeez, Kadence, you can't get more cliché. Hot teacher spends her weekends reading sexy erotic novels." She laughs and I throw my pillow at her head.

"Shut up, Holly. I read for educational purposes too," I argue.

"Oh, yeah? Like how to hit your G-spot? I have no idea how you read them. Seriously I can't get past how the guy will blow his load into the woman bare, and she gets up and walks a fucking mile without that shit falling out." She rolls her eyes. "Seriously, Kadence, it's bullshit. Some dude with super sperm blows his load in me, that shit is still coming out hours later." She laughs, shaking her head. "Lies, it's all lies, Kadence," she yells passionately, before rising from my bed. I roll my eyes at her dramatics but can't argue with her.

"Breakfast is almost ready," she sings, exiting my room. "We have big plans today," she yells out as she makes her way back down the hall. Yeah right, the only plans I have are with my trusty Kindle.

Ignoring her is always the best route. Instead of biting, I make my way down to our shared bathroom. I use the toilet first, and then brush my teeth.

When I first moved in with Holly, she was living uptown with her older brother Sam. In the beginning, it was temporary. I had just lost my house, and it was going to take time to get me back on my feet. We soon realized my life was going to take a while to get on track. The surgeries, the money, it was all adding up. As much as I love my mom and dad, I didn't want to live with my parents outside of town, so Holly decided we needed our own place, like back in college. We moved out, got a place closer to town, and also closer to work, and I focused on moving past the shit Zane had done.

At the time, I had no interest in going back to work. My life was falling apart around me; half my house burnt to the ground; my safety was in jeopardy and my body was fighting to heal. I didn't know who to trust. My fiancé had cleaned out my savings; a group of very dangerous men were after him, and he simply left me to pick up the pieces. It took time, but eventually, I came out on the other side stronger for it.

Finished with my morning routine, I walk down the short hall to the kitchen ready to argue with Holly about our so-called plans. Our unit is small but still has a kick ass kitchen with state of the art appliances, open plan living and an amazing view. Furthermore, living on the third level in the building makes us a little safer than the lower levels; something I was adamant about when looking for a place. I needed to feel safe, knowing that people can easily tear down your defenses.

Holly is frying bacon at the stove as I make my way straight to the coffee machine.

"So tonight I'm heading into the new club Liquid that just opened," she mentions as I pour cream into my coffee.

"Mmmhh," I say, turning to face her, looking over the rim of my cup. I know what she is about to say next. It's the same thing she asks every Saturday morning.

"Wanna come?"

"No."

"Wow."

"What?'

"I wasn't expecting that answer."

I roll my eyes and tell her, "You know it's not my thing."

"Kadence, nothing is your thing," she points out. I know she's right, but hey, I'm a hard one to please.

"Just come for a few hours, a few drinks. Then we can go home and you can spend the rest of your night with your book boyfriends."

I don't know why I agree but I do, and then I regret it the moment she starts planning the rest of our day with shopping and lunch. As much as the thought of walking around all day shopping for a new outfit sends me into an instant headache, I could go for a new pair of heels. Oh fuck it, I need to get out of the house and stop thinking about Nix.

"Oh, and I booked you an appointment at the salon. I'm thinking a new do for you," Holly calls out as I walk out of the kitchen. I groan at Holly's idea for a new do.

Once we finished college, Holly decided to put her degree in child psychology to good use and become a hairdresser. I don't even know what happened. One day she came home and told me she was going to cut hair, and she did. She's always on me about changing my style. I'm not sure how I've managed to do it, but I've seemed to keep her at bay with chopping my locks off. Color? Well, that's another story. I like the way my hair is at the moment, but a change might be nice. I wonder what Nix would say if I changed it? *Who the fuck cares what he would say, Kadence.*

Heading back down the hall, I again remind myself that I need to get my head on straight. I can't let him get to me anymore. I need to keep our relationship completely professional and not bend over at his every request, *especially over my desk*. Thinking about him as more than a parent has got to stop; in fact, thinking about him altogether needs to end. Turning the shower on, I realize that the task is going to be one hell of a mission. Nix Knight has a way of staying with you.

TEN DAYS.

Ten motherfucking days since I've seen Kadence. Ten days since I had my fingers inside of her, my hand coming down hard on her ass, and I still can't stop thinking about her.

Fuck.

Fuck.

Fuck.

I don't date; sure as fuck don't go back for seconds, but something about the sexy, dirty-talking teacher has me wanting to break all my rules. After seeing her again in the classroom, I didn't want to leave but I had to come up with something to get the stubborn teacher to open up to me more. A lot of fucking help that did. I can't believe I walked away from her bending over waiting for my cock.

Pulling up into the forecourt of the Knights' compound, I cut the bike's engine and watch Jesse walk out with the blonde from last night. The boys partied late, like they do most Friday nights; however, after the week I've had with thoughts of Kadence, I went home early, my head too far gone thinking of that damn woman.

Jesse bends down, kisses the blonde and smacks her on the ass as she walks to her car. Looking over at me, he throws up ten fingers, nodding his head up and down, impressed with his night. I just flip him the finger, letting him know I'm not interested. The man is a whore, fucking them and leaving them. *Shit, that's me in a nutshell. Or was me.*

Making my way inside the clubhouse, I nod to some of the boys hanging around playing the tables. We have several of the boys live here full time, taking residence in the apartments out the back. They are the ones who don't have a home outside of the club, but on weekends, we have a full house from Friday afternoon till Sunday night.

I'll stay a couple of times a week. I have my room in the main clubhouse, which makes it easier when I don't have Z, but I like to go home to my own bed when he's staying with me. We run a clean club but sometimes it can get wild, something that a pre-teen shouldn't be seeing. Walking up to the bar, I signal our latest prospect Hunter, to grab me a beer. We're not a strict club with prospects, but with our history, we like to keep the club on low numbers. Hunter is Brooks' old lady's nephew. So far, the boy is doing good and looks set to patch in a few weeks from now.

Cheers sound around the large open area in the clubhouse

as Jesse walks in after me.

"What's that about?" I ask Brooks, sitting down next to him.

"Apparently, Jesse had a screamer last night," he replies shaking his head. I grin, thinking only Jesse would be gloating about a screamer.

Thoughts of Kadence come creeping in and the many times I made her scream. The woman is a knockout in bed. Shit, the stories I could share. The woman goes off like a rocket and is so damn responsive. I keep my mouth shut, not even sure I'm gonna see her again after the way I left her, but I fucking know I don't want anyone to know how amazing she is.

After Addison, I lived it up, banging anything and everything, not the slight bit interested in settling down. The last eight years I've lived the bachelor life, loving it even, but one night with Kadence has me questioning it all. I need to keep repeating to myself that one night doesn't equal a relationship, and relationship? *What the fuck.*

Beau pulls up a stool beside Brooks. "Hey, man, we might have an issue," he reports quietly. Looking over at my VP and best friend, I take in his concerned face.

"What's up?" I question, hoping this weekend isn't gonna cause me problems. Z's with his mom for the weekend and I was looking forward to a few stress-free nights. After our meeting with Kadence, things have been tense, and I'm starting to get concerned. Kadence is right. My boy is holding on to some serious anger, and no matter what, I can't get him to open up to me.

"Sy ran into some problems last night closing up Ink Me."

Sylas is the newest brother, who earned his cut, and an old

friend. He's the quiet fucker of the bunch and rounds out the main group of brothers who handle the business side of things. I've known Sy since I was a kid, but he pissed off when school finished. No one knew where he went and we still don't. His pops was a brother alongside my dad, one of the originals. When he got sick three years back, Sylas came home to look after him and never left. After hanging around, seeing the way the club now ran, he wanted in. It didn't take long for the boys to decide he would fit in.

"What happened?" I ask, wondering what sort of problems the new ink shop's gonna bring me. I wasn't too keen on the shop, adding another business means more work, especially one I knew nothing about, but we soon learnt Sy apprenticed in tattooing and piercing while he was away. He manages the store and works the needle most days.

"Says there's been some of Kings' men hanging around at the front of the store last few nights. Then last night, there were some of Gunners' men."

Our county has been home to two motorcycle clubs over the last thirty years. My old man ran this town the way he wanted back then, not afraid to get bloody, which caused most of the problems for the Knights Rebels Originals. Back when Pops started getting into the guns trade, he moved in on the Warriors of Mayhem territory, causing a conflict between the clubs. For years it ran deep, causing a lot of blood loss between them, only ending after we got our revenge for my mom.

The Mayhems were the bigger club, but the Knights still put up a fight, until my pops and the Mayhems' Prez, came to an agreement; we held to our own town, dealing in whores and some small drug running gigs, while their club would deal the weapons and run the rest of the county. It wasn't until years later when and I was voted in, that I could begin to fade out the drugs and women. We've managed to keep to our business, living legit, and they've kept to theirs. As long as drugs don't hit Rushford streets, we keep our distance, and they keep theirs.

"Why the fuck are the Mayhems in town?" Brooks asks, knowing this could spell trouble.

"Rumor has it, their club's been having some problems within their own members. A change within ranks has stirred up some bad shit, plus Gunner Jamieson, is setting up on their territory," Beau speaks up, filling me in on the bullshit that comes with the territory.

"Set up a meeting with T," I say, wondering how the old VP, now Prez, will respond. T never did like the truce between the two clubs, thinking it would be bad for business on both sides, but when we went clean, it opened them up to more business, so I guess it worked out for everyone.

For five years now we've kept the truce. While I wouldn't put it past him to drag up some bullshit, my guess would be on Gunner Jamieson. The bastard has been inching closer and closer the last few months and gathering momentum. Transporting and distributing methamphetamine, cornering the market, we gave up. We've kept an eye on it, but it might be time to take the next step, secure what's ours and make sure the Warriors of Mayhem are with us. As the saying goes, an enemy of an enemy makes you a friend. We might not be on the illegal side of things, but when you push, we will push back. My pops earned our club's position here, and respect comes with that.

Beau nods his head and takes off to take care of setting up

a meeting. Turning around, I look out of the clubhouse and start to feel restless. I need to get my head straight. Pushing off the bar, I make my way to my office; getting my head stuck into some paperwork instead of the feisty woman might help.

Six hours later and I'm done with the day. If it weren't drug gangs creeping into our territory, it was drama after fucking drama. Fuckups after fuckups. The new club we refurbished and opened last month, Liquid, has been taking all the brothers time. It's not my fucking scene, but the money it's pulled us has been worth the chaos.

Now with the new ink shop, I'm beginning to wonder if we're stretching ourselves thin. Running my hands over my face, I decide to call it a night. Closing up my office, I go downstairs to the club bar ready to knock back a few and maybe get my dick wet. I've decided I'm gonna try to fuck Kadence out of mind. I've been fighting it for too long. Unless I tie her down to get her to admit she wants me, there's no way I'm gonna get through to her. Sliding up to the old oak bar, I call out for a beer and search out the talent for the night.

"Hey, Nix," Christina, one of the club whores, says coming up to the bar five minutes later. I don't normally like to touch the free-for-alls. Some can get a little crazy and no one needs crazy constantly following you around. After Addison, I'm not interested in crazy. After Kadence, I'm fucked up, so who knows what I want.

"Hey, Chrissie," I say, giving her one of my come-and-ride-my-cock smiles. Fuck it, tonight I need easy, and she's the one standing in front of me. She looks up, searching for my approval. Leaning in, I hook my hand around her neck and pull her sticky pink lips to mine. My dick stirs, but not enough for me to stay interested. *Well, that's a fucking first.*

Shit, the teacher has ruined me.

Deepening the kiss, I'm silently pleased to hear my cell sound in my back pocket. Pulling back, I turn, dismissing Christina to answer the call.

"Yo," I say, signaling Hunter for another drink.

"Prez" Sy's voice rings down the phone.

"What's up?"

"You might wanna get down to Ink Me. That piece of tail who's got you in that mood just walked in." He hangs up before I answer.

Shaking my head at his jab, I put my phone in my back pocket. The boys have been giving me shit all week about my bad mood. Those fuckers have got no idea. After taking a sip of my new beer, I walk out to my bike, ready to come face to face with a teacher who's been on my mind for the last few weeks. I know this is a sign I need to prove that the woman is meant to be in my life. I'm hoping the lesson I taught her last week has gotten through, and she's willing to give us a go. 'Cause there is no fuckin' way I'm taking no for an answer this time.

11

Kadence

"I CAN'T BELIEVE I'M ABOUT TO DO THIS," I BREATHE
out. A swarm of butterflies fill my stomach at the anticipation
of it.

"Have you picked yet?" Holly comes up beside me, leaning
over and looking into the glass cabinet.

"Yeah, I'm going to go with a plain gold one," I say,
pointing to the eighteen-karat-gold belly ring I'm about to
have pierced through my skin.

"Great," the scary-looking guy who's standing in front of
me mutters in a not too impressed voice. His dark hair is
shaved short, and what I can see of his body is covered in
tattoos. He looks familiar, but I can't remember where I've

met him before.

"Geez, what a ball of fucking sunshine," Holly snaps, leaning into my ear.

"Shhh," I tell her, hoping scary-tattoo guy didn't hear. Too late, the scowl he has been rocking deepens, if that's even possible. She's right. I have to wonder who stole his candy? Holly just shrugs and I roll my eyes at the crazy bitch. She started giving him lip the moment we walked through the doors.

Don't ask me how I ended up here. We began the day at the mall. Holly found me the hottest outfit, then ten more that I didn't need, and let's not forget the couple of pairs of shoes. Shopping with that woman is an art, and one I still can't perfect.

We spent the rest of the afternoon getting pampered. Holly and I fought over my hair. She thought it would be a great idea for something short and funky. I flat out refused, only allowing a few low lights and a slight trim. I decided I love my dark locks, and no one will ever convince me on the big chop. I was ready to collapse by the end of the day, but I couldn't let Holly down. When we finished dinner at our favorite Thai restaurant, we went straight to check out the club Holly has been going on about for weeks. After waiting in line for over forty minutes, we were finally granted access behind the red rope that separated us. Liquid re-opened its doors over a month ago. Whoever took over the old club refurbished and upped the cover charge. We had to push our way through the busy crowd to the long, lit-up bar. With the music blaring with all the latest tracks, I could barely hear myself think. The balcony upstairs had booths that were cut off for VIP. Downstairs, there were lounges sectioned off for a private party. The scene was totally Holly. I much prefer a bar atmosphere, but being the good friend I am, I sucked it up.

Halfway through the night I could have sworn I saw my ex-fiancé Zane hanging back in the corner near the bar, but I brushed it off as a coincidence. I wasn't prepared to let my mind wander off to what I would say or how I would react if I came face to face with the asshole again.

As the night wore on, and the alcohol wore off, the more I began to think what if it was him? I contemplated why he would be back. He left town in a hurry after the fire. Zane never came to bed that night, leaving me alone in the house. The police found him sleeping off his hangover at his brother's house. He wasn't at all concerned about the fire destroying our home or even me in surgery. He told the police that we had a fight and that we were over.

I was destroyed.

By the time I was paid a visit by one of the members of the Warriors of Mayhem MC, letting me know that Zane owed them some serious money, he had cleaned out my bank account and left town. For a long time, I thought he would come back or eventually feel safe enough to get a message to me, but three years later, I've still not heard anything.

After a few or more cocktails, some dancing and continually brushing off guys who wouldn't take the hint, I was restless to go home for the night. Convincing Holly was another story. She had met up with some guy she hadn't seen for months and begged me to hang around with her for a little while longer. I finally persuaded her to leave, letting her know I was walking home with or without her. She agreed to come, not at all okay with me walking on my own. She exchanged numbers with the guy and left on a high. I, however, was sober and ready for bed.

Walking the several blocks to our home, we passed the front of Ink Me, one of the few tattoo and piercing shops in town. Holly got an ingenious idea to get a tattoo, and after looking in and seeing the hot tattoo artist, she decided it was the perfect time. Fortunately, the cranky tattoo artist denied her request, telling her she was too drunk to get the ink, so now she is sporting a new belly ring. How I ended up choosing a ring and agreeing to have it pushed through my skin, I'm still not sure.

Before the fire, back in my college days, I used to have my belly pierced, but with the surgeries and prolonged recovery, it closed over. I never thought at twenty-nine I would be re-piercing it but the idea that I can take back my body after letting it control who I've become has me wanting to reclaim that confidence.

My night with Nix reminded me about living in the moment. After the fire, hell, even before the fire with asshole Zane, I found myself lost, shying away from taking risks and letting go. Sure, I'm still quick to snap back and I can hold my own in a confrontation. I'm strong and resilient, but letting go, letting people in to see that hurt, has been the hardest.

Nix gave me permission to relax, made me feel alive again. Even if sleeping with him was a bad idea, I'm glad that I could open up to someone. It was pretty deep for one night with a guy, sure, but one night with Nix was more than just amazing sex. I was fooling myself thinking it wouldn't mean anything. Seeing his response to my scar, I knew I was in trouble and now, after our moment on the desk, him calling me out on my indifference, I have no idea where my head is at.

I opened up to him more than anyone in the last three years. He didn't judge me but made me feel adequate in my own scarred skin. No one has managed to push past my insecurities but him. No one else has looked at me, seen past the repulsive skin and instead of showing me pity, made me feel beautiful. I've tried to discount our one night together, but no matter how hard I fight it, he's inspired this awareness in me, something that I lost long ago and I can't let that go.

The scary tattoo guy clears his throat, obviously pissed off he now has to deal with another girly request.

"I'll take that one, thanks." I smile up at him while pointing to the chosen ring. He gives me a form without a sound, and I move to the chair to fill it out. Holly hangs back and tries to engage with the man who isn't big on small talk. He is a real ball of laughs, that's for sure, but something in his expression, the way his eyes follow Holly, taking her in and silently looking pissed off about it, makes me wonder if my crazy friend might be hitting a nerve.

Standing back up, I hand my form back over as the bell above the door signals another customer. Cranky tattoo guy nods his head and I casually look back at the person behind me.

"Where the fuck are the rest of your clothes?" Nix barks out behind me. My head gets lost in the question, my body grounded in his presence. I hear Holly giggle to the side but I don't have a second to react before he inquires again, "Kadence, where the fuck are the rest of your clothes?" The greens of his eyes shine dangerously, letting me know he's pissed.

Shit, not again.

My body comes back to life, my mind back into focus. Oh,

God, just seeing him again makes me want him. I don't know if I'm strong enough to resist this pull. Images of him leaving me spread out on my school desk flash before my eyes and I remember what a douche bag he can be.

"Hello, Phoenix, nice to see you again," I greet him, willing my raging heart to calm. How the hell does this man manage to affect me like this?

"Cut the bullshit, Kadence. Your little prim and proper act is getting old." My eyes narrow to his, and he smirks like he has me all figured out.

"What do you want, Nix?" I give up my indifference. The bastard can see right through it.

"I wanna know where the fuck you have been wearing that." He points down to my outfit. "Why you're in my shop, pissin' Sy off in the process, and I wanna know why the fuck you ran the other night?" His last question is directed with more authority.

Holly lets out a sigh and then announces to no one in particular, "That was so hot."

Sy, aka scary tattoo guy, scoffs while I'm left processing his words.

Looking down at my skirt and black top that exposes a small amount of skin, I address his first question.

"What are you talking about? I've got clothes on." He leans into my space and runs a finger down the exposed skin between my breasts,

"Babe, you're coverin' less skin than you're showin'." I roll my eyes at his Neanderthal views.

"Shut up, Nix. Her outfit is smoking hot. Don't be a pig," Holly comes to stand at my side, saying the words on the tip of my tongue.

"I know it's fuckin' hot," he agrees with her. "So does every other fucker who's seen her wear it tonight."

I scoff, not about to get into it with him over his caveman views, or the fact he can get fucked; what's it to him? He doesn't own me.

"I didn't know this was your shop," I say truthfully, addressing his second question. Maybe that's why cranky tattoo guy looks familiar. Was he at the bar that night? I don't remember. Pushing away the feeling that I know him from somewhere else, I think back to when he talked about his businesses. I don't think we discussed the tattoo shop in detail. If we did, I was probably thinking of Nix and what we were going to be doing later that night.

"And," I continue, "Sy here," I point to scary but still hot tattoo guy, "was already in a pissed-off mood before we got here. I'd like to think that two young, *single* women coming in would brighten his night. Clearly, that's not the case."

Nix smiles and his dimple appears, the same one I found handsome on our one-time date last week. *Shit, don't get caught up in his alluring looks, Kadence.*

"And the last?" he pushes, so intent for me to admit what he already knows. I let out a breath, knowing he isn't going to let it go.

"Like we said, our one-time deal turned into a three-time deal." I shrug, not wanting to get into with him, especially in front of Holly.

Sy, or cranky biker as I could refer to him, clears his throat, "Hate to break up the love fest, but are we piercing that belly or not?" His voice sounds pissed off, but I can hear a hint of teasing.

"Yes." "No," Nix and I both say at the same time.

"Nix, just because you've had your mouth on my pussy doesn't mean you own it," I blurt out and instantly regret it.

Jesus, the man makes me crazy and now makes me blurt out inappropriate things.

He smiles again as Sy grumbles and Holly laughs. Turning back around, I tell Sy, 'Yes' and watch as he looks past me to Nix. Rolling my eyes, he looks back to me and nods, obviously getting approval. Spinning back to face my new apparent keeper, I put on my sweet voice. "Oh, thank you so much, Daddy, for letting me get it done. I'll promise I'll be a good girl." Nix and Holly laugh out loud and as I turn I see Sy's lip slightly lifted in amusement. *Ha! I knew he wasn't so badass.*

Nix leans into my ear. "You can thank me later, babe, when I'm spankin' your ass, and then you can call me daddy all you like." Heat floods my cheeks; a dull throb makes me squeeze my thighs together. He quietly chuckles when he notices it. *The bastard.*

"Right, come on," Sy grunts and I walk past Holly to make my way back to the piercing room. Holly hangs back but Nix follows close behind.

Stopping in my tracks, I look back at him. "What are you doing?" I ask.

"Comin' with," he replies, like he just told me he'll walk me to my car.

"Umm, no," I say, shaking my head.

"Umm, yes," he imitates me back, and I bite my lip to hold in a laugh at watching him do that. He looks down at my lips and shakes his head.

"Babe, I'm not real comfortable with you lyin' on the bed in that mini skirt, your top hiked up with Sy's hands on you."

"Wow, jealous much? Last time I checked, it wasn't your concern, Nix," I inform him but he just shakes his head.

"You have no fuckin' idea," he mumbles under his breath.

Not inclined to argue anymore, I continue down the hall, Nix close behind. First things first, I need to get this over with and then I can think about what I'm going to do with one possessive bossy man I seem to have on my hands.

12

Nix

I NEED TO GET A GRIP. FAST.

Walking in and seeing Kadence with her long fucking legs in her sexy-as-fuck heels, I had to take a minute to compose myself. The woman is a walking wet dream. Her blonde friend saw me first. I gave her a wink, and brought my finger to my mouth, motioning her to be quiet. She nodded and didn't give me up. I think I have a supporter in her.

Once again, Kadence and her smart mouth made my dick hard and my head hurt all in the space of sixty seconds. The woman would fight with me over the color of a red pen, but boy, do I fucking love it. Her throwing her attitude and being sexy as fuck while doing it is more than I can ask.

Two minutes in her presence and I knew I had to have her again. I don't think it will take too much to convince her. After watching Sy put his gloved hands on her, I need to find some release. I sat there grinding my teeth as his fingers touched her skin.

I'm pussy-whipped. I know it. I shot daggers the whole time at Sy, and the bastard fucking kept pushing me. With her top pushed up, he took great pleasure in trying to get a reaction from me.

The fucker will pay later.

His eyes skimmed over her scarred side, his hand a little too close for comfort. For reasons I don't even know, it made me feel protective of her. I don't know the story behind it, but I will find out soon enough. I kept waiting for the asshole to say something so I could rip him a new one. Kadence somehow sensed my stress and reached out, taking my hand in hers. Sy's eyes came to mine, a silent question, but I just shook my head in warning to leave it. I don't know what I'm going do with this woman, but whatever it is, I'm sure as hell going to enjoy finding out.

Kadence now sits behind me, her pussy pressed up against my back, her arms tightly around me. Sy took Holly home after I realized the girls planned on walking home. I was not fucking down with that idea and told them both just that. It took a bit of convincing, but after Holly had declared she couldn't wait to ride on the back of Sy's bike, Kadence had no choice.

After throwing a little of the Kadence attitude I've come to appreciate, I told her she would end up like she did the other night on her school desk. She quickly shut up and agreed to ride with me. Holly demanded to know why the hell she didn't know anything about a school desk, which earned me some more daggers from Kadence. Sy, on the other hand, didn't seem too impressed. Don't know why; Holly seems to be into him and she isn't sore on the eyes, that's for sure.

Pulling up to the front of my house, I shut off my bike. The ride was uncomfortable after I got a glimpse of Kadence's lace covered pussy as she climbed on the back. I've been riding with a semi hard-on for the last ten minutes. Kadence sighs and I feel a sense of gratification that she enjoys riding on the back of my Harley.

Getting off my bike, and before helping her off, I move in and crash my greedy mouth to hers. She melts into it as I push past her lips, her taste like a drug that I seem to crave after each hit. Pulling back, I help her off and take the helmet from her head. Snatching her hand, I drag her behind me, in a hurry to fuck her again.

"Let's go inside," I say, walking up to the front porch. Unlocking the door, I push her through, impatient to claim her. Slamming the door shut behind me, I spin her to the wall next to us and crash my mouth to hers, my tongue desperate for contact. Her hands come to my belt, just as wild as I am.

My cell rings in my back pocket and I ignore it, hungry for her touch. Pulling my jeans down, she laughs when she sees I'm not wearing any underwear.

"Laughin' at my cock won't make it happy," I warn.

"You want me to kiss it better?" she asks in her husky voice. Her hand wraps around my hard cock, stroking me in her tight grip. My cell sounds again from the floor as she drops to her knees. Fuck.

Trying to block out the ringing phone, I hold my breath as I watch her pink tongue come out. She licks the drop of pre-cum collected at the bulging head of my cock. *Jesus, that's fucking hot.*

My cell rings again and I ache at the thought that I might have to end this.

"Fuck, babe, as much as I want that hot little mouth around my dick, I need to get this. It must be urgent if they keep ringing." *Fucking better be or the assholes are gonna pay.*

Taking a step back, I watch as her face drops in annoyance. *Fuck, I'm with you there.*

Picking up my pants, I reach in my back pocket and grab the offending piece-of-shit phone, just as it rings again.

"What?" I snap into the phone. Holding my hand out for Kadence, I pull her up, bringing her to her feet.

"We got problems," Beau's tight voice reports.

"Talk to me."

"We got reports a Molotov went through Ink's shop window."

Kadence walks through the hall to the kitchen, and I follow.

"We only just came from there," I tell him. Thinking back to Kadence standing in the front of the shop only twenty minutes ago.

"Yeah, Sy dropped that woman home, and is on his way back now. Meet you there?"

"Yeah," I agree before hanging up.

Pissed that this has now ruined my chance of getting blown, I do my belt back up.

"I gotta go."

"That's okay. I'll just call a cab," she tells me, reaching for her purse.

"No, you won't," I immediately snap. I need to be careful with my words here, but at the same time, I'm not prepared to get into it about her running again. "You're gonna stay here and wait till I get back."

"Nix, it's fine."

"Jesus, woman, I gotta deal with club business. I'll be back once I sort it out. Will you just do as you're told for once?" I can feel myself starting to lose my temper as I watch her try to control hers.

"I'm capable of looking after myself," she bites back. If I wasn't worried about the shop, my dick would be coming to life at her firing up at me.

"I know you are, Kadence. It's not about that right now. I got shit I need to deal with. Just humor me, will you?" I ask her, not short of pleading. She looks at me quietly and must see I'm serious and not in the mood to get into it.

"What happened?"

"Fire at Ink Me."

"Fire?"

"Yeah, a Molotov cocktail through the window," I tell her and watch her pull in a sharp breath. Her face whitens, and I don't miss the small flash of panic that she quickly hides.

"What is it?" I ask her.

"Nothing, it's fine."

I know it's something but I don't have time to get into it with her right now. Pulling her to me, I ask her one more time.

"Just stay here and wait for me till I get back? We can finish what we started." Leaning down, I lightly brush my lips over hers. It's nowhere near enough, but I'll wait till later.

"Okay," she complies, and I feel better knowing she will

be here safe.

"All right, I'll call you when I'm on my way home. Give me your cell." Reaching into her purse, she pulls out her phone passing it to me. I program my number and call my cell so I have hers on mine. Angling my head to hers, I kiss her one more time, turn and walk to the door. "Make yourself at home, and don't answer the door for anyone," I call out, opening the door.

"Yes, Dad" she calls back and I look back at the little minx.

"Woman, I'll spank you for that."

"Can't wait," she replies and I reward her with a smile, letting her know I'll keep my promise.

Closing the door behind me and locking it, I head back to Ink Me, hoping the damage isn't too much to deal with because I have one hot and willing woman in my bed waiting for me.

13

Kadence

NIX HAS BEEN GONE FOR OVER AN HOUR AND I'M starting to fall asleep. After snooping around downstairs, I made my way upstairs to his room. Remembering his large tub from our night together, I decide to run a bath. Running the hot water, I find some bath oil, pour it in and submerge myself, contemplating what I was going to do with Nix. His showing up at the tattoo shop sent a spark through me. I wasn't sure after our last meeting how I would act, but ending up on the back of his bike to his bath was not on the list of logical outcomes. I know he wants more, more of what I'm not clear on, but I do know in the short time I've known the man, he won't give up. After reasoning with myself on my actions for twenty minutes in the hot water, I am no better off.

Stepping out onto the fluffy beige bath mat, I reach for a matching towel. For a man, he has impeccable taste. I cover my body in the soft towel. Its smell reminds me of his body, and I catch myself breathing in his rustic scent. God, he smells good.

After searching through his drawers for something to wear, I find one of his T-shirts. The black club shirt looks worn but calls to me, so I put it on over my black panties.

I don't know what I'm doing here. I'm supposed to be staying away but I'm obviously not doing well fighting off his advances. We both want each other, and we both can't seem to keep our hands off each other, but I can't help but wonder how much more he wants. I didn't realize how much his presence calmed me. Having him sit next to me while Sy could see some of my scars made it bearable. I could sense his irritation when Sy kept pushing him. I thought it was funny for a bit, but when his eyes went to my scar, and then straight to me, I knew Nix was about to lose his cool. He doesn't even know what happened, doesn't know how I got so badly burnt, but he is already defensive over me. Before he could say something to Sy and make me feel uncomfortable, I reached out, his eyes finding mine, a silent promise that he would protect me. I felt it from just his touch, knowing in that moment I didn't want to fight him anymore. This man has proven he will stop at nothing to get what he wants while sheltering me at the same time. Do I want to keep carrying on denying it? No. But the next steps are unknown for me. I can see myself getting lost in a man like him so I need to tread carefully. A man like Nix has proven he can give me what I've been missing, but I fear the moment he takes it away, I'll lose more than what I started with.

Turning his TV on, I climb into his bed, remembering the last time I was here. Visions of us lying naked, my head in his lap as he silently ran his calloused fingers along my skin, his mouth between my legs teasing me with his talented tongue while stretching me wide with his fingers, come easily. The scene leaves me hot just thinking about it. After leaving me wanting in the classroom, I refused myself any release. A punishment for allowing my body to react to him, but now, lying in his bed, the need coils through me, edging me closer to the height of urgency. My hand moves to the juncture of my thighs. I brush my fingers lightly over the lace of my panties, feeling the fever burn up in me. Just being in his bed has me craving him. Reaching for my phone, I send him a text.

> **KADENCE**: I'm in your bed, my hands were busy, but they took a minute to text you.

I second-guess myself as I await his reply. Shit, I hate feeling so insecure. It's alarming how much I want to expose to him.

I must have drifted off, as some time later, the sound of the front door closing wakes me. Keys being placed on the kitchen counter lets me know he's home. Throwing off the covers, I straighten his shirt, pat down my hair and make my way down the stairs to finish what we started earlier. Turning the corner at the bottom of the stairs, I see him leaning over, head deep in the fridge. His position gives me the perfect opportunity to check out his firm ass. The man has an amazing body. Sneaking up to him my arms coming around his waist, hands under his shirt, his tight abs contract under my fingers.

"Hey, honey, you told me you would call me," I say, pushing my front to his back before he suddenly comes back fast.

"Whoa," he shouts, spinning around and surprising me. His movements are so fast that my mind doesn't register that the voice isn't his. Looking up, I'm meeting a man who isn't Nix but is wearing the same cut. I let out a scream and back away.

"Hey, it's all right. Nix sent me," he quickly explains, trying to calm my frantic state. My mind slowly recognizes him as one of the men I saw with Nix the other night at the pub, his patch telling me I'm safe.

"He tried to call to let you know I was coming." He looks down at me before he turns away. "You wanna put on some pants?" he adds uncomfortably, and I look down and realize I'm only in my panties and a Knights Rebels shirt.

"Oh, shit," I burst out, pulling down Nix's shirt, trying to cover my exposed legs while backing away slowly. I know he's not looking at me like that, but his gaze turns back to me and is fixed on the scarring. Questions fill his eyes, but I'm not prepared to see the pity in them. Making my way upstairs, I find my skirt and throw it on, leaving Nix's shirt in place. I make my way back downstairs, grabbing my cell along the way. Looking down, I see a text message.

> **NIX:** Don't you dare fuckin' touch yourself! I'm sending one of the boys to get you. Now.

Shit, I mustn't have heard it go off.

"I'm Brooks," the man informs me when I walk back into the kitchen. "And if it's okay with you, can we keep that little greeting between us? My missus wouldn't appreciate the jabs the boys would throw. Though she might be more okay with it than Nix, I'd like to keep my balls," he admits laughing a little.

Oh, God, I would die if Nix found out about my slip up. I nod, thankful he won't go and tell the 'boys' about me rubbing up on him. I only know Jesse, and if they are anything like him, I won't hear the end of it.

"I'm Kadence by the way." I smile, and he smiles back. His dark hair is as short as Nix's, but now that I'm facing him, I realize he looks nothing like Nix. Where Nix is tall and built, Brooks is slightly shorter and a little broader. His short beard hides most of his face, but by his warm smile, I can see he's handsome. I find myself staring and shake myself out of it, already feeling awkward at my slip earlier.

"Where's Nix?" I grab a glass off the sink, filling it up with water from the fridge door.

"Club business," he states. I don't know what he expects me to do with that vague explanation.

"Should I go home?"

"No," he replies a little too fast. "I've been told to come and take you back to the clubhouse."

"But if Nix is busy working, shouldn't I just head home?"

"Just doing what the boss tells me," he says.

"What if I don't want to go?" I ask, putting my hands on my hips, ready to take him on.

"I'd prefer you came willingly, but I was warned you might say that." He smiles this time, knowing how much I must piss

Nix off. "If you don't come, I'll have to stay until Nix can get to you, and I really just wanna get back, sort out some shit and get home to the wife and kid."

As much as I don't want to go, I feel sorry he was sent to look after me, so I nod and go to get my purse.

"I don't know why Nix would send you to babysit me when you have a wife and daughter to worry about," I say, walking up to him ready to leave.

"That's the only reason he assigned me," Brooks mutters under his breath. I don't know what that means and I don't bother asking, probably some club rule. Locking up behind me, Brooks walks me down the path close to my back. Stopping short of the drive, I'm surprised he doesn't have a bike.

"No bike? What sort of MC are you a part of?" I ask playfully.

He lets out a laugh. "The bastard made me bring the truck."

Having been on his bike two times now and getting better, it clicks why Nix sent the car, not the bike. Damn possessive man.

The drive to the compound is short. Brooks talks about his wife and daughter and makes me feel comfortable. He's nothing like Nix with his bossy and alpha nature, but he still maintains a presence about him that you know you wouldn't want to mess with him.

My phone beeps and I grab it out of my bag to check the message.

Nix: Do as you're told.

I roll my eyes at his bossiness and type back my response.

KADENCE: HA. I was well behaved. Brooks is a gentleman. On our way.

NIX: Gentleman my ass. C U soon.

His response comes back instantly, and I place my cell back in my bag, excited and nervous to be heading inside the gated compound. Five minutes later, we pull up to a large property. A young guy walks out from the dark, unlocking and sliding the gate open, letting us drive through. The long, loose gravel drive winds around to the left and we follow it until we come to a large warehouse. Pulling up next to at least twenty bikes, I get out, ready to see Nix and the inside of his club.

Brooks meets me at my door; his hand comes to my wrist, gripping it in his large grasp.

"Keep close. We have some friends come to stay," he warns. I don't know what that means so I simply nod as he guides me to the front double doors. Two older men stand near the door, smoking cigarettes in the cool air. The red tips, glow bright against the black night, their expressions hidden behind their kick-ass beards. Their eyes assess me but nod at Brooks when we walk up to them, letting us pass without a word. Brooks pushes us through the doors into the dimly lit hall and walks us down to a large open area. The smell of leather and smoke fills my nose, and I look out around the large area. The long wall along the back holds pictures of members in their cuts, some mug shots, but more family shots. The Clubs insignia carved in a large wooden display sits in the center of the wall, Knights Rebels inscribed above the skull head. A few young men standing around the pool table look up as we pass through the open area.

"Is it always this quiet?" I ask as we walk down a hall.

"No, the party's been moved down the back. They got a bonfire set up," he explains.

Brooks' grip releases my wrist as we come to an open set of double doors at the back of the club. Stopping at the threshold, I see Nix before he sees me. I stand and take in all of him. His appearance is powerful, his character electrifying. The long solid timber masterpiece he sits at captures my attention. The same carved emblem that hangs out on the clubhouse wall is inscribed in the middle of the timber table.

"Prez," Brooks calls as he raps on the door. The three men sitting at the table turn and focus their attention on us. Jesse winks at me and Sy's eyes narrow. The third man with longer dark hair pulled back, is one of the guys at the bar the first night Nix kissed me. His blue eyes shine in laughter before letting it out in a loud bark. Feeling a little exposed, I second-guess the shirt. *Shit, was wearing it the wrong thing to do?*

Nix's eyes rake down my body, smiling when he notices the shirt I'm wearing. Standing from his seat at the head of the table and ignoring Brooks, he walks straight to me, pulling me into him. The heat from his body warms me before he pulls back. Angling his head down, he presses his lips to mine. It's a quick kiss, not demanding, but I still feel a light blush rise to my cheeks.

"Sorry, babe," he says close to my ear. "Club business, I couldn't leave."

"It's okay, Nix, but honestly, I can go," I say, worried that having me here can complicate things with not just us, but his club. I don't know what's happening between us, but being in his club, around his friends, is a little daunting.

"You're stayin'. Let me show you to my room," he orders, leaving no room to argue. Moving past me, he grasps my hand, leading me away from the guys. Their conversation obviously over, he walks me down the hall to the left, stopping at a closed door. Reaching down, he turns the handle and pushes it open, dragging me in and slamming the door shut.

My shoulders crash into the wall when he spins me around and backs me up, pressing himself into me.

"Gotta say darlin', seein' you in my shirt, in my club, is a major turn on." He tugs on his T-shirt and I smile up at him, glad he isn't angry. Going up onto my toes, I reach around his neck pulling him down so I can kiss him softly.

"I missed you in bed," I say, feeling bold. I can't help it. He brings it out in me and makes me feel comfortable. I'm weak when it comes to him, and I'm done fighting it.

"Did you touch yourself?" he asks, pushing further into me. I shake my head no and reach down, rubbing my hand along his bulging crotch.

"Don't be a tease, baby. I gotta go back," he groans, resting his forehead to mine, clearly as frustrated as I am.

"You wanna come and look around, or you feel more comfortable in here?"

"I'm pretty beat." I'm not sure if I want to leave his room wearing what I am. He nods, and then kisses my nose.

"Okay, I got shit to deal with. Take your panties off before climbing in my bed, and I'll meet you there later when I'm done."

His request floods me with want, and he catches my flush.

"She likes it when I boss her," he mumbles more to himself than me. I smack his chest and he grabs my hand. He's right. I love it, but he doesn't need to know that.

"Can't wait to have my tongue in your sweet pussy," he

teases, and I feel my stomach tighten in response. "Been dreamin' about it every night for the last ten nights."

My stomach does a flip on that announcement; the throb I've been fighting since he walked into the ink shop now beats erratically. I want him, badly. Leaning in, his lips come to mine one more time. His tongue swipes along my bottom lip, teasing me with his taste.

"Be back," he says, stepping away. "Don't you dare touch yourself." I hold his gaze before nodding my agreement. Then he's gone, leaving me alone in his personal space.

Making my way to his bed, I consider disobeying his request, before thinking better of it. Images of waking up to his head between my legs leave me feeling ready and wanting. Stepping out of my panties and pulling his top over my head, I climb under his sheets. His smell blankets me. Burrowing further under them, I breathe them in. Breathe him in. Closing my eyes, I force myself to sleep before my sexy biker comes back to wake me.

121

Nix

"TELL ME HOW THE FUCK THEY GOT IN?" I ASK MY Sergeant-at-Arms.

"They went in through the back door and worked smart," Jesse answers, still filling me in on the fucked-up bullshit the Kings have got us into.

"And the ink shop?" I ask as I feel the start of a headache coming on.

"Just the front."

Fuck.

Fuck.

Fuck.

The fuckers not only hit us at the tattoo shop right after

we left, they got into one of the bars downtown, injuring one of my workers in the process. It was a warning; we just don't know why.

Knights Rebels territory is protected, and those fuckers are just begging to create a war.

"You get a hold of T?" I ask Beau, trying to calm myself down so I can think straight.

"I put a call out, but still waiting for him to get back to me. Word is there was a shipment that got held up; some assholes intercepted it, and he was cleaned out."

"You think they're thinkin' we're responsible?"

"Don't know why they would," he responds. "Those fuckers have been in our town, know the way we run things. We don't want their drugs." I nod 'cause I know he's right, but why the fuck would they make a move against us?

"We secure the shop?" I look over at Sy, his usual pissed-off self more volatile than normal. He nods his head; no spoken communication needed. We're used to it.

"Get some eyes on Z, just to be safe," I tell Beau. It's not my weekend, but if there's a shit storm brewing, I want him safe.

"Yeah, prospect is heading there now. I'll head over after here." I nod, hoping like hell Addison doesn't cause shit. Last thing I need is her being a bitch to my boys.

"Right well, you know what we gotta do, keep our eyes open, and until we hear from T, or Intel comes in, let's play it safe," I say, standing from my chair.

"So Kadence?" Beau drawls, ready to move on to more pressing matters. I give him a look, warning him not to go there. "Fuck, boss, you got it bad." Jesse shakes his head and crosses his arms.

"Don't even start," I warn them, even though they all start laughing.

"Should have seen him earlier, so pussy whipped already." Sy shakes his head like he's disappointed.

"Fuck you, Sy. Don't think I've forgotten about your little act earlier."

"What act?" Beau questions.

"Just laid claim, nearly come out of his skin at me touching her," he tells them, laughing.

"You were pushin' it brother, and you know it."

"Couldn't help it. That woman has a mouth on her. That night at the bar was nothing compared to what I've seen." He shakes his head, a smirk tugging at the corners of his mouth.

"I'll say, I think Nix has found his match, boys," Brooks smirks, rising from his chair.

Jesse sits, watching me quietly; I can see the concern in his eyes, the unspoken words on his face. I know he has some connection with Kadence but he has nothing to worry about. I know how I feel about her, and after tonight, she'll know I've laid claim.

"We got a problem, Jesse?" I come right out and ask.

"She told you about the burns? Everything she had to go through?"

"None of your fuckin' business." My temper rises a little; I don't want to get into it with him but I will if I have to.

The guys stay quiet, the playful teasing a few minutes ago now tense. I'm not about to discuss Kadence and something that is private to her in front of them, and I'm getting pissed Jesse even brought it up. It pisses me off more that I don't know what happened.

"Jesse, I know you're lookin' out for her. I get that, but

I'm claimin' her as my woman. She's mine, therefore my responsibility. You can play the big brother act. I'll give you that, but don't mistake it for anythin' more. What Kadence and I discuss will only be between us." He holds my stare, but I don't back down. I stand by my word; it's none of his damn business, and the last time I checked, we didn't grow pussies and start braiding each other's hair wanting to talk about this shit.

"Your woman?" He smirks like I don't have a chance. "Good luck with that one," he laughs. Asshole.

"Fuck off." I ignore him and walk out, leaving them all laughing with each other. Fuckers know that I'm a goner.

My woman? Yeah, I'm calling it. The moment she walked into my club, wearing one of my shirts with the club's insignia on it, I knew she was the one for me. Now, I've just got to convince her. God, help me.

Finding one of the boys to pick her up was a hard one, especially after the fucking text she sent. I swear my dick must hate me with how much that woman makes it hard.

I chose the man least likely to try to hit on her, or not give her shit at least. Happily married, I know if Brooks fucked around on Kelly, there'd be hell to pay. Walking down the hall, I wonder if Kadence obeyed my order about the panties. I've seen the way she responds to my dominating side. Her eyes hold the battle she has within herself, and I love watching it, waiting to see if she is going to fight me or submit to me. It's going to be fun seeing how far I can push her.

Quietly opening my door, I look to the bed and see her asleep on her side. Her left leg bunched over the sheet exposing her dark and raised scar. She went to bed naked like a good girl.

Making quick work of my pants, I toe off my boots and take off my cut. Once naked, I quietly climb in behind her. She stirs briefly, and then settles back to sleep. Her sleeping body, naked in my bed, and her dark hair splayed out over my white pillow strengthens my need to taste her. Pulling the sheet down, I expose her sexy little tits. I'm not a tit man. It could go either way, but her small handfuls are just perfect. It's her nipples that do it for me. The pert buds always respond to my touch. Leaning down, I take one in my mouth.

"You're back." She stretches, waking from her sleep as I release her from my mouth. Leaving a kiss on her nipple, I pull back and run my hand down her body, cupping her between the legs.

"I see you've been a good girl." She smiles and nods her head. "I knew you could do as you were told," I say, leaning back down thirsty to have my tongue around the pale pink buds again.

"Did you sort everything out with Ink Me?" she asks as I slide my finger into her slick wet heat.

"Yeah, the boys are on it." My eyes watch her mouth gasp at my touch. The pleasure I'm giving her is written all over her face.

"Why would anyone do that?" Her question comes out unsteady as I insert a second finger.

"Babe, I've got my fingers inside of you. I don't wanna talk about club business while I'm finger fuckin' my woman."

Her legs close together, trapping my hand between her thighs, my fingers still inside of her.

"One, I was just asking, Nix. You don't have to be an ass, and two, your woman? When did I become your woman?"

"Babe, you became my woman when you walked into my

club wearing my clothes straight from my bed." I try to pull my hand out, but her legs tighten.

"Well, it didn't seem like I had much of a choice," she retorts. Loosening her grip, I sense an argument coming on, and as much as having my fingers in her when we are about to argue could be hot as fuck, I remove them and sit up.

"You could have told Brooks to fuck off. You have no problem telling me to. You could have even hightailed it out of there after I left, but you didn't. You walked into my club wearin' my fuckin' clothes," I remind her, glad that she didn't run and stayed just as I told her. She sits up, pulling the sheet with her.

"Why did you stay?' I ask.

"Because you asked me to."

"Exactly!"

"What are we doing, Nix? What is this, because I thought we were just having fun and now? Now I just don't know. I don't want to label anything, but if this is going to be more than fun, I'm going to need to know."

I laugh at her interpretation of what's happening between us. "This is more than just fun, Kadence."

15

Kadence

"THIS IS MORE THAN JUST FUN," HE SAYS.

The concept fascinates me but at the same time frightens me.

"I haven't been able to get you out of my mind, woman. Your attitude, your body, from the moment I had you on the back of my bike, I knew I was in trouble. You feel it too, Kadence. I know you do. Stop denyin' it." He leans over me, stripping the sheet off my body.

He's right; I do feel it. I just didn't realize he was feeling it that much. Sure, he's persistent, but I thought it was more about how amazing our night was, rather than wanting another slice of the pie.

"I want to know everythin' there is to know about you, Kadence," he declares, crawling over and covering his naked body to mine. "I want you in my bed." He kisses my lips softly. "On the back of my bike." His lips move to my ear. "I want to bury myself inside of you and stay there for days."

Every word he speaks settles in a little further, and I grasp at them, savoring them, memorizing them. Is it smart? I have no idea, but listening to him admit he wants more from me makes me defenseless, leaving me open to want more of him.

"Nix, we've only known each other for all of three weeks. We've spent a handful of times together. Don't you think this is moving a little too fast?"

"Fuck no," he disagrees. "Kadence, just relax. I'm not askin' you to marry me, woman. I'm just tellin' you to stop running and let me in."

"You're telling?" I ask.

"Yes and if you don't start listenin', I'll tan your ass like I did earlier last week."

His reminder brings back memories and I cover my face with my hands. "God, why did I let you do that?" I ask, embarrassed at the thought of it.

He pulls down my hands. "'Cause you wanted me to. You know it. I know it." He holds my gaze, his eyes searching mine.

"Fuck, babe, it was one of the sexiest things I've seen." He informs me, smiling. "No more fightin', okay?" he asks, and I make my decision to let go and stop holding back to see where this thing between us goes.

"Okay, but let's take it slowly," I respond. I'm still not sure if I'm ready for his world, or his authority and the way I react to it. If this ends, when it ends, it'll probably ruin me.

He laughs at my slow comment. "Kadence, I don't do slow."

"Well, you will if you want me." I hear the lie in my own ears.

He shakes his head and leans in, nose-to-nose, his erection lying against my stomach. "Baby, I already got you."

I can't deny it. He's right. So I do the next best thing: I roll my eyes and backhand his hard chest. "Don't be smooth. It makes you sound lame," I say, not really meaning it.

"Lame? Kadence, lame is not what you were callin' me the other night while I had you bent over your desk"

"Don't be rude," I say as heat floods my cheeks. I think about how I loved every second of his large calloused hand coming down on my ass. I throb just thinking about the sting of the slap, followed by the soothing of his caress while he teased my pussy. Just thinking about it now makes me wet.

"You like my dirty mouth. Don't lie. I can see it in your eyes." I shake my head, denying his accusations.

"You want me to prove it?" he pushes, and I'm already getting excited just thinking about what he'll say and do next.

"Get on your knees, dirty girl," he demands, rolling off me, his voice a controlled deep rumble.

"Why?"

"Don't ask questions, Kadence. Just be a good girl and do as you're told." I want to fight it. The need pulsates through me to argue back, but as strong as that feeling is, the want of what he is about to give me is stronger.

My center aches at his instruction as I come up onto my knees, facing him. He lies down on his side with his elbow propped up, his head in his palm while he rakes his eyes over my body. "Time to pay up, Kadence. Your hands aren't busy now. Touch yourself," he commands, throwing my text message back at me as I kneel there watching him. "Show me how much you need me to touch you," he encourages me, and I do as he asks, more turned on than the last time we were together.

I part my lips and run my finger along my wetness. I'm in tune with myself. I've never shied away from masturbation before, so with him lying there watching me, I relish in the knowledge he's being turned on by it. "Taste yourself," he continues to order. The authority in his voice doesn't stop me from hesitating at his demand. Now this is something I wouldn't normally do. Sure, I've tasted myself on another man's lips after he has gone down on me, but sticking my finger in my wetness, and putting it in my mouth? No.

"Kadence are you wet?" he asks me, my reservations not lost on him. I nod my head, trying to keep my gaze on him as self-doubt slowly creeps its way between us. "Show me how wet you are just from my dirty mouth," he pushes, ignoring my shyness. I hesitate at first, but then bring my finger up, showing him the glistening wetness. "Now put it in your mouth and enjoy how wet I make you."

His words wash over me, and I can't control the power my body wants to give him; bringing my hand to my mouth, I watch him watch me taste myself. His eyes flash with desire, need, and his hand starts to touch himself.

My eyes catch the movement and I'm drawn to it. Watching his large hand circle his aggressive arousal and stroke himself sends a tightening sensation through my stomach. Nerves singing, blood rushing, I lose myself to the erotic act.

"You want my cock, babe?" I nod breathlessly, eager to

have him. His delicious voice is making me dizzy.

He brings himself up to a sitting position, me still on my knees, his head in line with my breasts.

"Where do you want my cock, Kadence? In that tight little pussy of yours, or in that smart mouth?" Thinking about having him in my mouth makes me shake; watching him come undone by my mouth would be a sight to see. With no other option, I shamelessly reply, "Mouth."

He growls his response, sliding his fingers into where I am wet and desperate. "Fuck, Kadence, you're soakin," he rumbles before moving off the bed to stand. Lowering myself to my ass, I turn and face him, letting my feet fall to the floor in front of me. His thick hardness sits directly in line with my ready mouth. Taking him in my hand, I stroke him once before leaning forward and licking the tip clean. His fingers glide through my hair, gently pulling it, proving his impatience. I tighten my grip and blow a warm breath over the wetness I left behind. Stroking him harder, I stop to run my tongue up along the inside of his dick.

"Don't lick at it, woman. I want you to suck it."

Pulling back I look up at him. "Oh, is it not fun when someone is teasing you with oral?" I ask him, remembering his little bullshit game he did with me that first night.

"Fuck," he mumbles, and I have a laugh at his position. "I'm serious, Kadence. Don't push me or I'll take you hard and won't let you come. The only person in this relationship that controls the bedroom play is me," he threatens.

Is that what this is? A relationship? Pushing that aside, I think of him taking me hard and not letting me come. Would he? I wouldn't put it past him; the words ring true in my mind. Shaking off the dreaded thoughts of not releasing, I lean forward again and I wrap my lips around his width. I take him whole the first time, before coming back up. Nix's hands grip hard in my hair as I begin my oral assault; the pleasure of the sting makes me tremble more. Working him with both my mouth and grip, I reach down with my free hand and cup his balls, rolling them over in my hand. He groans his approval and it sends a rush straight to my core. Hearing him lose himself spurs me on and I suck deeper and harder.

"Kadence, if you want my dick in you, you have to stop or I'm gonna blow." He grinds out after a few minutes, his control slowly slipping. I fight the internal battle of taking him to the brink or letting him relieve the ache between my legs.

"Kadence," he warns again and I let the power of being able to make him come undone rule my decision. Relaxing my throat, I take him deeper as he tightens his grip, holding my head in place as he begins to fuck my mouth. The thrill and the forcefulness of watching him come undone before me floods my body with desire. I reach down, yearning to ease the growing ache between my thighs.

"Don't even fuckin' touch it," he snarls at the same time he blows his load down my throat. My hand stills, his command turns me on even more. He is right; I love his dirty mouth.

Swallowing all that he delivers, I hold back the urge to gag and let him finish. When he slows and releases my hair, I take over sucking him clean.

"Fuck, we are so doing that again," he insists after I let him fall from my mouth, and I look up at him. I smile and nod, agreeing it was one of the hottest things I've ever done.

"Now lie back. It's my turn," he orders, pushing my shoulder, before falling to his knees. I let the fall take me and feel his tongue lap up my wetness. As much as I love what we just did, I think I'm going to love my turn more.

The rays of the morning daylight sneak through the parted curtains. The sun coats my skin, warming me. The heat at my back lets me know Nix made it back to bed. Last night, after giving Nix the best head job I had in me, he returned the favor, ending in me riding him hard. We were interrupted halfway through, making it quick, but still so goddamn hot. Afterwards, I was left alone while he went to sort out whatever Jesse came and got him for. I don't know what's going down with the club. Nix wouldn't tell me but he did say not to worry.

I shift my naked body, trying not to wake him, and gently turn to my side, untangling my body from his. Nix mumbles something unintelligible and curls further over.

Grabbing my phone and his shirt, I quietly make my way to the connecting bathroom. After putting on Nix's shirt, I dial Holly's number to let her know I'm okay. I know she will be worried I didn't text last night. Placing the phone to my ear, I sit on the toilet and wait to hear her voice yell down my phone.

"Why hello, hussy," she answers after the third ring.

"Hello." I keep my voice low, careful not to wake Nix.

"I see from your bedroom door that you didn't come home last night," she laughs.

"Yeah, I stayed at the clubhouse."

"YOU WHAT!" she screams at me, and I pull the phone away at the loudness of her voice. "You lucky bitch." Lucky? I guess I can't argue with her on that.

"Well, while you got the sexy bossy biker, I was left with Sy, aka cranky moody biker. Did you notice what a barrel of laughs he was?" She continues on her rant, "He mumbled two words to me after dropping me home. Two words, 'See ya.' That's it, but I swear to God, Kadence. He could bark at me like a dog and I would still want to get inside his pants." She growls in frustration and I believe her; the woman knows what she wants.

Sy is a serious man. The thought of him barking at Holly makes me laugh. She huffs down the phone, not impressed.

"Do you need me to come pick you up?" she asks, moving on from Sy.

"No, I'm gonna hang out for a bit. Nix had some club business to deal with last night so I'll be home later."

"Oh, ditching our standing lunch date for a man?" she sighs, and I let out a small laugh at her blatant jealousy.

"I'll make it up to you, promise. I have to go," I say when I hear Nix call out through the door.

"Have fun with all that male hotness," she calls back before hanging up.

After using the bathroom, I wash my hands and place some toothpaste on my finger and do a quick brush to get rid of my morning breath. Walking back out of the bathroom, I see Nix sitting on the end of the bed.

"Morning," I say, placing my phone on the bedside table and walking up to him.

"What the hell you been doin' in there?" he asks me, standing up to do the button on his dark wash jeans. Geez, cranky much?

"Just talking to Holly," I tell him. He bends down, takes my face in his hands and kisses me lightly. His whiskers tickle my face as I deepen the kiss; my tongue comes out, ready to dance with his. The groan I swallow from his mouth gives me the reaction I was hoping for before he pulls back.

"I gotta go. Got a meeting to sort this shit out." He steps out of my embrace, reaching down for his shirt and pulling it over his head. The muscles of his chest and the tightness of his abdomen are immediately hidden. The man has a magnificent body.

"Oh," I say, feeling disappointed that he keeps having to run off.

"Hold that thought. Give me an hour and I'll be back. I'll eat you for breakfast and then I'll feed you," he promises, leaning back down and kissing me deeply. I sag against him, my body molding to his. Drawing back, he brings his arms around me, his embrace strong, his scent making me weak. His hands roam further down, the roughness of them grazing my bare skin. "Fuck, Kadence, you're not wearin' any underwear?" I shake my head and watch as a pained expression fills his eyes. "Make sure you wear panties if you leave this room." His eyes tell me he's not joking, but of course, I like to tease.

"Oh, really, Nix? I thought it would be a good idea to walk out wearing your shirt as a dress, you know, let all the boys get a glimpse of what I have." His hand comes to my hair, tugging it in a sharp movement. I don't know what feelings course through me more, the stinging pain coming from my head as it comes back at his pull or my throbbing pussy at the total act of dominance.

"Swear to fuckin' God, woman. Do. Not. Push. Me." His mouth attacks mine, his tongue showing me more than words can say. I guess teasing him like that would be a bad idea.

I lift my leg and hike it up over his thigh, drawing him closer into me. His hands cups my ass, lifting me up he walks me back, my shoulders reaching the coolness of the wall. My body is suspended between him and the wall. Keeping me steady, he moves his hips, his arousal finding the spot.

Matching his rhythm, I let myself build. A whimper escapes as he moves his mouth down the side of my face continuing down my cheek, slowly descending toward my neck. He nibbles and sucks at the softness of my skin right near my collarbone. My head in a haze, the closeness of his body, and him trapping me to the wall, leaves me panting for more. I reach down, working the buckle and button as fast as I can. My soft fingers dive in and wrap around his rapidly growing erection.

"Kadence," he warns, my name coming out as a sigh.

His cock jumps at the pressure as I squeeze him in my hand, telling me he wants me just as much as I want him. His lips work their way back up to my mouth, while I pump my hand up and down his cock.

"Fuck, woman, don't think I don't know what your game is. If your hand didn't feel so fuckin' good squeezin' me tight, I'd take you over my knee for the shit you keep pullin'." He makes a sound, which comes from the back of his throat, before his mouth comes down hard on mine. I open, allowing entry as his tongue comes out stroking me to ecstasy. My movements become harder, faster, rocking in unconscious time against him. He pulls back, eyes full of desire, breathing ragged.

"Fuck it," he laments giving into the pleasure. He carries me back over to the bed. Throwing me down, I bounce on landing. My hands go to my shirt, ripping it over my head. I have no shame. How I can go from hiding away embarrassed to ripping my clothes off in two nights? I have no idea. It's like the need is taking over.

His body covers mine; the heat instantly has me craving more. My hands grip the sheets as his hot wet tongue circles my nipple and his fingers work the place I'm most desperate. With his thumb and forefinger, pinching and pulling at my sensitive clit, my head falls to the side as I feel the waves begin to build with each roll of my hips. His calloused fingers are rough against my bare core. Moaning his name, I reach down and grab hold of his hard length, keen to have him inside of me again. He moves his hand, taking it up to my lonely nipple while his mouth works the other.

Bringing his knee up between my legs, he pushes in, his upper thigh right where my burn is. "Rub yourself up against me," he commands, as the momentum of rolling myself up against his thick thigh takes over. I've never dry humped anyone before, but the wild waves of pleasure hitting me right now is enough to make we want to savor the intensity of it.

"Eyes, Kadence," he warns, moving his mouth onto my left breast. He looks up at me as I look down, our gazes locked. Goose bumps break out over my skin as his teeth latch onto my nipple, rolling the erect bud over the sharpness before biting down hard. The orgasm hits fast, starting from my toes and ripples through me. My grip tightens around him; grinding my hips against him as a tidal wave of enormous power sends me over in a final shattering release.

"Fuck," he hisses before releasing himself into my hand, the warmth of his cum coating my fingers as I squeeze him dry. His approval, a harsh cry of raw masculine satisfaction, tells me his release was just as intense as mine.

"You're gonna kill me if we keep acting like fourteen-year-old horny teenagers," he pants in short bursts.

I don't know about horny teenagers, but the chemistry is intense for grown adults. Even masturbation between us is as hot as the real deal.

"You've made a mess," I laugh, looking down at his pants, my hands covered in him.

"Let me clean up. I'm gonna be late, but fuck, that was worth it." Pulling back, he plants a gentle kiss to my mouth, stands and walks to the bathroom.

I lie naked, the orgasm aftermath still floating through my body. My limbs are heavy and relaxed, but the need to have him is nowhere near filled. Knowing that's all I'm going to get, with Nix needing to sort out club business, I follow him into the bathroom.

After we both clean up, Nix makes me promise that I'll wear my panties out in the club. I roll my eyes at his command but agree I'll be on my best behavior. Kissing me senseless, he leaves me alone with a vow to be back and ready to take me again.

Flopping down on the bed, I let out a frustrated sigh at my now boring morning. I'm not keen on leaving the room without Nix, so I guess I could go back to sleep. My phone beeps next to me as I settle back in under the covers. I reach over and grab it from the bedside table checking the screen.

> **UNKNOWN**: Kadence, we need to talk. Urgently. You're in danger. Call me. Zane

Zane. I freaking knew I saw him last night. What a freaking asshole, dipshit motherfucker. I should have gone looking for him and given the man a piece of my mind. Still in bed, I stare at my phone, emotions raging through me. I can't understand why after three years, he finally contacts me. My heart beats rapidly in my chest. The urge to see him again and wanting to punch him in the junk is tearing me apart. I don't know what to say, how to answer. I don't have a chance to respond as another text comes through.

> **UNKNOWN**: If you don't want what happened to our house to happen to Holly, you will meet me.

What the hell? Was that a threat? He is the biggest asshole I've ever met. I can't believe I was going to marry him. Rage now replaces any notion that he finally came back for me.

> **KADENCE**: What do you want, asshole?

I text back, already regretting it. Engaging with him will only spell trouble.

> **UNKNOWN**: Meet me down by our old house. At the park on Old Bay Road.

I contemplate not going, telling him to go to hell. I don't even know if I'm going to be able to get out of the clubhouse, but the idea of Holly's place ending in the same fate as mine makes me have second thoughts.

Shit.

> **KADENCE**: What time?

UNKNOWN: One hour.

While texting Holly there's a change of plan and I need her to meet me at the front of the Knights Rebels compound, I race around the room searching for my panties, skirt and shoes. My phone beeps again. I pick it up quickly to see if Holly can pull off my request.

HOLLY: On my way.

She's so good to me. Running my hand over my bedhead, I take a large shaky breath. Am I really going to go do this? Maybe I should text Nix. Pushing that thought away, I steel myself ready to handle Zane myself. The asshole took too much away from me. I'm not going to give up a perfect opportunity to let him have a piece of my mind. Quietly, I make my way out of Nix's room. I know Nix asked me to stay, but he didn't say I had to stay. If he were here, I would probably do the same thing. Wouldn't I? Either way, I'm leaving. I need to sort out my dipshit ex and hope whatever he has to say doesn't end in me wanting to murder him.

16

Nix

BACK **WHEN MY DAD AND THE K**NIGHTS **R**EBELS Originals ran the drug trade of Rushford, Nevada, they would never even think about doing what we are about to do. Things were a lot different, and riding freely onto Mayhem territory is something that just did not happen. Even with the truce, I don't like what we're about to do.

Pulling into the parking lot fifteen minutes outside of town, I prepare myself for the shit storm that I can feel brewing. Today is a friendly gathering: three boys each. I brought Sy, Brooks and Jesse with me, leaving Beau back at the compound.

T and his boys sit in the back corner and I make my way

to their table. The boys hang back, keeping our meeting relaxed.

"Nix," T says, nodding his head. I can see he's pissed that we called this meeting but fuck if I give a shit.

T is a large bastard. His shaved head shows off his tattooed skull giving him a menacing look. A scar that runs from his temple to his jaw takes me back to the night that my pops gave it to him. The Knights Rebels had intercepted some of their men on our territory and took them to the warehouse. My father had a huge barn set up out the back of a brother's farm where they held most of their illegal dealings. That was the first mistake that changed the course of our lives. Being so close to town, so close to civilians, he didn't realize how open it left our loved ones.

Mayhems were on our territory and that's all that mattered in the war between the two clubs. My pops was still pissed at me, still unsure what I wanted to do with my life, and this one particular night, he took me out to the barn to show me how they ran the guns. I wasn't prepared for what unfolded. I witnessed them torture two men for walking over some imaginary line they had made up.

Watching my father slice open the side of T's face sealed the fate of my mother; only at the time, no one was to know that. T was a runt, a prospect for the Mayhems, and only a year older than me.

My father let the men go that night, a warning for all not to fuck with Red Knight and the Knights Rebels; that was his second mistake. I learnt not long after that an outlaw MC doesn't take too kindly to a threat, and the retaliation that followed cost my sweet mom her life.

Shaking away thoughts that won't help me now, I take a

seat opposite T. The scowl on his face leaves no question that he's just as excited about our meet as I am.

"Wanna tell me why the fuck you're wagin' war with Gunner Jamieson and why we're in the middle of it?" I get straight to the point, no time for idle chitchat. After Beau had got a hold of him last night, we learnt that the Mayhems weren't responsible for the attacks on the two shops.

"Wanna tell me why you intercepted our shipment?" he replies with his own question.

"What the fuck you talkin' bout, T?"

"Our weapons shipment, word out is some of your men were in on it. Now, I know our club has the truce, but you double cross me, Nix, we got fuckin' problems. I had a big marker on this one, and I'm not taking it lightly that you got your fuckin' hands in on this. You want in, then this makes it fair game, guns and drugs," he declares, and I feel my temper slowly rising. T and his boys don't like the truce for the simple fact that they run a different way than us. Where we keep it clean, they are prepared to get as dirty as possible. But now that we're out of the game, T and his boys benefit more than we do.

"The fuck, T? You know our hands are clean. Our history speaks for itself. If I wanted back in, you sure as hell would know it."

"Don't give a shit about history or respect. I've got a fuckin' truck load riding on this," he responds.

"You should care about respect, brother. You've got a lot more ridin' on this. Don't know what the fuckin' deal is, but your info is wrong. We got nothin' to do with it. You're dealin' with Gunner Jamieson and his crew all the way on this one. Our hands are clean, and you know it," I inform him.

"And don't forget, T, you start pushin' drugs in Rushford, you'll need to prepare yourself for shit to go down. You have my word," I tell him, meaning it. The market of Rushford is off limits, and we've made it our job to keep it safe. The Knights Rebels and the Mayhems made that deal five years ago, and that still stands solid. They keep their shit out of our town, and we leave them to run shop how they see fit in their territory.

He holds my gaze searching for some tell that I'm bullshitting him. I'm not. We both know drugs in my territory are not taken lightly.

"I'll sort out Gunner. Don't worry, that fucker and I go way back," he assures me.

"Well fuckin' sort it quick. We've got break ins and fires happenin' on our side of town. As far as we are concerned, this is your mess you need to clean up. The last thing we need is Jamieson stickin' his nose in our business. This shit lies on you. If you can't deal with him, we're gonna step up and you know that won't be a fuckin' fun fair," I threaten. I don't want to get involved; the boys and I work hard to keep out of the shit that gets thrown around, but we will if they can't contain it.

"I told ya, we fuckin' got it," T barks, and I don't miss the warning in his tone. Nodding my head, I let it go. Last thing we need right now is pissing each other off, especially with Gunner sniffing around.

After talking for another ten minutes about the issues they've been having with Jamieson, we agree to keep the lines open. I'm not sure if T and his crew are going to be able to handle the asshole by themselves. Impatient to head back and see Kadence, we leave T and his boys in the diner and make our way back out to our bikes.

"Boss man," Jesse calls out as I mount my ride. I can feel a headache coming on after dealing with T and all the shit that comes with it. I hope there is no more shit to deal with.

"Kadence left."

Fuck me, I spoke too soon.

"What the fuck do you mean she left?" I ask, my headache now throbbing. "Where the fuck did she go?"

"Her friend picked her up outside the club twenty minutes ago."

Pulling my cell out of my pocket, I see a text.

> **KADENCE**: Sorry I had to go, explain later.

I dial her number. She ignores the call, letting it go to voicemail.

"Kadence, call me back," I demand. Hanging up, I send her a text.

> **NIX**: Jesus, you're a pain in my ass. Call me.

"Did Beau get eyes on her?" I ask Jesse, hoping he did as I asked when I left. I didn't think she would run, but fuck, I must have known she would.

"Yeah, Hunter's on her. Says she stopped off at her house, but left in her own car five minutes ago."

Pocketing my phone, I look to the sky asking the big guy why he thinks it's funny he sent me the most testing woman on earth. Brooks laughs beside me, telling me to get used to it.

"What way did she go?" I yell over the roar of the pipes,

wanting to know what direction to start heading.

"South," he tells me. My mind is already trying to figure out where she could be going. We pull out of the diner's parking lot and head back south in search of my woman. The same woman who needs to learn that no matter how many times she runs, I'm gonna keep finding her.

17

Kadence

PULLING INTO THE OLD STREET THAT I USE TO LIVE on, I start to second-guess my choice of meeting Zane. My exit of the clubhouse didn't go to plan. To say Beau wasn't too keen with me just leaving would be an understatement. After pleading that I had an emergency, he gave me the choice of waiting for Nix, or letting him take me. None of those ideas worked for me, so I conceded and went back to Nix's room to come up with another idea.

I had to not only get past Beau, but also make it out through the gates to get to Holly. *I was screwed.*

I ended up sneaking out through the back and creeping around to the side. Fate was on my side. As I made it to the gate, there was a commotion with some guys about to ride out.

Somehow, the guy at the gate wasn't where he was supposed to be and I walked straight out and into Holly's car before they noticed I was gone. I kept the text from Zane and what I was going to do from Holly. I didn't need her following me and going all badass on him. I needed to get this over and done with before Nix found out I left.

My phone rings as if on cue and I look down and see Nix calling. Ignoring the call, I throw my cell in the back of the car. I can't be tempted, and I need to get this over with.

My palms sweat and a wave of nausea grips me as I drive past our old house. No signs of the fire that destroyed my home, but I know different. The memories of the flames and the smell of the charred remains will always stay with me. Pulling up in front of the old park, I spot a figure sitting on the park bench.

Getting out of my car, I walk the short distance down the old path. Zane stands and walks forward, his dark hair now longer and pulled back into a short ponytail. He looks so different from the last time I saw him. His expensive cut suit fits his body like a second skin, and I can't help notice how well he looks. The thought makes me angry; he took something away from me and left me broken. *Not broken, Kadence, just scarred.*

The last time I saw Zane, I had gone to bed defeated. His behavior in the weeks leading up to the fire was out of character. He was acting strangely, snapping at me one minute and then being over-attentive the next. He was fidgety and secretive. Holly suspected drugs but I put it down to stress; working for an impressive architect firm here in Rushford wasn't what he wanted anymore.

He worked hard to move his way up, and that hard work paid off. Their sister company had just acquired a bid for a new development in California, his dream job, and we had to make a decision if we were going to pack up and move closer or try the long-distance thing. I'd just secured a full-time position at Rushford Elementary and wasn't prepared to give up my dream of being a teacher in my hometown, but Zane wanted me by his side and it was something we fought constantly over.

That night Zane had received a call that he took outside; we were going out for the night with some of his work friends to celebrate his promotion. I put the night down to being a bust after that phone call. He came back inside with a mood and snapped at everything I did, what I was wearing, how I had my makeup, even the way I smelt. We had been together for three years, only recently engaged, and he stood there and tore me to shreds. I tried to ignore the words he spewed at me, but the ugliness of them was too much. Each insult broke me down with every blow he dealt. I was pathetic. He could do so much better. He wasted three years of his life.

I tried everything not to believe them. I was lost and thought the man I was going to marry was having a hard time dealing with the stress of work, the uncertainty of where we were going, and I wasn't making it easier for him. It was only natural that he would take it out on me. I wanted to be there for him. I wanted to be his partner and stand by his side through it all, so I brushed off his abuse hoping once we made our decision regarding his job, everything would go back to normal.

The whole night he continued being in a foul mood, his

work buddies not once looking uncomfortable with his constant digs at me. By the end of the night, I was beaten down. I realized, in between listening to the venom he spat out at me and the looks he was giving other women, that Zane was no longer the man I agreed to marry. I didn't know what was happening to him. I was concerned for him, for me and for us. I made it in the front door back home before unleashing my anger on him. We argued for over an hour, me accusing him of anything and everything. He was accusing me of being paranoid, not supporting him. I went to bed exhausted and drained, with no idea what I was going to do. When I woke up in the middle of the night to our house burning around me, I had no clue that it was because of Zane. I only later found out Zane wasn't coming back.

Determined not to fall down the hole of why, I straighten my shoulders ready to meet him.

"Kadence," he greets me, reaching for my hand. I pull back, not wanting his fingers touching mine.

"Cut the bullshit, Zane," I snap back at him. "What the hell do you want?" He looks taken back for a moment. His blue eyes look shocked, not used to my attitude. He wouldn't. He missed the phase of me dealing with my anger after I almost died.

"I need your help—" he begins before I instantly cut him off.

"Do you think I'm dense? Do you honestly think I'd believe you've come back to town for my help?" I laugh, knowing I won't fall for his shit.

"Is this how you greet your fiancé after three years, Kadence?" His question angers me, but not as much as his disregarded that it has been just *that*. Three years.

"After everything you have done to me? What you put me through? Yes, I would say that's just about right," I manage to fire back without clawing his eyes out. What is wrong with this man? What is wrong with me for even thinking I was in love with him?

"Kadence, cut the dramatics. Yes, I did a shitty thing, but you're okay. You're fine. I've seen you the last few weeks. If anything, you've bounced back well."

"I've bounced back? My life isn't a fucking ball game, Zane. You destroyed it; took it all away from me. I can't believe I even agreed to come here." I begin to feel more stupid with each second that passes.

"You don't mean that, baby." He steps forward, giving me the look that used to get me.

"Baby? Jesus, you are fucking dumb. I'm done. Leave me alone. I'm not getting involved with whatever bullshit you have gotten yourself into." I turn to go, ready to be out of his presence. I know he threatened me with Holly's house, but standing in front of him, that terror that he once placed in me is now replaced with pity. The man is pathetic. I don't know that he won't follow through, but standing here, listening to him telling me I'm being dramatic proves it wouldn't matter what I did. He is going to do what he wants.

"Kadence," he calls out, as I walk away. "I need my money from the house," he tries again, and this time I bite.

"You what?" I ask, wanting to double check what I just heard, hoping I heard different, 'cause there is no way in hell he just asked me for money, considering the asshole cleaned me out.

"The money I put into the house. It's mine, and I want it back."

I laugh in his face. The guy has a screw loose that's for sure.

"Zane, the house sold last year. It has been three years of no contact from you, and now you want money? Do you even care that you left me alone in that house to die? Do you understand the surgeries I went through and the pain? You missed it all." The memories of feeling lost and alone slowly seep their way out. I've kept them so deeply locked away, having them surface again feels foreign to me. "You never returned any of my calls. Do you even care that I could have died, that I nearly did?" I shake my head, knowing it's all lost on him. He doesn't care, doesn't give a shit.

"You stole from me. Cleaned me out. You no longer have the rights to anything that came from that house. You had a chance to come home. You didn't. What did you expect? That I was going to wait for you? You left me to burn, all over an unpaid debt to a motorcycle gang," I scream, finally losing it. Fuck him and his indifference. A rage boils within, my hands itching to lash out at him. Every moment I lived through because of him comes to the surface as I let everything out.

"Step back, Kadence," someone demands from behind me. His voice that controlled anger I remember back at the school with his ex.

Nix. Shit.

"No way, Nix," I argue, ignoring his demand, ready to take both of these men on.

"I'm not kidding, Kadence. You need to move behind me right now." The tone of his voice plunges into a low and fierce level, but it's the way he barks my name that puts me on alert. We've come to blows a few times now, but this? This is a whole new level of anger. I look at him, slightly afraid and not sure if I'm scared for my safety or if I'm scared that I have made him mad. I like to push him to frustration, but to anger boiling over, I'm not too sure. I move to the side and slide in behind him. I notice Jesse come up behind me with Brooks closing me into the side.

"What's this, Kadence?" Zane yells out. For a second there, I forgot the asshole was here.

"You speak to me and only me." Nix walks forward, getting into Zane's space. Two guys wearing black walk out from behind some trees, closing in next to Zane. What the hell is going on?

"You wanna tell me why the hell you're talkin' to my woman, Edwards?" Nix spits out, calling Zane by his last name. What the hell. How does Nix know Zane?

"Your woman? Guess you'd be the type to go for another man's woman," Zane fires back smiling.

"The fuck you just say?" Nix walks further up to him. Zane holds his ground, but I can see by the look in his eyes he's holding back some fear. He must grow some confidence or have a death wish because he responds.

"What I should have said is that your 'woman' is my fiancée and that sexy mouth of hers has been around my cock plenty of times," he smirks.

I don't know what universe I've stepped into, but I'm standing frozen, listening to my ex-fiancé describe to my current lover, who is now looking every bit the scary biker dude, that I've had my mouth around his cock. Oh, shit.

"Kadence, get in the car," Nix addresses me. His stare is still firmly on Zane.

"Nix—" I begin.

"Kadence, get in the goddamn car, now!" he bellows out,

and I shrink back at his harsh tone. "Jesse, take her," he demands, still not looking at me. Jesse grabs my hand and pulls me to follow him. Looking up at Zane, I see the bastard has a smile on his face, clearly enjoying the show.

"Bye, Kadence, it's been great catching up. Shame you've turned into a biker whore—" He doesn't finish his sentence because Nix throws a punch, hitting him square in the jaw.

"Shut your fuckin' mouth," I hear Nix say as Jesse drags me further back to the car.

"Jesus, woman, what the fuck is that all about?" Jesse asks when he opens the car door for me, my hands too shaky to get the keys out of my handbag.

"I have no idea, Jesse. Zane is my ex; the one I told you about. He sent me a text and told me he needed to talk, threatened me if I didn't come."

"Sweetheart, you need to get it together and drive back to the compound now." I shake my head, not liking that idea, with Nix and his anger.

"I'm not sure Nix will want that, Jesse," I voice my concern.

"Kadence, I'm telling you now, it will be a whole lot worse if you don't get your ass back to the club. Trust me." I nod my head, not prepared to discuss with him.

"How does Nix know Zane?" I ask, afraid of the answer. My whole world feels like it has just been turned on its axis, and I feel like I'm missing something.

"You might know him as Zane sweetheart, but around here, he's known as Edwards, and that bastard holds the second highest position in the drug cartel organization. In other words, your ex is a very dangerous man. Now go. We'll explain it all when we get back." I slowly nod and get into the driver's seat, hoping my shaking hands calm enough for me to drive.

"Straight back to the clubhouse," Jesse repeats, leaning into the car.

He closes the door and watches me take in what he just told me. Zane Edwards, the man I was engaged to, wasn't a part of any organization; he was an architect. We lived in a four-bedroom home, and we were in the middle of planning our wedding. No way was he into drugs. I would have seen it. *Wouldn't I?*

Starting the car, I force myself to relax and keep myself together. The need to get away, away from Zane and away from Nix is too much to ignore. I know Jesse told me to go back to the compound, but facing Nix, knowing that he knows I was with that man, makes me turn home instead.

I need Holly.

I need her to tell me what to do. I've got bigger issues than I first thought. If Zane is this big drug thug who runs with bad people, why does he want money from me? He can't be that hard up for money, could he? Or is he playing me for bigger things?

Driving past our old house, I have to wonder how it all came to this. We were in love. The man I saw today was not the man whom I was prepared to give my life to. That man is long gone. If only I had seen that sooner, maybe I wouldn't have had to go through everything I had. The fire, the nightmares, it all comes back, and now I'm hanging by a thread and barely keeping it together.

I force myself to push the pain that I've long forgotten down, and not allow the darkness to creep in. When I'm back in the safety of my home, the safety that Holly gives me, only then will I allow myself to break.

18

Nix

POCKETING MY PHONE, I LET OUT A FRUSTRATED SIGH. Kadence was engaged to that fucking asshole? It's too fucked up to process. Talk about twisted. This guy is dangerous, and as second to Gunner Jamieson, I have no doubt this little meeting was set up.

"What's happening, boss?" Brooks asks, and I turn looking at him and Sy. I sent Jesse to follow Kadence 'cause I knew she wouldn't go back like she was told. *Stubborn-ass woman.*

"The damn woman didn't go back to the clubhouse."

"Figured," he smiles, shaking his head. "Get used to it, brother. Been with Kelly for ten years, and the wife still doesn't listen to me."

I shake my head, not thinking of the next ten years. I don't know if I'll last a month without that woman doing my head in. That's a lie; the thought thrills me. What pisses me off is knowing that the asshole has had her. Had what's mine.

"You stupid fuckers are mad, thinking you can't control a woman," Sy informs us. He doesn't normally give us his opinion, but lately I've noticed a slight change in him. I've grown to like the silent Sy. This new one is a little strange to get used to.

I shake my head knowing he's right, but even if I never control Kadence, even if I have to give her my balls on a silver platter, I know it would be better than anything I've ever had. When I ended things with Addison, I never thought I would find myself wanting a relationship again. Kadence is different. Her fucking mouth is always fighting me, pushing me, and pulling me. I can't get enough.

I nearly killed that asshole for speaking that way about Kadence. He had it coming, but calling her a whore, fuck. I turned red with fury. No one calls my woman a whore. After Jesse pulled her away, the asshole Edwards took the blow I delivered. He stood there with a smile on his face as he wiped the blood trail from the corner of his mouth; the guy is whacked. After telling him to not contact her again, I made it very clear where we stand on territory. Letting him know about our meeting with the Mayhems earlier, he didn't seem so smug. The fucker is trying to play us and knowing that alone gives us a one up. Something about the club has him running scared. I only hope he doesn't grow some balls and come running back. We gave him a message to send along to his boss, Gunner: under no circumstances will we ever allow their business to hit our streets. I don't give a fuck what I have to do, even if we have to go above the law. This bullshit territory war they've got going on with the Mayhems needs to end.

"Want us to follow you?" Brooks asks, knowing I'm in for some fun.

"Fuck no. I'm not ready for my boys to see me get my balls handed to me," I tell them, watching them laugh. Fuckers have no idea. "Head back. I'll stay with her tonight, or head back to mine. Either way, she's with me." Brooks and Sy nod before taking off on their Harleys. I don't know what fucking game Gunner is playing, but using me as a pawn in his war with the Mayhems is one thing. Using my woman is a whole other story. Pulling out onto the street, I make my way to Kadence's house. I need answers to why she ever thought meeting with Edwards was a bright idea. Surely, she knows how dangerous and crazy the fucker is?

"Open the goddamn door, Kadence" I bang for the fucking tenth time. The woman is stubborn; I'll give her that.

"Go away, badass biker daddy. She doesn't want to see you," her friend Holly calls back.

"Swear to Christ, woman, open the damn door or I'll kick the fuckin' thing down," I yell out, my patience wearing thin.

"Nix, can you just give me tonight? Please," Kadence calls through the door, her voice soft and quiet, letting me know she's right there at the door. So close, yet I can feel her already pulling away.

"Babe, whatever you've got goin' on in your head, get it out." I move to the door, resting my forehead on the dark wood. "Let me in, Kadence. I'm not leavin'." The silence is deafening before the latch on the lock clicks, and I step back waiting to see her. The door opens enough for me to walk through, and I enter, kicking it shut behind me. Not noticing the apartment around me, my eyes zero in on her. She stands in front of me, her dark hair in a knot on top of her head. Loose strands hang free, framing her face. Even in a tight cami with matching pajama bottoms, she looks amazing. Every bit of her screams sexy and fuckable. I walk forward, but her hands come up, stopping my pursuit.

"Don't," she orders me, but it's not the command that stops me. It's the tone in her voice. I'm taken back by the coldness of it, of her. Looking into her eyes, I see the same look of vulnerability I witnessed when she showed me her scars back at my house.

"Don't what, Kadence? Don't comfort you when you're standin' over there all in your head, overthinkin' some serious fucked-up shit? If you think I'm gonna let you push me away, you got another thing comin'." I move forward and pull her into my arms. Her vanilla-smelling shampoo invades my senses, reminding me of her scent on my pillow back home. Her body sags against me, the fight in her escaping.

"Wanna tell me why you're meetin' with your asshole ex in the middle of fuckin' nowhere?"

"Nix, it was fine."

"No, Kadence," I warn, my tone leaving no argument that I want the details.

"He's in bed with a fuckin' drug kingpin, babe. You weren't fine," I tell her, stepping back to look at her face creased with concern.

"Nix, I didn't know that. I swear. He wasn't selling drugs when we were engaged." The words leave her mouth, but with her teeth biting down on her bottom lip in worry, I know she's starting to question it.

She has every right to question it. That asshole has been around for the last four years and has only recently worked his way up to be Gunner's right-hand man.

"What did he want?"

"What did you do to him?" She ignores my question, asking her own.

"What did he want?" I repeat, not prepared to let her know I used my fists while he ran his mouth. I already know her feelings on using your fists.

"He wants money. He lent me money to put into the house, and now he wants it back."

"He doesn't want your money, babe. He has plenty; he's just testin' the waters. His boss controls the drug trade in two counties and is movin' in on ours. He has the Warriors of Mayhem in his sights. If he gets their territory, then we got major problems here in town." I feel myself getting worked up at the thought, but I don't miss the ghastly whiteness spread over her face. "What is it?" Her body stiffens at my question.

"Do you know the Warriors of Mayhem?" The question comes out like she's shocked.

"Yeah, babe, I do." She pulls back abruptly, moving out of my arms.

"What is it?" The color of her face makes me uneasy. The fear and anger mixed in with a tortured look doesn't sit well with me.

"Are they your friends?" She takes another step back further away from me, like she's frightened.

"I wouldn't call them my friends. We keep out of each

other's business. We have an agreement and sometimes have to do things for each other, why?" She shakes her head, not letting me in.

"What is it, Kadence?"

I'm starting to wonder if she knows someone in the club. The anger in her eyes tells me it's bad.

"They were responsible for the fire," she says quietly before continuing, "Zane owed them money, and he didn't pay. That's what the police told me. I lost my home because they wanted their money."

Fuck me. My day just got a whole lot more messed up.

"He owed them a lot more than money. He used their money and tried to set up his own distribution in town. That is a big fuckin' no," I try to explain the situation. "The Warriors of Mayhem and our club have an arrangement: no drugs in Rushford. We've kept it clean for the last five years. Edwards has been around that whole time, tryin' to break through that law."

She shakes her head not accepting what I'm telling her. She walks over to the living room, planting her ass down on her leather sofa. "I'm serious, Kadence. He started out small time, got into some serious shit with Gunner and fucked with the MC. I'm tellin' you now that shit falls back on him settin' up in town."

"It doesn't matter what it was, Nix. They are responsible for what happened to me." I walk toward her, squatting down in front of her.

"I don't doubt your anger, Kadence. Knowin' they did that makes me see red, but that anger and that fear needs to be directed at your ex."

"So you think it's okay that they set my house on fire, just because it was a warning?"

"Fuck no," I quickly reply, sensing things are getting way out of hand. It's not fucking okay, but fuck, I have to explain how dangerous these men are. I have no doubt the Mayhems threatened her; this is how they run. I feel conflicted in wanting to agree with her, but at the same time, I don't. "Kadence, just let me get my head around the fact that you were even engaged to that asshole."

"Don't bother. It sounds to me like you're defending them. Is that what sort of club you run?" She's not listening to what I have to say and I have no idea how to get through.

"Kadence, don't fuckin' put words in my mouth. All I'm sayin' is you obviously don't know the truth. All this anger should be directed to your ex. Goin' to a fuckin' secluded park with a man like Edwards is not smart. What were you thinkin'?"

"He's my ex. I was fine," she dismisses my concern, pissing me off.

"Yeah, so I've been told. That and how much you loved working your warm mouth on him. No wonder you're so good at it," I lash out and regret the words before I finish saying them. Her hand comes across my face, the slap stinging my cheek, the sound echoing in the quiet living area, shocking both of us.

"Get out."

"I'm not goin' anywhere."

"I swear to God, Nix, get the fuck out of my house. I've got nothing to say to you."

"Well, I've got a lot to say to you. Be pissed. That was a shitty thing to say, but fuck, listenin' to him tell me about you workin' his cock wasn't on top of my list of things I wanna fuckin' hear. I told you to stay put. I don't fuckin' have time to be chasin' your ass cause you decide to get a wild hair and fuck off." I can feel my anger rising and I can see hers bubbling under my gaze.

"Nix, just go. I don't want to see you anymore. This thing between us will never work if you're in bed with those types of people," she repeats my words about her ex back at me. I know she's angry, but so am I. I don't wanna leave her, but I sure as fuck don't wanna play games. I think about leaning and taking her mouth, claiming it to show her I can see past this bullshit argument. I know she's freaking out and trying to push me away.

Deciding to do just that, I lean in and slam my mouth on hers. She fights it, her hands coming to my chest pushing me back. I push further, intent to taste her, to calm her. I just want to make her see that I'm not what she thinks I am. My hand cups her neck, pulling her closer to me. Her soft lips open slightly, and for a second, I think I've got her, my tongue sliding into the wetness, seeking to entwine with hers, until she latches onto it and bites down hard.

"Fuck, Kadence, why'd the fuck you do that?" I ask, pulling back from her lips. My question comes out as a lisp. A warm, metallic, salty taste mixes with my saliva. Her hands come to my shoulders, pushing me back. I fall flat on my ass but watch her stand and walk to the front door.

"Go, Nix. I've got nothing to say to you." Her face holds no emotion. It's like she's just mentally switched off from me. Holly walks into the room watching our exchange carefully, but not saying anything. She looks to Kadence and back to me.

"Kadence," I sigh, rising from the floor, wiping the blood

on my sleeve.

"Save it. You have no idea what you're talking about, Nix. You weren't there. You didn't experience what I went through. For you to sit there telling me I'm misdirecting my anger, you're no better than Zane, and that just proves it. I've got nothing to say to you." She draws in a hard breath.

"Kadence."

"Get. The. Fuck. Out."

I walk up to her realizing I've totally screwed this up. The fun, flirty, sassy woman I've come to know over the last couple of weeks is gone, and standing in front of me is a cold replacement. Smartass Kadence is hot, but pissed off Kadence is something else. I know I'm not going to get through to her right now. Her ability to act indifferent doesn't surprise me; she's been like this from the moment I met her. But I've also seen her open up, seen the other side of this cold indifference.

"You think I don't know what I'm talkin' about, Kadence? That same club that you hate so much took my mom from me. I know exactly what you're goin' through. If you would just calm the fuck down, you would see I don't condone any of this shit, so don't play that card with me." My words register to her and understanding washes over her features before she hides it. We both stand quietly watching each other.

"I realized I fucked up here and you're angry. I get that. So I'm gonna let you calm down, let both of us calm down, but make no mistake, I'm comin' back and we *will* talk about this," I tell her when she doesn't say anything. I lean down to kiss her lips, but she turns her head, giving me her cheek.

Fuck me.

I walk straight out and then listen to her slam the door

behind me. My fist connects to the wall beside me. Pain radiates through my hand, taking my mind off the fucked-up shit that just happened. Looking back at the door, I stand for a few minutes hoping she changes her mind. When the door doesn't open, I walk away, pissed that I'm not with her right now, pissed that I fucked it up and even more pissed Zane Edwards is the cause of it all.

Motherfucker is gonna pay.

19

Kadence

THROWING BACK ANOTHER SHOT, I LET THE BURN take over and allow the warmth to soothe me. *Good God, I needed that.*

Turning around from the bar, I scan the club trying to find something to take my mind off the emptiness that has taken residence in me all week. Holly and I are back at Liquid, and if I'm going to be stuck here for the night, I may as well make the most of it. Holly dragged me out kicking and screaming after sulking all week at the way things ended with Nix. I keep replaying the whole scene in my head, and each word, each action leaves me cringing. I fucked up. Bad.

Taking my drink, I make my way back to our table. I

stumble slightly, the fifth shot making its way through my system. Yes, just what I was looking for, total oblivion.

"Whoa there, sweetheart," a familiar voice breathes over my ear while reaching for me before my ass lands on the floor.

"Jesse? What are you doing here?" I ask as I look up and gain my feet, walking the rest of the way back to my chair.

"What? Didn't you know?" he barks out a short laugh and sits down next to me. "Kadence, the Knights Rebels own this place." He shakes his head.

What the hell? How did I not know that? I need to pay more attention.

"Tell me he isn't here." A spark ignites for a second, and I look around hoping to see him but praying I don't.

"God, no." He shakes his head. "He sees you wearing that dress, you'd be out of here before you'd even see it coming." Like hell, I would be. I wouldn't give up without a fight. Besides, Nix and I are done. I haven't heard from him since I tossed him out last Sunday; it's now Friday. He did tell me he would call me, but I haven't heard from him since he texted me later that first night, telling me he wished I was with him, in his bed. I ignored him, my stubborn ass pushing him further away. Am I hurt that he hasn't called? Yes and no. What girl doesn't want a guy to call and sweep her off her feet, but at the same time, I've been hanging onto the anger all week. Holly's pissed at me because I met with Zane without her and that my stubborn ass is refusing to contact Nix. To top it all off, after the way I acted, she is siding with Nix.

"Wanna tell me what you've done to our Prez?" Jesse elbows me, taking me out of my alcohol-induced fog.

"What are you talking about, Jesse?" I act unaffected. I

don't want to get into it with him.

"He's been sulking around all week, and I haven't seen you around. Put two and two together." He sits back, his booted feet crossed at the ankles. I ignore his question and the pang of guilt I feel at hearing Nix is having a shit week like me. I look out at the dance floor trying to find Holly. I spot her dancing with a different guy than the one she went out there with. I wish I could be like her. I wish I had the freedom and the confidence not to be weighed down with my past worries. Nix was the first person who allowed me to do just that, and now after seeing Zane for ten minutes, I feel like everything is coming down around me. I've screwed things up. I bet he realizes what a raging bitch I am.

"What do you want me to say, Jesse?" I finally give him an answer. "He was an asshole. He said some shitty things. I responded with some shitty things, and then told him to leave and he did. I haven't heard from him all week. End of story." I take a sip of my drink, washing the lie down. It burns worse than the truth.

"Not end of story, Kadence. Don't feed me your bullshit." I narrow my eyes at him and his ability to see through my bullshit. I've known Jesse for three years, and sitting here across from him, he looks like the same blond-haired, blue-eyed pretty boy I met on my first day in group therapy. I'd just come out of my last surgery. I hated the world, hated myself, and I didn't want anyone's help. The only person I let in was Holly, and let's be honest, that's only because she wouldn't leave me alone, even after telling her to take a hike. I was a single, twenty-seven-year-old woman whose body was deformed. I didn't want anyone's pity; I didn't want to meet with a former Marine, ex-firefighter trained counselor. I didn't want to hear him tell me how lucky I was that I survived. I wanted to feel sorry for myself and be left alone. I walked into the session all anger and attitude. I didn't realize how far I was lost in my head.

Until Jesse pulled me firmly out.

Being in therapy, listening to Jesse's stories of what he lived through over in the war, made me realize how lucky I was. I had survived my burns. I could move on. Listening and learning about other people's stories left me heartbroken for them. While my injuries were extensive, and rehab and recovery was taking everything out of me, they by no means impaired me from living my everyday life. My self-loathing was for nothing. I survived, and the pretty-boy firefighter was the one to help me understand that. By showing me what he survived, what he endured and how he dealt with it, I was able to find the old Kadence and learn to accept what happened. Without Jesse, who knows where I would be. Having him come back into my life, by association feels right. He's like a big brother I never had.

"Just leave it alone, Jesse, okay? It was nothing," I tell him, my tone leaving no room to argue.

"If you say so, sweetheart," he smirks, shaking his head.

"So how long you been a part of the MC?" I ask, curious to know. I would never have guessed Jesse was part of the MC.

"I patched in when I came back from my last tour." He smiles. The man never stops smiling, always so happy.

"And you like it?" I ask, wondering what he gets out of being in a club like the Knights Rebels. I know Nix talked about brotherhood, but I wonder if Jesse feels the same way.

"It's the closest thing to a family I've had in a long time.

Nix saved me from a dark place, Kadence. I would do anything for that man."

Of course he did. Another tick in the Nix-is-amazing column, and I remember what an idiot I am. A redhead walks over, whispers into Jesse's ear, and plants her skinny ass on his lap.

Are you serious?

Rolling my eyes, I stand from the table not interested in watching Jesse pick up, and I'm over speaking about Nix. I've thought about him enough over the last six days, and I'm trying my best to leave it at what it was. I make my way through the crowd to the dance floor, leaving Jesse behind. He calls out, but I don't turn back. The last thing I want to do is show him how much I'm struggling with my argument with Nix.

Bodies push into me as the tempo of the music slowly rises. Holly is dancing with a new guy, his hands roaming her body as she sways in time with the song. I move to her, ready to dance and forget about the shit week I've had. The alcohol running through my veins help me let go, my inhibitions a little relaxed.

My body moves to the beat of the music. Swaying my hips, I let the song wash over me. My arms take on a life of their own. Embracing the beat, I feel it resonate in my soul.

When was the last time I danced freely?

Hands come around me, settling on my waist. I freeze up for a second before forcing myself not to be tense. I push up against the person at my back, moving my body further into him. His hard chest is plastered to my back. The song changes, taking the tempo slower. The guy behind me grinds his hips into my ass, and I push back, molding my back to his front.

"Wanna get your fuckin' hands off my woman?" Nix's voice crackles with anger behind me. The body behind moves away, the heat I was feeling now gone as a new presence moves in. Damn, I didn't even see the guy's face. I go to turn, ready to tell the asshole I'm not his woman, but his tattooed arms come around my front, pinning me to his chest.

"Give me one good reason I shouldn't take you over my fuckin' knee right now?" His breath comes to my ear. My body is instantly turned on by his dirty words.

"Nix—" I begin, but he cuts me off.

"Don't, Kadence. It's bad enough that you're in my arms wearin' this dress with those sexy fuckin' heels after not havin' you for five fuckin' days, but that you let that guy touch you, touch what's mine?" The gravelly sound of his voice sends a thrill down my spine. The breath of his voice brings goose bumps to my skin. For a moment, I forget I don't like him anymore, forget that he has ignored me all week, and just enjoy that he called me his woman.

"You didn't call," I accuse him, trying to get out of his embrace, but he holds me steady, pulling me closer. God, even to my own ears I sound whiney. *You didn't call? Jesus, Kadence, grow a pair would you.*

"I was waiting," he replies as an explanation. "Thought I would give you some space. Though seeing your reaction to seeing me, I'm thinkin' that was the wrong move."

I'm pissed my body feels more alive than it has all week; my heart finally has that extra beat in it, my stomach full of butterflies that he's here, touching me. My body begins moving to the music and my mind is unable to tell it to stop. I grind my backside into his hard length as his hands loosen their hold to move down to rest on my hips. Our bodies are swaying in a sensual rhythm.

"Babe, you gotta stop rubbin' that sweet ass up against me," he gripes, spinning me around to face him. My arms go up around his neck, and his smell invades my senses, the mixture of leather and his cologne pull me right back to our last night together.

Shit, all that hard work ruined by one sniff.

"What are you doing here?" I ask his chest. I can't bring myself to look up at him.

"I fucked up, Kadence," he admits, bringing his hand to my chin and lifting my face to look at him. His forehead creased in concern as he waits for me to respond.

"Nix, I was a bitch. Seeing Zane again… I don't know, seeing him again brought up all these memories," I immediately apologize, feeling like a brat. During the week, Holly and I did some digging and found out not only was Nix right about Zane, but also he was telling the truth about his mom. I felt like a real bitch.

"I get it, babe. I do. I was an ass, and I shouldn't have said what I did," he counter-apologizes. We both stand, watching each other. I didn't see my night ending up like this, and now that he's here in my arms, I don't even know why I was ever so angry. Okay, I still remember what he said, but knowing what I know of Nix, it was a natural reaction to anger, like me slapping him. His eyes sparkle with mischief like he's thinking something dirty and I can't help the smile I give him. He leans down, and I come to my toes, his lips to mine. The roughness of his tongue pushes through like the last time he was on my lips, but this time, I don't fight it.

So much for me holding my own.

I grant him access, his taste covering my tongue, our mouths connecting for forgiveness. Being in his presence again sets me on fire. The slow burn I've been feeling immediately ignites by one kiss. He pulls back, ending the hot but brief kiss. Running his eyes down the length of my body, he grabs my hand and pulls me off the dance floor. Taking long strides, he drags me behind, walking straight past Jesse, who still has the redhead on his lap, her breasts pressed up to his chest. He catches my eye and just shrugs. *Traitor.*

I scowl over at him letting him know I know that he is the one that ratted me out. He just laughs and gives me a wink. Nix pulls me around the corner and pushes me against the wall.

"Fuck, Kadence, I don't know if I'm gonna make it all the way back home. I need to fuck you so bad." His knee comes between my knees, spreading my legs further apart. The dirtiness of his words washes over me, and I've never felt more alive.

"On one hand, I wanna hike that barely-there sexy-as-fuck dress up and bury myself balls deep in you right now against this wall for every asshole to see that you're fuckin' mine." His fingers slide slowly up my leg, coming to the hem of the dress. "But, on the other hand, I wanna take you home, fuckin' make you wait for being a tease wearin' this outfit in public." I look down at the black dress I'm wearing. It's nothing too sexy, but the way Nix keeps looking at me, you'd think I was naked.

"Take me home and fuck me," I tell him. The dampness in my panties becomes uncomfortable after each word he grunts out. Anticipation builds, and all thoughts of my shitty week have left. His harsh words about Zane and the fire replaced by the dirty words he now speaks.

All that anger directed at him the last five days is now forgotten, because I know whatever he has planned will be something to be excited about.

20

Nix

PULLING UP INTO MY DRIVE AND HELPING KADENCE
off my bike takes all the self-control I possess. I'm working
hard at reining it in. The overpowering need to take her right
here on my bike is almost too much. Seeing her move her ass
up against some asshole snapped something in me. I really
fucked up on this one. I didn't want to ignore her all week but
after what went down, I just wasn't sure she was ready to hear
what I had to say about Zane Edwards.

Gunner has been fuckin' us all around, even starting in on
Mayhem Territory now. T and his boys have yet to detain him
or any of his crew. I know he's waiting now, and I have a bad
feeling that shit hasn't even begun. T's called in their

neighboring chapters while we all prepare for shit to go down. Gunner's using Zane's relationship with Kadence to go up against the Knights Rebels. We've been busy keeping everyone at bay, and trying to get a lock down on him while making sure I always had eyes on Kadence. I didn't trust that Edwards would leave her alone, and even if she was pissed at me, and I at her, I couldn't leave her open to a threat by Edwards.

I messed up with how I reacted to Kadence and Zane. She apparently is still working through some of that shit, but I still stand behind what I think. Zane Edwards is dangerous. The asshole got himself into some messed up shit before he got into bed with Gunner. Owing the MC money, and then trying to get himself out of it, he went from one shitty situation to another. Do I agree with T and his boys threatening her? Setting her house on fire? Fuck no, but the Mayhems are one percenters; that shit wouldn't bother them. They've done a hell of a lot worse and gotten away with it. Fuck, I've done worse. With her being the only connection to him, that threat had to go to someone. Once they realized he didn't give a fuck what happened to her, they let her be. Now that Kadence is with me, none of that will fall back on her. I protect what's mine and no one fucks with what's mine.

Kadence pulls me out of my thoughts as her hand comes down and squeezes my throbbing cock.

"You going to fuck me on your front lawn or are you going to take me up to your bed?" Her smooth voice is challenging, but her lips, soft against my neck, are inviting. Jesus, I nearly take her right here but I'm sure the neighbors don't want to see that show. Picking her up, I walk her to the front door. We've got five days to make up for and I'm not about to waste any time.

★★★

"Wow." Her breath comes out shallow and fast above me, her bright smile infectious, lighting up the room. "I might have to instigate another argument if that's how we make up," she laughs, rolling off me.

"Fuck no. A week without your sweet pussy is not worth it," I admit. Her smile deepens at my admission. Not seeing her, touching her, or even talking to her was bad enough.

"I'm sorry, Nix. I wish you didn't have to see that." She shakes her head, reliving our messed up Sunday afternoon. "You were right; my anger should be at him. I knew that he left me there, left me without a backwards glance, but I guess I was holding on to the hope that something else happened. Maybe he didn't want to leave me." I lean down and kiss her swollen lips.

"I didn't want you to learn that lesson, babe, not that way anyway." I kiss her lips again, not getting enough of the softness of them.

"I know, Nix, but I realize now I was holding on to something that wasn't there."

I nod, glad that she can finally see that. "The Mayhems, they run a lot differently to us," I begin, wanting this to be out there between us.

"It's okay, Nix," she interrupts me before I can even begin.

"No, Kadence, this situation is fucked and I need you to understand that I would never be okay with what they did to you, but you also have to know our relationship with that club is based on keeping the town safe. Both clubs have done things to hurt each other, but we've come to a point where it's not worth it. I can't just go in and seek revenge for what they did."

"I'm not asking you to do that, Nix."

"I know that, but I need to lay it out for you, okay?"

"Does your club do those sorts of things now?" she asks, her voice barely above a whisper, unsure of my answer.

"I'm not gonna lie. We sometimes have to do things that you're not gonna like; that's just the way it is. We do our best to keep out of that shit, but if we have to, we will go above the law." She nods, not saying anything.

"You still with me here?" I ask, hoping this isn't a deal breaker.

"I don't think I'm ever going to be okay if you break the law, but I think I can deal," she admits, turning to me, and pulling the sheet up with her to cover herself. I stop her, pulling it off.

"Nix," she argues, pulling it back up again.

"Don't hide away from me." I reach down, throwing the sheet off her again. I don't like it when she shies away from me. Sometimes she can just let go, forget about the scars, while other times, she'll hold herself back. I want her to feel confident and comfortable in my bed.

"I don't want you to look at it," she confesses. Her voice wavers and her hands cover the marred skin. I reach down and run my finger along the scar.

"Kadence, don't ever be ashamed in front of me. You're fuckin' beautiful. This scar here," I move my finger along the rigid surface, "simply means you're stronger than that asshole."

My finger moves to the piercing that Sy gave her. It looks

almost healed and so damn sexy; the soft glow of the bedside table lamp hits the golden bar. I play with the barbell, and watch as her belly contracts.

"Will you tell me what happened?"

She rolls onto her back, a breath escaping her in frustration at me asking. "It's really not that exciting," she assures me, but I doubt that. Something like this is huge.

"Try me," I push.

"I woke up in the middle of the night to an empty bed. Zane and I had been fighting that night, but I didn't think anything of it until I woke up to a noise." Her head turns to the side, looking directly at me. "I went looking for him, thinking he was still up. I didn't think it could be anyone else. It was the smoke that hit me first. The smell was almost choking me." She takes a deep breath still looking at me. The silence in the room is eerie: me waiting patiently for her to speak and her trying to gather strength to continue. "When I made it down the hall, I couldn't even comprehend that half of my house was burning in front of me. For a moment, I wasn't sure what to do or where Zane was. It all just happened so quickly; there was an explosion, and when I tried to get out, the door was stuck and the smoke was too thick." She stops for a moment, letting the details wash over me. Reaching down, I entwine my fingers with hers. She seems so detached, like she is reading from a script, but I know reliving it wouldn't be easy.

"I woke in the hospital the next day after having the first surgery. The police told me the fire was started with two Molotov cocktails through the windows. Zane was nowhere to be found and I was severely burnt to ten percent of my body."

Fuck me.

"They told me my skin was too damaged; that it wouldn't be able to regenerate on its own, so the first surgery I went through was to protect the most damaged parts before they could graft it." She shows me the smoothest part of the burn. The pale skin is taut, not red and raised like the rest. You think that would be the least burnt area.

"Fuck, Kadence," I say, trying to get my head around it.

"Yeah it was a lot to take in. The second surgery was a grafting; they took skin from my backside and I really wasn't prepared for the pain of that." A shudder runs through her as she relives the pain.

"After three weeks, fluid built up underneath the donor skin, preventing it from attaching to the wound. It failed, so they had to re-graft more skin. That time they grafted from inside my thigh. I'm not sure if you've ever noticed," she says, pointing to the slightly different patch of skin. Leaning forward I scan the area. I must admit I haven't noticed it. My eyes have always been on the prize between her thighs. I had seen the faint area on her ass, but she never acted like it bothered her, so I never commented.

"I stayed in the hospital for three weeks after that one. I wasn't healthy enough to be able to go home. I gave up, mentally and physically. Looking back, I can see the weakness, but laying in the hospital, I didn't see it as survival, only how much I had lost."

"You're one of the strongest women I've ever met," I interrupt, not sure if she understands the honesty of my words. She shakes her head in disagreement, a blaze of indignation burning furiously in her eyes.

"I was so worked up over losing my home and Zane,

angry that it was all taken away from me. I didn't want to think about how lucky I was or how strong I was. People around me in that burn unit were dying, fighting for their lives, and I was complaining about this small section of my body. I was selfish and had no idea about being strong until I met Jesse."

She turns her body to mine, lifting her leg over mine. "That's how I met Jesse. He was the one to show me what it truly meant to survive. I was feeling sorry for myself and he helped pull me from the darkness," she admits and it all comes together why Jesse is so protective of her. Even though I hate Jesse had that with her, I know she needed him at that time in her life.

"You survived it Kadence and you're stronger for it," I tell her. Hearing her story, knowing what she went through burns something inside of me, something I haven't felt in a long time.

"I know, but it's a struggle sometimes. Opening myself up to you is scary, Nix. My insecurities leave me feeling so unworthy. I've never let anyone in." Her voice is quiet with the truth.

"I get that. Believe me I do, but hiding your body from me is something you don't need to do. I swear it. I look at you and I don't see what you think. I see you, Kadence, the woman who survived that, and if that doesn't make me want to know more about you, I don't know what does."

She shakes her head, still not getting it. "Don't tell me that if you could choose between a woman with no scars and me, you would choose this." She points to her burns.

"Are you fuckin' kiddin' me, Kadence? Believe me, there is no one I would chose over you," I tell her, hoping she can hear the honesty in my words. Fuck, this woman is dangerous to me.

"If you say so, Nix." She rolls her eyes, not trusting a word of it.

"Do you know how beautiful you are?" I ask, concerned she doesn't.

"Nix," she says, trying to move her leg off me, but I stop her, holding her to me.

"No, answer me."

"I'm not ugly," she laughs, but nothing about this conversation is funny.

"Do you know the moment I laid my eyes on you, I felt the wind knock out of me, like someone just gut-punched me. I was pissed that Addison threw the meetin' on me, concerned for Z, and I walked in, and fuck me, I nearly fuckin' fell over. I couldn't even look you in the eye at first. I had to calm myself down, or who knows what I would have said. Then you threw your attitude and set me on fire."

"Yeah, when I was fully clothed." She shakes her head still not getting it.

"Then a week later, you stood in front of me baring this." I touch her burns again. "Not once did I think any differently. If anything at all, it made sense. You feelin' unworthy is the biggest load of crap I have ever heard. If anythin', it's me who is unworthy. You stood there vulnerable, and fuck if that wasn't beautiful. As much as you hate your scars, I love them, 'cause they make you, you. The person who stood in front of me, and for the first time ever, let me in. Me. If anyone is unworthy of that, it's me baby," I give it to her, letting her see the truth in my words. The first teardrops fall, and for a second, I think I've fucked up.

"Don't cry." I wipe at her face. Fuck, I have no idea how to deal with tears.

"No one has ever said anything so nice to me before," she hiccups.

"What, no one?" I ask in disbelief.

"I was going to marry a man who never once said anything as sweet as that."

"Babe, Zane is all kinds of asshole, I can believe that, but the shit he's put you in is beyond asshole. He's a fuckin' fool for not treasurin' you. I don't ever want you to meet with him again," I tell her, adding that in, hoping she listens. I couldn't handle her getting hurt once again at his hands.

"Trust me, Nix, I never want to see him again." She wipes at her face, the tears no longer falling.

"I think it was a setup, him comin' back in town," I say, treading carefully. I don't want to scare her but she needs to know.

"I'll be careful," she promises.

"Good, and next time I see him, he and I are gonna have serious words."

"Nix, don't go and do something stupid. It's not worth it. *He's* not worth it," she pleads, her sad eyes now gone and replaced with concern.

"Oh, it will be worth it, Kadence." I don't tell her that I've already got the boys looking for him. That asshole is going down. She rolls her eyes at me, another thing I have missed all week. Rolling her back over, I cover her body with mine. The urgency to have her again, to worship her body, and prove to her just how beautiful she is, scars and all, pulls at me. This woman consumes me, and it's time to show her just how much.

★★★

> **NIX**: Got held up meet me at the club.

I send the text to Kadence once I realize how late it is. We were meant to be staying in for the night, but after another fuck around with one of T's shipments, he called a meeting to keep us up to date with their new plan regarding Gunner. The sooner they sort this shit out, the better.

> **KADENCE**: Okay. Be there in ten.

It will be the third time she's been here, and each time she gets more comfortable. If only I could get her to agree to come clean to Z. I'm sick of hiding this from him. Even though it's only been three weeks since that night she opened up to me, I feel like we're slowly getting somewhere.

"What the fuck you smiling about?" Beau asks, kicking at my foot resting out in front of me.

"Not what, who," Jesse smiles across from him. Beau looks concerned for a moment before hiding it.

"What the fuck is your problem?" I ask, noticing he is the only one who hasn't taken to her.

"Don't like that she's got ties to Gunner," he shrugs

"Fuck off. You had a problem with her before that."

"He's just pissed she got out under his nose." Brooks laughs, taking a sip of his beer.

"Fuck you." He stands and goes to leave.

"Sit the fuck down, you pussy," I tell him. Ignoring the fact that Brooks is right, Beau has some serious trust issues.

"She knows what we're about, brother," I tell him,

knowing it will take more than words to get him to trust her. It's just gonna take time. He nods, knowing what I'm saying. I trust Beau more than anything, and he's only looking out for me.

"You staying for the party?" Jesse wiggles his eyebrows up and down. The fucker is crazy. He's already got a blonde bitch on his knee, no doubt he will have another soon.

"Love to see Kadence's face when she sees one of those parties," Beau laughs.

"Fuck off. She'll deal," I defend her.

"Deal with what?" she asks, walking in wearing her hot teacher get up.

"Especially wearing her uppity clothes," Beau keeps going. Her eyes narrow to him, but she doesn't bite. She knows she pissed him off that day she snuck out.

"Hey, baby." I pull her down on my lap when she gets close enough.

"Hey," she sighs, not caring we're in front of all the guys in the middle of the clubhouse. Yeah, my woman fits right in.

"Hey, guys." She pulls back and turns her body to face the table.

"How was work?" I ask when they get through their hellos.

"Meh, work is work. Glad the week is over." She goes to stand from my lap, but I hold her in place.

"Want a drink?"

"Are we staying?"

"Was gonna have a few with the boys," I tell her, waiting to see what she's gonna do. She needs to get used to the clubhouse lifestyle.

"Okay, yeah, I'll have a beer," she smiles, pushing up from

my lap.

"Hunter, get my woman a beer," I yell over to the bar, taking my hands to her waist, and planting her back where she was.

"If I knew you were going to yell at him, I would have gotten up to get it myself," she whispers so the others don't hear.

"That's his job, baby. He likes gettin' me beers," I tell her, smiling, but she just shakes her head.

"You ready to see yourself a real Knights Rebels' party?" Jesse asks her a few minutes later.

"I'm sure it's not that crazy, Jesse." She rolls her eyes, not understanding just how serious these boys like to party

I laugh on the inside; the woman has no idea.

21

Kadence

HOLY SHIT.

That's the only thought I have lying in Nix's bed at the clubhouse the next morning. Jesse was right. The Knights Rebels sure know how to party. My head throbs as I try to roll out from under Nix.

"Don't move," he groans into his pillow.

"Need bathroom," I say, beginning to sound like Nix. I need the bathroom and I need it now. He rolls to the side releasing me from his body. I barely make it to the toilet to bring up who knows what. Fuck. I drank way too much. After Jesse explained just how much the Knights Rebels like to party, I decided I need a few drinks if I was about to witness something like that.

"Fuck, baby, you sick?" Nix asks from behind me, his voice still full of sleep.

"Go, Nix. You don't want to see it let alone smell it," I moan, my head still in the bowl. He ignores me of course and pulls my hair back as I empty my stomach into the bowl.

"Oh, God," I moan as he places a cool washcloth over my forehead.

"You feelin' better?" he asks after a few minutes of reprieve.

"Yeah, I think I got it all up," I say, standing to wash the funk out of my mouth.

"I'll get you something to eat," he says, walking away. The thought of eating after what I just threw up makes me dry heave, but I don't argue. I already know he won't listen. Cleaning up and making myself presentable, I make my way to the kitchen.

"Kadence," Jesse booms from the table as I walk straight to the coffee machine.

"Shhhh," I whisper, turning away from him. I don't know how in the hell Jesse can even be up and about this morning after the things I witnessed last night, let alone be in a happy mood. He laughs louder, seeing how I pulled up from last night.

"Fuck, girl, you sure know how to party with some of the big guys," he laughs into his coffee cup.

"Oh, look what the cat dragged in," Sy smirks from the door. "Didn't think we would see you this morning," he says as he makes his way to get his morning coffee.

"Ease up, guys. It was my first clubhouse party," I whine into my coffee.

"Here, baby," Nix says, passing me a piece of dry toast. "Eat," he demands, pointing to the spot next to Jesse.

"Gah," I grumble, sitting down next to a smiling Jesse.

"You did good," Jesse nods. I don't know how he thinks I did good. I got drunk off my ass and now I'm paying for it.

"He's right. You did do good. Told all those bitches who was boss," Nix laughs and I drop my head to the table.

"Can we not talk about it?" I ask, hoping they'll drop it.

"Hell, no, that shit was funny," Brooks says as he walks in to the kitchen. "I knew you had it in you," he winks, walking past me.

"You were so hot, going all possessive over me," Nix whispers into my ear.

"Is it really like that at every party?" I ask, hoping it's not. I don't know if I could handle knowing these skanks are trying to get into my man's pants. They all laugh, not answering my question.

"Don't worry. You made it known not to fuck with you," Nix says, putting me at ease.

"Though she hasn't met Chrissie yet," Brooks adds.

"Oh, yeah," Jesse laughs, making me worry more.

"Who the fuck is Chrissie?"

"Forget her," Nix says, putting me at ease. "The bitch will hear how you laid Tina out." At the mention of Tina's name, the boys all start laughing. I feel kind of bad that I did that, but I was sitting right there and the woman just rubbed her tits along his arm. *Hell the fuck no.* I don't know what came over me. Okay, that's a lie. I know what came over me; my temper getting the best of me. Once Nix told her to fuck off, she still didn't listen so I had to do something to get her to listen. I wasn't expecting to have to pull her off him. I'm mortified while the guys think it's epic. Great, now I'll never live this one down.

"Next time I see her, I'll tell her I'm sorry."

"Like fuck you will," Nix warns. "The bitch had it coming. Forget it, Kadence. She'll now know not to fuck with you. You wanna survive in the club against women like her, they need to know you won't back down." All the boys nod, agreeing with him.

"Okay," I say, taking a bite of my toast. I didn't really wanna say sorry anyway.

"Eat up, baby. We're going for a ride," he says, watching me slowly eat my breakfast.

"Where?" I ask, not sure I can handle a ride today. I need a bed, a bucket, and some Tylenol.

"It's a surprise," he says, not telling me.

"I hate surprises," I say, swallowing large bite of toast.

"You'll like this one."

"Dinner at your place tonight, Prez," Jesse says, standing from the table.

"I'll bring the beer," Brooks says, also standing.

"I'll get the steaks," Beau adds, walking in and joining our conversation.

"I'll bring myself," Jesse laughs.

"Make sure you have a fucking shower before you turn up," Sy says, standing next to him. "You fucking stink like sex and pussy," he says, shaking his head. The thought of Jesse smelling like that has me standing from the chair and racing to the bathroom to throw up the half-piece of toast I just consumed, leaving the guys laughing their asses off. Assholes.

The sunlit clouds drift across the blue Nevada sky. Commanding my eyes to stay open, I take in the sight of them. Fresh air fills my lungs with every sharp breath I take. My heart beats furiously out of my chest at that the thrill of what we're doing. The chance that we could get caught in the middle of the day heightens the level of adrenaline coursing through me. He's building me with every swipe of his finger and every flick of his tongue. I force myself to stay quiet, biting down on my arm as the desire to cry out becomes too much.

"Don't hold it in, Kadence," Nix growls from between my legs, his grumbles vibrating my pussy.

"Nix," I pant, wanting to explode, but the thought of getting caught holds me back.

"Babe, you either come on my mouth, or you come on my cock. Either way you're comin'," he dictates before dragging his rough tongue through my soft flesh again.

Shit.

His finger enters me again, finding the place he knows will take me over. A blistering heat swells from my core, slowly gathering momentum as he works my clit and massages my G-spot. The yearning to sensor myself long forgotten as the wave of encompassing pleasure spreads through me. I thrash my head, back and forth. My thighs squeeze shut, locking his head between my legs. His strong hands go to my knees pushing them apart as he continues to assault my most sensitive place.

"Nix," I cry out as the heat sears over my whole body; the most marvelous sensation prickles at my skin as my body begs for it never to end. Seized by a rush of awareness so intense, I scream out with unabashed abandon.

Nix slows his talented tongue as the wave subsides, the last of my orgasm rolling through me. My hangover long forgotten, I marvel in the aftermath of my orgasm.

Oh, God, did I just let him do that in a public place?

Sitting up from the picnic blanket, I push down my skirt and watch Nix lick his fingers clean. He looks so freaking delicious kneeling in front of me with his chin covered in my arousal and his eyes shining with a devilish glint.

"Fuck, sweetheart, I love it when you go off like that," he states, coming back up to me and capturing my mouth with desperate urgency. The taste of myself mixed in with his taste, unfortunately, turns me on more. Jesus, I need him again.

My hands come around his neck; falling back down to the blanket, I pull him with me. His weight crashes to me. The hard pulse of his arousal in his pants rubs against the inside of my leg.

"Want me to take care of you?" I ask, smiling against his lips.

"Oh, baby, you've got no idea what I have in store for you." He smiles wickedly before moving back up to his knees and hiking my skirt back up to expose my bareness. He took my panties off when we sat down for our picnic, pocketing them and told me I was not getting them back. Typical Nix.

"You're gonna get up and you're gonna turn around and show me that sexy ass of yours." He says it so calmly like we're in the privacy of our bedroom and not out in the open

"No, Nix, someone will see us," I flat out refuse. We've already done way too much today, and we're lucky we haven't been caught yet. I look around seeing if anyone has stumbled upon our little hiding place.

Last night, when I was drunk off my face, I made a

comment about public sex. Somehow, Nix thought fulfilling that one thing I'd yet to do would go to the top of his list. I wasn't too keen to try, but after him convincing me, or should I say just taking me, I now know that it is indeed very hot.

It's been three weeks since I opened up about the fire, letting him in to understand my whole ordeal. I knew for us to move forward, I had to let him in, but I wasn't expecting it to be so soon. I don't know if we're moving too fast, but we've spent every night together at his house, in his bed and even a few nights at the club. Even the nights he had Z, he wanted me there, me only agreeing if I snuck in after Z went to bed and leaving before he woke. Every night, he proves to me just how much he thinks I'm beautiful, how much he craves me, and every night I feel like I'm giving him a little more of myself.

His eyes find mine, anchoring me to my spot on the picnic blanket he brought along for our impromptu picnic, Nix told me we were going for a ride. He didn't tell me we would be stopping for a public sex session.

"Yes, Kadence," he argues, reaching down to release his erection from his jeans.

"Geez put it away, Nix." I look around again, making sure we're still alone.

"The only place I'm gonna put this," he stops to look down at his hand stroking his rigid shaft, "is in that tight pussy of yours."

"You're such a romantic," I accuse, but the action he's doing draws me in, mesmerizing me.

"You want romance, baby? You want roses and sweet nothings whispered to you as I worship your body gently?" The smoothness of his words caresses me. The image of him fisting himself still captures me.

"Well, it would be nice," I lie, knowing I love his dirty mouth. No other man has been able to get me ready with one sentence.

"Fuck that. I'm hard and fast and I'm anythin' but fuckin' gentle. Now get on your knees and point that sexy ass in my face."

"Do you even have a condom, Nix?" I ask, looking up from his cock.

"Don't need one," he states.

"Is that right?" I cock my brow at him, just waiting to hear this one. We've always used a condom, and as much as I want to say yes, we haven't had the talk about it.

"I'm clean, babe, and I've seen those pills you take. Today, I fuck you bare," he answers my worries, while still bossing me.

"Do I even get a say? Geez, Nix, could you get any more caveman? Me fuck you bare, woman." I roll my eyes at him.

"I fuckin' love it when you're a smartass, makes me wanna fuck you harder." He smiles, still stroking himself. Fuck, why does that turn me on.

"Why don't you ask instead of demanding me all the time?"

"Hmm, that's not fun, but let me try," he smirks, leaning in and kissing my parted lips.

"Kadence, I'm gonna take you raw. I'm gonna fuck you so hard and you'll scream so loud, you'll be lettin' the fuckin' birds know how much you love my cock, and then you're gonna sit here with my cum leaking down your legs while we eat lunch, okay?" he says it so calm, like the thought of it is perfectly normal.

The corners of my lips start to lift and I try to hold in my laughter.

"Nix, that was worse."

"What? I thought that was good. I like that idea." He acts like he's offended. "Okay, how about, babe, please let me sink my thick cock into your tight pussy and feel your snug heat like I haven't before. I want to feel you tighten around me for the first time with no barrier, Kadence. Then when I finish, I want to watch my cum spill from your cunt while I eat my lunch."

"NIX," I yell, "don't say that word. It's gross."

"Nothing gross about it, babe," he smiles, kissing me again. His tongue seductively reclaims my mouth.

"You gonna let me fuck you bare?" he asks against my lips. This time the question is tender and intimate, all teasing aside.

"Do I have a choice?"

"You'll always have a choice, Kadence. I'll just let you know when you make the wrong one." His eyes sparkle with mischief and I give in to his dirty yet sweet words. Wrapping my legs around him, I feel the warmness of his cock at my center. I embrace his smoothness as he tenderly enters me. The connection of our bodies on a deeper level suspends me for a moment, the touch of his skin, the warmth of his body all brings me apart.

Does it frighten me that we seem to be getting in so deep with each other? Yes, but I can't fight it. We can't get enough of one another, the attraction heightened by every moment we spend with each other. I've known this man for seven weeks, and every day he tears at my perfectly constructed armor. To say I'm not feeling anything for him would be a lie.

"Kadence?" he whispers as our bodies move together, his

rhythm intense with each slow, deliberate thrust.

"Yeah?" I answer as I feel myself begin the climb. The heat that gathers from the base of my spine rapidly builds momentum.

"You ruin me, woman," he breathes, before taking my mouth in his. I want to tell him he ruins me too, more than I care to admit, but right now, it's like the warmth he's filling me is enough. It's building quietly inside of me waiting to devastate me.

Closing my eyes, I let the sweet depth of his movements take over me, knowing more than anything that this man has the power to devastate me. I'm just not sure I'm ready to admit that to him, let alone myself.

"Kadence, how the fuck did Nix score you?" Jesse asks later that night sitting on Nix's back deck. I take a sip of my drink and shrug. More like how the hell did I score him.

I knew the boys were coming over for dinner, but after my day of fighting a horrendous hangover and our little rendezvous in the park today, I wanted to eat in and just be with each other.

"What about you, Brooks? How did you end up with Kelly?" I ask, taking the pressure off me.

"It was love at first sight." He smiles back at me. You can see the man is smitten with his wife. Over the last few hours, I've come to learn Brooks is the oldest of the bunch. He was a prospect when Nix was still in high school. I wonder if the shit he's lived under Red Knight influenced him in staying on when Nix stepped up. Last night, he introduced me to everyone in the club, from the main set of guys who help run the businesses, to the weekenders, the men who come in and hang out over the weekend. I really did have a good time. The club, the people, all made me feel welcome.

"Kelly and Addison used to be best friends," he explains, and I don't miss the past tense reference. It still rubs me the wrong way hearing her name. I know she's Nix's ex and Z's mother, but ever since that afternoon in my classroom, I don't know what it is, but something about her doesn't sit right with me.

Nix and I have avoided talking about her. I feel like it's one of those conversations I'll never be ready for.

"She walked in one day with Addison and I fell in love," he continues.

"Just like that?" I question, trying to hold back my disbelief. I am a strong believer that a person can't fall in love in an instant. People fall in lust, often confusing it for love. That desire makes your heart beat faster, your palms sweat all the while leaving that overwhelming urge to want to be with them. All those things are important when finding the one, but until you fall in lust with those intense feelings, only then can love grow.

"Just like that," he repeats. I nod my head, not about to get into it with him. The man believes he fell in love at first sight; who am I to tell him that it's impossible.

Nix catches my eye from across the decking; he's been in deep conversation with Beau for the last five minutes. Beau's still holding onto his annoyance that I outmaneuvered him back at the clubhouse a couple of weeks ago. He's barely said a few words to me, and I'm beginning to worry he might not like me.

"You lookin' after my woman, Brooks?" Nix questions

from across the table.

"You bet ya," he calls back, tipping the neck of his beer his way.

"Keep her away from that asshole," he jokes, pointing to Jesse. I laugh aloud and Jesse fakes a pout. The guy is a massive flirt, no wonder Nix doesn't trust him. Hell, I don't know how I feel about the traitor, ratting me out to Nix. I level my gaze at him, realizing I never called him on his play last week.

"What?' he asks, seeing my frown.

"I just remembered I'm angry at you."

"For what?"

"For ratting me out to Nix, that night at Liquid." I don't tell him I think of that night only for the unbelievable make-up sex and the night Nix made me feel beautiful.

"Oh, please, he already knew you were there. He had eyes on you all week." He laughs and I immediately recognize what a fool I am. I honestly thought he would have just let me be for a week. Of course, Nix had his boys follow me. I turn, looking at him, and the man just shrugs. Shrugs.

"Babe, I've had a man on you every second you've been out of my sight," he admits, looking smug.

"You what!" I come to stand. I can't believe I never noticed. How did I never notice?

"It's for your own protection, Kadence," he explains without explaining.

"It's a bit much," I argue, sitting back down, feeling awkward in front of the guys. I can go head to head with Nix, but having an audience of all the boys is a bit too much for me.

"Your dipshit ex is still sniffing around. Until we find him and make it clear that you're off limits, you've got a tail," he explains coming to pull a chair up at the table.

"I can take care of myself, Nix. Zane won't bother me again."

"Kadence, he will. Trust me. It's best this way."

"But I'm sure the guys have better things to do, right?" I ask, looking at Jesse, trying to get Nix to see.

"Not me. I love it when you and Holly go shopping, especially in Victoria's Secret." He bounces his brows at me.

"Jesse," I gripe, listening to Sy and Nix growl. "Did you just growl like a dog?" I ask Sy, trying not to laugh remembering Holly's reference to him barking. He narrows his eyes, his lips tightly sealed.

I look to Brooks, hoping I have an ally in him. "That coffee shop you go to in the morning is my favorite." The bastard winks. Rolling my eyes, I turn to Sy; he looks at me as if the question is stupid. Of course, he hates it.

"He doesn't count. The fucker is a cranky asshole," Nix replies before I can use him as an example.

"Fine," I huff out defeated, "Beau?" I ask, not hopeful with him still being pissed. Last night he didn't warm up to me.

"I'll let ya know next week, Kadence, when I'm on duty," he smirks, and I finally give up.

"Nix," I plead, hoping I can at least get him to ease up a little. Shopping? Come on.

"It's for your own protection. It's that or lock you down." My body freezes for a second at the thought of lockdown. Yuck. No way.

"Didn't think so," he adds, seeing my disdain for lockdown. "As soon as we find the asshole, we'll ease up. Until then enjoy your entourage." He smiles his smug-ass smile.

What a nightmare.

"Do you believe in love at first sight?" I ask later that night, not even realizing how that could sound until it's out of my mouth. After thinking over what Brooks told me earlier in the night, I wanted to know what Nix thought.

"I think anything is possible," Nix responds behind me, reaching around to cup my breasts under the bath water.

"Well, that settles that then," I reply. My smartass tone not lost on him.

"Watch it, Kadence." He pinches my nipple in warning.

"Well?" I push, wanting to know.

"What do you want me to say? I don't think I've ever loved anyone but my mom, dad and Z," he admits.

"Didn't you love Addison?" I ask, and cringe as soon as the question leaves my mouth.

"I thought I did. I tried hard to, but I soon learnt it's not meant to be hard. You either love them or don't. There ain't no learnin'." I nod, agreeing with that statement.

"But you asked her to marry you. You must have had feelings for her."

"Didn't ask her. We just did it when we found out she was pregnant with Z. Lookin' back, I know that wasn't the right thing to do, but I wanted somethin' better for my son. I wanted him to have a mom and dad."

I nod, understanding his reasons. I can see where he was coming from, but I don't agree.

"What about you?" he questions, throwing it back at me.

"No, I don't believe in love at first sight."

"Are you sure, Kadence? I was there when you first met me." He laughs, and I elbow him in the stomach.

"Ha ha. No, I think people fall in love with the idea of it, but lust is what you fall into, and love can only grow from that," I answer honestly. Do I think I can fall in love with Nix? Yes, but right now what we have isn't love, because honestly, can someone love another after a short time? For me, this feeling was like the beginning of an intense journey. A spark ignites with every kiss and every touch, his words fueling the flame further. I can see myself catching fire, burning incandescently for him.

"Are you in lust with me, Kadence?" he teases, pinching my nipple again.

"I'm in something with you," I retort. *Oh, God, did I just admit to that?*

"Did you love your asshole ex?" he asks, ignoring my slip, bringing the washer over my stomach.

"I did. I gave everything to him, but even then it wasn't enough," I confess, feeling like a fool, and I hate myself for it. I loved him more than anything. I was the idiot who loved someone more than they loved me.

"As much as I don't wanna talk about that fucker while I'm layin' naked in the bath with you, I just have to say, I'm glad it wasn't enough. 'Cause if it had been, you'd never have given me a chance." He kisses my temple.

"So what you're saying, Nix, is that you're glad I'm not good enough?" I laugh, teasing him.

"Kadence, if you only ever give me what you've given me so far, it will be more than enough." I lean back and twist my head to look up at him.

"Are you sure, Nix? You strike me as the type as all or

nothing."

"Oh, baby, I am, but I'm also the type to know when he's got a good thing, and you, Kadence, are a good thing." He leans down, our lips finding each other.

I want to relish in the feeling of now, of in this moment, knowing it's something I'll want to remember. That pivotal point when you know the man you're giving your body to just took a little of your heart.

Lust my ass, my heart sings.

22

Nix

I STIR AT THE SMELL OF COOKED BACON COMING UP from the kitchen. I don't even need to open my eyes to know she isn't in bed. Looking over at the clock, I see it's half past nine. I groan in frustration that once again I haven't woken up with Kadence naked in my bed; she keeps disappearing on me. Rolling out of bed, I grab my boxers and make my way downstairs. I need to have a word with my woman telling her a few house rules. Number one rule: no leaving the goddamn bed before I wake up.

She's standing at the stove, my T-shirt hanging low on her thighs, her bare feet looking fucking amazing in my kitchen. What is it about her feet in my house? Walking up behind her,

I push the loose strand off her neck and plant a kiss on her soft vanilla skin.

"Mornin'."

"Good morning." She turns around to face me. Her smile nearly knocks me on my ass.

"Fuck, you're beautiful," I tell her, and I've never spoken more truth before. A slight pink blush floats across her cheeks as she shakes her head in disagreement. The woman just doesn't see what I see. It's been two months since I walked into her classroom, and she looks more and more beautiful to me every time I see her.

"Gotta tell ya, babe, as much as I like seeing you barefoot in my kitchen, I'd much prefer to have your naked body layin' next to me when I open my eyes for the day."

"You've got to eat, Nix."

"I was gonna eat you," I confess, leaning in and brushing my lips against hers. She rolls her eyes and smacks my chest, a move she seems to have perfected, and it seems I've grown to like it, a lot.

"Don't be vulgar," she responds, and it's my turn to roll my eyes.

"How many times do I have to prove to you that you love my dirty mouth?" Leaning down I kiss the softness of her lips, I can't seem to get enough of her mouth. "And you love my dirty mouth on that pretty pussy of yours," I tell her and kiss her again, stopping her from arguing with me. "Come back to bed," I plead. She melts into me, but the smell of burning bacon brings her back.

"Shit," she shrieks, turning around, trying to save our breakfast. See, eating her would be much easier.

"What's your plans for today?" I ask, walking over to the

coffee pot, frustrated that I'm not getting her back to bed.

"I don't know. At some stage I'm going to have to go home. I have to work tomorrow." I'm happy she doesn't fob me off, wanting to rush home. The last two months have been fucking amazing, but we've been going at a slow pace. I want more. I want her in my club, by my side. No more hiding. I understand we need to tread lightly with school, but my patience is wearing thin.

"We're havin' a club BBQ this afternoon, a family affair. I want you there," I tell her, watching her closely for a freak-out. She looks up at me, not showing any tells to what she is thinking, so I continue. "Z's gonna be there. It's my four days startin' today. You okay with that?" I push, hoping she doesn't argue and we can just go about our day. We have a date in bed, my mouth buried in her pussy.

"Do you think that's a good idea?" she challenges, turning away to break an egg into the pan.

"Why not? You know what I want, Kadence. I'm not in the habit of fuckin' around. If you're with me, then you're with me. I'm not sneaking around at night anymore. I want you in my club, around my people. I'm done hidin' us from Z." I lay it out it for her. I'm thirty-seven years old. Three years ago, no way would I be saying this, but Kadence is different, and I'm a man who knows what he wants, and by God, I want this woman. This perfectly scarred woman, who pushes my buttons and argues over every damn thing, I wouldn't want her any other way.

"You with me on this? I ask her again, watching her break a second egg.

"Can I bring Holly?" she asks, still avoiding my question.

"Jesus Christ, Kadence," I growl, walking up to her, and

turning her around to face me. "Tell me you're with me on this."

"Do you think this is moving too fast, Nix?"

"Fuck no! You know me, Kadence. I don't mess around. I had you in my bed after one date. I like to move fast," I claim. She knows this and, besides, two fucking months is not fast. She's fucking lucky I've waited this long.

"And what happens when you've had your fill? Don't you think Z will be confused?" She turns back around to remove the eggs off the heat, saving them from burning like the bacon. What the fuck? Is this what she thinks I'm doing, just getting my fill?

"Jesus, woman, don't you get it? How can someone so beautiful and smart as you, be so clueless? Every time we're together, I feel it more. Stop fightin' it and start embracin' it. You know this shit deep down and I know I'm never gettin' my fill of you, ever." I pull her to me, away from the stove, and then turn her and walk her back to the counter. "If you don't tell me you're with me, I'll take you right here and now until you agree."

"You can't just fuck me into submission, Nix." My hands come to her waist turning her around to face the counter. I don't even respond to her statement. I will fuck her into a yes.

"Keep your hands on the bench and don't move them," I demand, my voice taking on the deeper menacing tone she seems to like. Ripping her lace panties down her legs I watch as she nods her head, her legs slightly spreading, letting me know she wants this.

I move my hands under the hem of her shirt, sliding them higher to cup her breasts. Her nipples pebble under my fingers, her arousal my main mission.

"Tell me you like it when I fuck you into submission, Kadence," I demand, squeezing her pert nipples hard between my thumb and finger. She nods in agreement, but I want words. Dragging my hand down her body, I run it along her raised scar and feel her tense under my touch. I ignore it, not giving her a chance to freak out. She'll soon realize that when I tell her I find every inch of her beautiful, I mean it. I drag my finger along her wetness between her legs, asking the question again, "Gonna need words. Tell me you love it, Kadence."

"I love it, Nix." My name's delivered breathlessly, just how I like it. My dick jumps at the sound.

"Good girl, now you want my cock or my mouth?" My fingers find their way into her, pumping her slowly.

"Cock," she pants as my fingers work her harder, pumping my frustration at every obstacle she puts up for me.

"You comin' to the BBQ today, Kadence?" I ask her, using my free hand to pull my boxers down my legs. My erection springs free, throbbing and waiting to slide into her heat. Wrapping my fist around it, I give it a few tugs, relieving the tension building in me. She's panting, meeting each of my finger thrusts.

"Yes! God, yes, Nix. Just fuck me."

"Good girl." I place my lips to her shoulder, trailing kisses along the sensitive skin. "Now you know what I told you about that pretty mouth and what the word fuck coming out of it does to me." I remove my fingers, trailing them along her smooth skin back up to her nipples while lining up my neglected cock to the heat of her pussy. I'm so glad she agreed to let me take her bare. The feeling of her snugness is like no other.

"You ready?" I ask her, my hands shaking in anticipation. She pushes back, her tightness gripping my hard length.

"Fuckin' impatient little thing, aren't you?"

"Quit fucking talking and fuck me, Nix," she grumbles

Jesus, her dirty mouth is the biggest turn on.

"Oh, Kadence," I grunt out with each hard thrust. "I'm gonna fuck your greedy pussy all right," I say, bringing my hands to her hips, my fingers digging in, ready to show her just how hard I can fuck her.

Pulling up to my old house that Addison and I once shared, I always get a sense of dread that I'm about to walk into one of her setups. Normally, it's either her forgetting she's still in her nightgown or asking me to fix something around the house, trying to get me to spend time with her. I have no clue why she pines over me when we haven't been with each other in years. That ship sailed a long time ago.

Z races out, his backpack slung over his shoulder. Opening the back door, he throws his bag in and then slams it shut.

"Bye, sweetie," Addison calls out from the front door. He ignores her, climbing up into the front seat.

"Hey, bud, how you doin?" I ask, looking over at him.

"Hey, Dad," he smiles, looking like he's excited to be coming with me today.

Pulling out, I notice Addison still standing there in her nightgown at one pm. "Your mom sleep in today?" I ask, pulling out of the driveway without acknowledging her.

"Yeah," he mumbles, looking down at his iPod. After a few minutes of driving in silence, I decide I'm gonna come right out and tell him about Kadence.

"So, bud, I wanted to talk about something that's important. You think you're up for that?" I ask.

"Sure," he says, looking up from the game he's playing

"Well, I guess there's no other way to say it other than, I've been seein' someone," I say, waiting for a response. I'm not sure what sort of response, but I'm expecting something.

"So you're not getting back with Mom?" he asks a little too excitedly. Okay, not what I was expecting.

"No, bud, why would you think that?" I ask, wondering what shit Addison has fed him.

"Mom said you guys were getting back together." He looks at me confused.

"Shit, Z, I'm sorry, bud, but we're not," I tell him truthfully. Fucking Addison is spinning her shit again.

"Good," he states.

"Good? You okay with that?" It's now my turn to look confused; the kid is confusing me now.

"Yeah, Dad, I'm okay with it." A smile breaks out over his face.

"Okay, so if you're cool with that, I hope you're cool with who it is then," I say, testing the waters.

"Do I know her?"

"Yeah, bud, you do. Miss Turner and I have been seeing each other for a little while now," I let him know, watching him closely.

"Cool." His excited voice bounces off the windshield.

"You okay with that too?"

"Hell yeah, that's wicked, Dad." He smiles over at me.

Well shit, there you go.

"She's coming to the BBQ today. I want you on your best

behavior, okay, bud?" I ask, knowing he'll be good; he always is when he's at the clubhouse.

"What do I call her?" he asks, already thinking ahead.

"Let's just start off as Miss Turner, and we'll let her lead us as to how we're gonna handle it. How's that sound?"

"Sounds good, Dad," he beams up at me. "Is she gonna be my new mom?" His enthusiasm is flowing out.

"Jesus, Z, calm down," I laugh. "You already got a mom to start with, and Kadence and I are a long way off from that. Let's just see how it goes, yeah?"

"Okay, Dad," he sulks. The fella is getting way ahead of himself. I hope he calms a little and doesn't scare her off. It was hard enough getting Kadence to the clubhouse today. I'd hate to think what she'd do if she heard Z start talking about that.

"Dad?"

"Yeah, bud?"

"I really like Miss Turner. She's funny and pretty." I smile over at him, agreeing with him. "And when you are ready, can she be my mom?" The question throws me a little, not the part about me being ready, 'cause I can see myself getting there. It's the prickly feeling I'm getting that he wants a new mom.

Pulling up to the clubhouse, I file it away for when we have some one-on-one time. Something is not sitting right with me.

"Let's just get through the BBQ today, and then we'll talk. Okay, Z?"

"Okay, Dad." He nods and opens his door excited for our afternoon. I'm prepared for this; ready for Kadence to be more a part of my life, a part of club life. I just hope today doesn't push us back.

23

Kadence

WE PULL UP TO THE COMPOUND JUST BEFORE FOUR P.M. After Nix had his way with me on the kitchen counter, proving how hard he could fuck me, we had breakfast and then spent the rest of the morning in his bed. After he had fed me lunch, he brought me home in his big-ass truck. I missed the bike, but I knew he was on his way to pick up Z so I didn't complain. Holly was home, but that didn't stop him from kissing me senseless, before leaving me to go pick up Z and get ready for the club BBQ.

The last few weeks have been a whirlwind. I've said all along, I'm not sure where this thing between us was going, but the turning point for me was the night I told him about my burns. I never considered that letting him in and revealing that part of me could bring us closer together, but it has. I feel like we are at a new phase in our relationship, but I also feel like I'm in way over my head. When it's just Nix and me, I feel comfortable, happy and content, but taking it further, letting Z see this part of us, freaks me out. How do I act? What if he hates this?

"So is Sy going to be here?" Holly asks, pulling me out of thoughts of Z having a massive fit about us.

"I'm sure he will be, Holly," I tell her as she slowly makes her way up the long gravel drive of the Knights Rebels compound. My head is already going through every scenario and I'm freaking the fuck out.

"Do you know what you are getting yourself into, Kadence?" Shutting off the engine to her beat-up Honda, she turns to look at me.

"I have got no idea, Hol, but there's something there. Nix has made me realize how much in the past I've been living," I tell her, turning to face her. "I don't know where this is going, but I'm ready to move on. I'm ready for some goodness."

She smiles, reaching for my hand. "I'm glad, babe. If anyone deserves it, it's you. Now, let's go have us a hot biker BBQ," she cheers, getting out of the car, her short skirt and tight tank sure to capture some of the guys' attention. I opted for jeans and a tank.

Walking up to the front door, I notice a few more bikes in the compound. My hands sweat knowing we're moving into new territory, and I'm not sure if my heart is ready for it. My head screams, telling me it's a good thing, but my heart is second-guessing if introducing us to Z is the right thing to do.

"Come on, woman. Suck it up," Holly says, noticing my

reservations before dragging me through the door, apparently eager to see inside the clubhouse.

Leather and smoke assault my senses and I drag a breath in, my body remembering the scent as all Nix. I'm beginning to love this place. Music beats out of the surround speakers making the framed pictures hanging on the walls next to us shake slightly. Children, women, and their men fill the room, their voices fighting to be heard over the music. Holly takes me straight to the bar, ordering us two Coronas from Hunter.

"This place is great!" Holly marvels, taking a drink from her beer.

"Kadence," Jesse calls from behind me. I spin on my stool to face him. He leans down and kisses my cheek. "Good to see you here, darlin'," he whispers to me, a slight grin on his lips. Jesse steps back and then looks over my shoulder. "I don't think we've formally met," he drawls. I turn back to Holly, watching Jesse bring her hand to his lips. Real smooth.

"Holly, this is Jesse. Jesse, this is my best friend, Holly," I do the introduction without much enthusiasm.

"Hello, sweetheart." He moves in close and I have to laugh. I think all these men have it bad for themselves, but Jesse takes the cake. The guy is the modern-day Casanova.

"Hi." She barely gives him a glance, not affected by his blatant flirting. Holly's disinterest doesn't deter Jesse. His play is only taken to the next level when he reaches out and pushes a loose strand of hair from her face.

"Geez, you're a pretty little thing, aren't ya?" he states, and both Holly and I roll our eyes. Watching Jesse with his blond messy hair and tanned skin standing next to Holly's similar coloring, you can't help see they would make a cute couple. However, I know the type of guys Holly goes for, and Jesse's good-boy looks are not her type.

"You done?" Sy's voice comes up behind me. A tremor slides down my spine at his dark, menacing tone. I don't turn to face him, but from the look Holly is giving him, I know he is pissed. I freaking knew he has something for Holly.

"Sorry, brother, am I stepping on some toes here?" Jesse pulls back from Holly. I slightly shift in my stool, the temptation too much for me not to watch this play out. Sy looks more pissed off. Whether at himself or at Jesse, I'm not sure, but if I have to guess, I will say he doesn't like seeing Jesse talking up Holly.

"No toes," Holly pipes up, her manicured hand reaching out and grabbing onto Jesse's massive bicep. The little vixen knows what she's doing. If I didn't know her so well, I would say she's playing it totally cool.

"Fuck me," Sy grunts out under his breath.

"Wanna show me around?" Holly asks Jesse as she stands from her stool, her eyes still fixed on Sy, holding his gaze. He holds hers back, his eyes narrowing and the tick in his jaw moving at a dangerous beat. He follows their movements as they walk past, glaring daggers at Jesse when he turns to give him the thumbs up.

"Have you seen, Nix?" I ask Sy after sitting with him for a few minutes in an uncomfortable silence. Shit, I have no idea what to say to him, and I'm nowhere near stupid enough to ask him what that whole scene with Holly was about.

"Out the back with Z," he supplies, taking a pull of his beer.

"Thanks, Sy." I smile awkwardly, leaving him alone. I'm not sure how his moods work, but I'd rather be out with Nix facing Z, then sitting with him. The guy is one scary man.

214

Walking through the club, I look around at the men and women here today. Most of the men have been around the last few times I've been here. I smile and wave as I pass them. Walking outside, I spot Nix and Z with a ball and mitt throwing back and forth between them near a large metal shed. There are a few kids running around, people standing around in small groups, but my stare is lost on Nix playing ball with his son.

Jesus, if that isn't a turn on I don't know what is.

Unsure what to do, I hang back and wait for them to finish up. I spot Jesse and Holly talking to Brooks and a woman who must be his wife; their daughter, a spitting image of her mom, bounces up and down on his lap.

"Hello," a woman with big hair and even bigger tits comes up to me before I can make my way over to them. The sway in her hips telling me she's not shy at all. "You're new around here," she remarks, clearly not caught up on who I am. I nod and smile before discreetly looking her up and down. I have no doubt in my mind that this piece of work is Chrissie. The guys have warned me of her.

"Miss Turner," Z calls out spotting me from his game. Dropping his mitt, he runs toward me. The woman narrows her eyes at me; I'm sure assessing me like I was just doing to her. I don't react, just step around her to greet Z.

"Hey, Z," I say, feeling less awkward than I thought I would. Z looks a lot older for his age. His tall frame stands a foot shorter than me. He seems happy to see me, and I can only hope today goes well.

"Hey, Miss Turner," he smiles.

"Hey, Nix," Big Tits behind me calls out as he makes his way to us. She walks past me to him as he gets closer. I'm somewhat dreading how I will react if she touches him.

"You know the fuckin' rules, Chrissie. It's a family get-together. Leave now." He steps out of her way, reaching out to grab me around the back of my neck to pull me into him. Bending at the neck, his lips seek mine in an act of dominance that I don't fight, but take it for what it is. A claiming in front of his club, letting them all know that I'm his. I open up. A soft sigh comes from my mouth earning me a growl. His hands come to my loose hair, fisting and then pulling my head back to give him more control.

The kiss takes over, and I get completely lost to everyone and everything around us. Nix consumes me, surrounds me while taking everything from me. The sound of cheering breaks through the haze of our passion. Pulling back, Nix brings his forehead to mine, our breathing heavy as each other's.

"Hey, honey," I say, smiling at his smile. The gentleness of his features melts me when he shows me his soft side.

"You came," he simply replies, no teasing; more disbelief.

"Of course I came. You told me to."

"You've been known not to do as you're told," he reminds me before quickly kissing me again and then pulling back, his smile this time teasing me. The cheers calm down, and I come to my senses remembering Z is standing next to me. Shit!

I pull out of Nix's arms and turn to face him, but he's gone. For a second, I worry we've embarrassed him or upset him at our public display of affection.

"It's okay. He's over by Brooks," Nix calms me, sensing my panic. I turn, looking for him. His eyes find mine before he's smiling over at me. I smile back, relieved that he isn't freaked out by me being here.

"Had a word with him before you got here." Nix leans down to my ear again so only I can hear. "He's fine with this," he tells me. A weight of worry lifts from my shoulders, relieved that he spoke to him.

"Want something to eat?" he offers, standing back from me. I nod, ready to move past the attention Nix just gathered us. "Come on. Beau is grilling today." He takes my hand, walking me over to Beau. I'm still not sure about Beau. I wonder if his issue with me is more than me escaping.

"Hey, Beau," I smile, hoping he warms up to me soon. He's Nix's best friend and things could get awkward, fast.

"Kadence," he replies in his way of greeting. Okay, so maybe not today. I grab a plate ready to move on.

"You speak with T?" Nix asks Beau.

"Yeah, he can't get a hold on him. Thinks he's gone underground." Nix nods, looking deep in thought.

"Still think they're planning something." He sounds annoyed.

"You okay?" I ask after a few moments of awkward silence. I don't know what they're talking about, but whatever it is has Nix worried.

"Yeah, just some club shit. Let's go find Z." He takes my hand and leads me over to where he's sitting with Brooks. After introducing me to Kelly, Brooks' beautiful wife, and their adorable little girl, Mia, I start to relax.

"What did she say to you?" Kelly asks, bouncing Mia on her lap. Kelly is the only old lady around my age. After eating, Nix had to go off and deal with some 'shit' so he left me with Kelly. She let me in on the gossip regarding me putting Tina in her place and filled me in on the woman known as Chrissie, aka big hair and bigger tits. Apparently, I missed the words

Nix gave her before I got there. Skanks like her aren't allowed on family days, only on club nights. Why she even tried, Kelly doesn't know.

"Just observed I was new around here," I tell her, not concerned about the woman.

Kelly nods her head. "I don't trust her," she shakes her head. "You should have seen her storm off after she saw that kiss. The woman is delusional. Really close with Addi too," she adds. "Which reminds me, how is Z doing?"

"Better. Since seeing the school counselor, I've noticed small changes in him. This morning, Nix and I talked about what could be bothering him and it all comes back to his mom," I admit before I remember she was her best friend.

"Yeah, I think so too," she agrees, making me feel less bad that I just blamed his mom.

Addison is one subject I don't like to get into, especially with Nix. Letting Z know about our relationship is a big step for me. I wanted to wait until the end of next month, when school is out and he moves up a grade. I feel bad that Nix feels like he's been hiding us from him, but the situation we are in can go either way. I'm Z's teacher and the school doesn't know about our relationship; I hope that if they do find out before the school year ends, they don't make too much of a deal about it.

As the afternoon progresses, Holly continues to piss Sy off, ignoring him while teasing him at the same time. They've got this kind of sexual tension that seems like they are familiar with each other, yet they've barely held a conversation. Even Nix notices that something is up. I try to talk to her about it, but she just keeps blowing me off.

Z shows no signs of feeling uncomfortable with my being

in his dad's clubhouse. He even hung out with us most of the time. The day was a success. It also solidified in my mind that I really want things to work out between Nix and me.

Until his ex-wife walks in.

I'm sitting next to Z talking with Kelly and Brooks when I realize something is wrong. Z freezes next to me. His happy, normal self sinks further in his chair and I'm instantly on alert.

"Are you all right, Z?" I ask, reaching out and lightly touching his arm.

"Bitch, get your hands off my son," Addison's voice yells out across the back courtyard.

"Addison!" Nix warns, calling out from across the huge area where he was talking with Jesse. He begins stalking closer with long steps.

"Sorry, Prez." Hunter comes up behind Addison, obviously the one to let her in. "She fucking said it was an emergency." He shakes his head, clearly realizing he fucked up.

"Z, come with me," Kelly says, jumping into action, standing from her spot next to me and holding out her hand.

"Z, it's time to go, now!" Addison yells, walking closer to us.

"I'm warning you, Addison," Nix comes up, standing in front of us.

Everyone is quiet around us, but my brain is trying to keep up with Nix and Addison yelling at each other and Kelly trying to convince Z, who refuses to leave, watching his father and mother stand up against each other.

"Z, go with Kelly, would ya, bud?" Nix turns to look at his son.

"Like fuck," Addison spits out, still being a pain in the ass and only pissing Nix off more.

"Z, look at me, buddy." Z's eyes find his dad's. "Go inside." He nods to him, letting him know that it's going be okay.

"Z, get your ass in the car. We're going, now. Get your shit together." Z stands locked in their battle, unmoving, stuck between who to listen to. Reaching my hand out to his shoulder, I squeeze it to get his attention. I feel sorry for him, standing there watching his parents go at it with each other and fighting over him. I've never experienced anything like it before.

"Get your hands off my son, bitch," Addison yells again and I watch Z flinch.

That's the second time she's called me a bitch, the temper in me slowly rising each time she spits it at me, but I ignore it for Z's benefit. He doesn't need to see this, bigger things are happening.

"Z?" I softly call. He looks up at me, his eyes pleading with me.

"I don't wanna go home with mom," he whispers, just for my ears.

"It's okay, Z. I won't let her take you, but you need to go with Kelly so your mom and dad can talk, okay?" He nods his head and moves forward with Kelly, Mia in her arms. Brooks moves in now, standing closer to me.

"Z, quit being fucking stupid. I'm not gonna tell you again, get your fucking shit and get in the goddamn car." She reaches out as he passes her. Z shrinks back like he's frightened that she is going to hit him, the ugliness of her words settling around everyone who's here.

"What the fuck, Addison?" Nix's voice takes on a coldness

that I've yet to hear. I step in closer to his side. I know he wouldn't hit her, but the tension in the air is so thick, who knows what's about to happen. Everyone is on alert, Jesse, Beau and Sy, all moving closer.

"You speak to my boy like that? What the fuck is wrong with you?"

Kelly takes Z's hand and walks him past his parents, away from the shit storm that's brewing.

"Why is Z's teacher getting comfortable with our son?" Addison immediately begins when Kelly closes the door.

"I'm not telling you anythin', woman. You think you can walk in, spewin' your fucked-up shit. The only reason my hands aren't on you, draggin' your sorry ass out of here is 'cause our son is sittin' in the next goddamn room scared out of his fuckin' mind," Nix grates out, his temper riding the wave of the anger we all are feeling at her words and the way she spoke to Z.

"Don't be dramatic, Nix," she scoffs, like it's no big deal she just tried to put her hands on her son.

"Fuckin' tell me why I shouldn't just do it? Speakin' to our son like that, the shit you're spewing is affectin' my boy. What the fuck is your problem?" He asks the question that's on everyone's lips.

I go to walk past them, not prepared to be a part of it. Watching Z shut down like that, it's not hard to see that his issue has to do with his mom. After meeting with them back at the classroom weeks ago, I would never have guessed that things could be this bad. Nix's hand comes out, grabbing my wrist in his fingers.

"You're stayin'," he firmly states.

"What the fuck?" Addison screeches. Knowing that I'm

not going to get very far arguing with the man, I nod, agreeing to stay.

"So you're fucking Z's teacher now? Is that it? You've got to be fucking kidding me."

I swallow past the urge to defend myself, to tell her it's none of her business, but I kind of know it is so I just shut my mouth, knowing things will only just get more out of hand.

"We'll talk about that in a minute," Nix says, letting go of his hold on me, and taking a large step into her space. "First we're gonna discuss why you're in my club. Then we're gonna establish why you think speakin' to my boy like that would ever be okay. 'Cause I'm tellin' you now, woman, I ever hear you talk to him like that again, we're gonna have fuckin' huge problems." He takes a step back but still stands in her space. Addison nods her head, swallowing loudly but with a scowl still on her face.

"What are you doin' here?" he asks again, seemingly calmer than me. How he can seem so controlled, while I stand here overwhelmed with anger and a need to protect Z, impresses me.

"Heard she was here." She points to me, hatred etched over her face.

"So? You think that gives you the right to walk into my club? What happens while Z is in my care is my responsibility."

"You fucking her?" she hisses with disdain.

"That's none of your business," I say, interrupting them, forgetting I should keep my mouth shut.

"I'm not talking to you, bitch," Addison spits out at me.

"That's the last time you call her a bitch. You speak only to me. We have enough problems, Addison. Don't create more."

Nix squeezes my hand, letting me know that he has this. Frustration and anger flow through me. Seriously, this woman is a piece of work.

"Go home, Addison. I'm not gettin' into it with you tonight in your state," Nix tells her.

"I'm taking Z with me," she continues not to listen.

"Like hell you are. After today, I'm not even sure I'm bringin' him back after my four days." I have to agree with that idea, knowing for sure that Z won't be safe at his mom's. I saw the fear in his reaction; something or someone has instilled that in him.

"You wouldn't dare," Addison scoffs, not getting how fucked she really is.

"Wouldn't I? I'm over this bullshit you keep pullin'. Z is my main concern, and this just seals the deal. You need to leave Addison, now, before I do somethin' I'm gonna regret. Somethin' Z doesn't need to see."

"This is all your fault," she seethes, taking her anger out on me. "You're a home-wrecker," she accuses.

"Right, you blew it," Nix snaps, signaling Sy and Jesse. "This conversation is over," he states, pulling me away from her. Sy takes one arm and Jesse the other, pulling her along. She doesn't leave without a fight, kicking and screaming.

"Fuck you, Nix. You're my husband. You're fucking my husband, bitch," she continues to scream as Sy and Jesse struggle with her.

"Are you okay?" I ask as she is dragged away around the corner.

"Who fuckin' told her Kadence was here?" he bellows out to everyone standing around. "We got a songbird on our hands," he sneers.

"Nix," Brooks speaks up, "it was probably fucking Chrissie, relax," he says trying to calm him down as everyone starts leaving, heading inside to give Nix some space.

"You right, brother?" Beau comes up, looking concerned.

"I don't know. Let's go find out how bad I've fucked up here." He rubs the tops of his eyes.

"Hey, this is not your fault, Nix." I take his hand. I can see the anger working behind his eyes.

"She's been speakin' to him like that when I'm not around. Who fuckin' knows what else she's been doin'?"

"We don't know that. Going in there angry might frighten him, okay?" I try to coax him off the ledge. I can see he's slowly slipping, can see how he might not get a grip on it, but he has to, for Z. He sits on a vacant chair as the guys leave us alone.

"Do you think this is what's been goin' on? Why he's been so withdrawn?" he asks after few minutes of silence.

I want to say no, maybe it was a one-off, but I see the fear in his eyes, hear his plea.

"I think so. The signs are there," I give it to him honestly.

"Why wouldn't he tell me?"

"Maybe he was scared, Nix. You saw the look on his face."

"Fuck," he breathes out, grabbing onto my hand. "I've fucked up badly here."

"How? This isn't on you," I tell him, even though I know he won't listen. I can already see his mind ticking over at what he missed.

This is on Addison. A mother's job is to protect her child, not abuse their trust. You can see in Z's reaction something isn't right. Something has broken that trust.

"Dad?" Z calls from the back door, his expression lost and

scared.

"Hey, bud, come and sit with me." He taps the chair next to him. I stand to give them some space.

"Can Miss Turner stay?" he asks, looking at me, so unsure.

"Yeah, she won't go anywhere," Nix assures him, knowing I won't leave if he wants me here. I move over one chair so he can sit between us.

"Am I in trouble?" his voice wobbles, looking up at his father.

"Why would you be in trouble? You haven't done anything wrong," Nix assures him, his eyebrows creasing.

"I'm sorry, Dad. I didn't know how to tell you." Z sounds so uncertain, I can't help but reach out. I take his hand in mine, trying to offer some comfort. He has nothing to be scared about, nothing at all.

"This been goin' on for long?" Nix quietly asks.

"Just really started to get worse," Z confirms.

"She touch you in anger like that before?"

I hold back the need to cry at Nix's question. I just feel so helpless listening to him confirm what I had feared.

"Sometimes, when she's really angry. Mostly it's just a grab or slap and yelling at me."

"Fuck," Nix curses under his breath.

"I was gonna tell you this weekend, I swear, but then we had the BBQ," he rushes out.

"Hey, Z, it's okay. You're not in any trouble," I try to reassure him.

"But I should have told Dad or the counselor you sent me to. I just didn't know what was gonna happen."

"This is not your fault, bud. We'll sort it out," Nix assures him. Reaching over, he kisses his head.

"Let's go home." Nix stands and waits for Z's response.

"Is Miss Turner coming?" They both look to me waiting for my answer. Shit. I want to go, to be there for both of them, but should I back off, let Nix sort this out? Looking up at Nix, he nods, giving me his answer.

"Only if you call me Kadence, but don't tell any of the kids at school," I smile, giving him a wink.

"I promise." He smiles, and for a moment I forget things are about to get a whole lot messier. I don't know what the hell Nix is going to do to Addison, and the thought alone scares me.

24

Nix

I SLAM THE BEDROOM DOOR SHUT BEHIND ME, THE RAGE BUILDING inside of me bringing me to the brink. The week has been the most fucked up I've had to deal with in a long time, but reading what I just read, I'm struggling to contain it.

I made an appointment with my attorney after spending the rest of Sunday afternoon talking with Z, trying to get him to open up about what's been happening. I soon realized that the shit at his mom's house is a lot worse than I first thought. I knew that Addison never wanted to end things; that decision was mine, but taking all her anger out on Z? That shit is fucked.

I can't believe I didn't see it sooner. The pain of watching my son express his fear of going back to Addison's tore at me. I want to take away the bullshit she put him through. I want to wring her neck at the shit she's been telling him, but at the end of the day, the only thing I can do is make sure this shit doesn't happen again. I've wanted to go over there every day this week, do to her what she's done to him, put my hands on her, but that's not going to help Z. After just coming from my attorney, and reading through Z's statement for CPS, I feel like if I don't get a handle on my burning anger, I'm going to do something I'll regret.

I pace the length of my room, willing my body to calm. Z doesn't need to see this; he's already witnessed too much hate.

My phone beeps from my pocket and I reach back and pull it out.

> **KADENCE**: On my way home. Want me to pick anything up?

Is it bad that hearing her call my home her home has me feeling all kinds of good?

> **NIX**: No, only want your pretty face in my presence ASAP.

> **KADENCE**: Yeah, yeah, Casanova. You just want my cooking skills. Lasagna?

> **NIX**: Okay, you got me. Your pretty face and your amazing lasagna.

After two text messages, she's managed to calm me

enough to be able to find Z and make sure he's okay. I couldn't even talk on the drive home. I probably scared him, but reading his recount of what she'd done to him, her hands on him, and the fact he was too afraid to tell me? Fuck, it was too much.

Walking down the hall to his room, I lightly tap on the door.

"Hey, Z, can I come in?"

"Yeah," he replies and I push the door open. He's sitting on his bed, his iPod in his hand.

"Sorry about that. I just needed to have a breather," I explain my behavior. He nods, looking back down at his lap. Leaning up against the wall, I decide to tell him the truth.

"Z, what your mom has done is tearing me up and I can't seem to get a handle on it," I admit. I wish I could, but right now, I feel like I'm swimming in so much hate.

"I didn't know what to say. What you would have said. I was scared." He looks up at me, his small voice breaking.

"I know and I'm not angry at you for that. I'm just trying to work through all this with you. You're my life. Anyone hurts you, they hurt me. I'm meant to protect you, Z. It's my job."

I walk forward and sit down next to him. Fuck, this kid is my life. The anger burning in my veins is for him, for what his mother did to him.

"I won't have to go back, will I?" Fear flashes over his green eyes, and it just cuts me more. Where I crave the chance to have more time with my mom, my boy is hoping he doesn't see his again. The woman is a fool.

"Not if you don't want to," I tell him. No fucking way will I make him go if he doesn't want to.

"I don't wanna go."

"Okay, buddy," I nod, agreeing with him. I don't blame him; she lost that privilege when she first put her hands on him.

My phone rings from my back pocket. Pulling it out, I see Kadence's name flash across the screen.

"Hello?"

"Hey, babe," she says. And a jolt runs through me when I hear her voice. "Is Z there?"

"Yeah, why?" I ask concerned.

"Can you put him on?"

"It's for you." I hand the phone to Z, feeling less wanted. I'm jealous of my fucking son. Great.

"Hello?" he answers. His mouth spreads into a smile at the sound of her voice.

"Yeah," he exclaims, his head bobbing up and down as he listens to her talk. "Okay, bye." He ends the call, handing the phone back.

"What was that about?" I ask, wanting to know what has him smiling so much, something that only seems to happen around Kadence.

"She wanted to know if I liked apple pie. Told me she'll make one from scratch and bring home ice cream." His mind is blown that people make them from scratch. I laugh at his reaction. I'd like to think I'm a good cook, but I don't do any baking and obviously his mother has never baked him one.

"She told me she would make lasagna again too," I tell him, more excited for supper tonight.

"Yes!" he fists pumps, his smile breaking out over his face again. She made it last Sunday night for dinner when I took them both home following the shit that went down with

Addison.

I love my brothers and the support they give me, but I needed to be with Z, and most of all, Z and I needed to be alone.

Kadence didn't have a choice, Z wanting her to come with us. I knew she wanted to be there for him, but watching her face as Z confessed to some of the things his mom had been saying and doing, I could say we both needed each other. She cooked us dinner while Z and I sat and talked. I wanted to know everything, but at the same time, I didn't want to push him. He opened up more with Kadence around, feeling comfortable with her.

By the end of the night, we were all drained and ready for bed. Before Z went up to bed, he told her that if she was staying the night, she didn't have to sneak out early like all the other times last week. A blush flooded her neck and over her cheeks as he laughed himself up the stairs. He had admitted during our talk that he knew someone was here last week, heard them talking when he had woken early one morning. He just didn't know who it was.

It was a moment that made a tense night feel like things were going to be okay. She stayed that night and every night since, and not once has she had to sneak out in the morning. In one week, we've created this routine that I don't ever want to break. Z has moments where I can see what the truth of this week has done, completely shifting his life around, exposing the secret he's hidden. He'll look lost trying to process it all, and then Kadence will walk through the door, and I'll have my son back.

"Come on. Let's go down. She'll be here soon," I tell him, standing from the bed. He follows, excited to see Kadence.

Even though that warms me, it also fills me concern. Pushing it away, I turn and face him. "Z." I stop and look down at him.

"Yeah?"

"I love you, buddy." I scruff his hair, knowing more than anything, he needs to hear it.

"Love you, too, Dad." He smiles, and for every smile he gives me, a small amount of that stagnant anger that lives in me leaves.

"Oh, God," Kadence whimpers as I place my hand over her mouth.

"Shhh, babe. You're gonna wake up Z," I tell her between thrusts.

"Well, stop fucking me so good then," she pants behind my hand.

"Never." I quicken my movements, as I feel her tighten around me. Her head thrashes to the side, her teeth biting into the soft flesh of her upper arm to soften her cries.

"You. Feel. So. Fuckin'. Good." I punch out with each thrust. Her orgasm takes over, her unique kind of blush making itself known as it creeps across her skin. Fuck, I love it. Her pussy tightens around me, milking my orgasm from me. My cum fills her as I release my frustrations of today with each brutal pound. She takes it all, every hard and harsh thrust while begging for more.

Fuck, I'm in— I love this woman. *Love?* Even if I tried to deny it, my head wouldn't let me.

I move my hand to the side of her neck and plant myself as deep as I can and let the orgasm ride out. Her head turns;

the warmth of her lips find the inside of my wrist. I'm lost in the moment, forgetting about the shit week we've had.

"Are you okay?" The softness of her voice and the closeness of our bodies make me want to tell her that I've fallen in love with her. But I don't. I know she's not ready to hear it, and with the shit going on with Z, I wouldn't be able to handle it if she pulled away.

"Yeah," I breathe out. Leaning down, I kiss her forehead and pull out, rolling onto my side.

She turns facing me. "It's going to be okay, Nix," she promises, and as much as I believe her, I'm still struggling.

"I know, Kadence. It's just being his dad is the most important job to me, and I can't help but feel like I've let him down."

Her head shakes in disagreement. "You've got to stop blaming yourself."

"I know. It's just hard when he responds better to you than me," I admit. Fuck, I didn't mean it like that. I just know Z feels more comfortable with her.

"Is my being here too much?" She comes up to her forearm, her eyes now concerned.

"No. No, I'm not saying that. I just feel like he's relying too much on you as a buffer to me. I feel like I need to connect with him, get right with him." My hand reaches out to soothe her soft skin.

"And you can't do that with me here," she finishes for me.

"I want you here, babe. I do. But I'm thinking of takin' Z up to my pop's cabin for the week. I think it would be good for both of us."

"I think that's a good idea, Nix." She smiles, reaching out to stroke my face. I fucking love it when she touches me.

"It will only be for a week, five days even," I repeat, hoping she doesn't think I'm pushing her away.

"Honey, if you needed a month, I'd give it to you. It's okay." She leans forward, bringing her soft lips to mine. I don't deepen the kiss; instead, I pull back to look at her. Her eyes open and meet my gaze. Behind her pale blue eyes, I recognize something that she hasn't given me before, something that I know she doesn't want to admit, but staring back at me, it's written all over her face. She's falling in love with me.

"What did I do to deserve you?" I wonder aloud, feeling like this woman just doesn't stop bewitching me.

"Nothing really. You bossed me into dating you. Fucked me good, and then you wouldn't leave me alone. Now you're stuck with me." She laughs at her own take of how things are.

"It's more like you're stuck with me," I tell her. Her eyes sparkle with happiness, like the thought of it couldn't get any better. Her mouth descends to my ear, and quietly she confesses, "I wouldn't want to be stuck with anyone else."

Yep, I've fallen in love.

25

Kadence

THE SCHOOL BELL RINGS ABOVE MY HEAD LETTING ME know that the long week I've just had is almost over. The kids pile out, happy their weekend is here, while I'm quietly dreading mine.

It's been four nights since Nix took Z out to his dad's cabin two hours away, deciding to have some one-on-one time together. Nix needed to make sure Z is handling the change. I understand his decision to go to his pop's cabin. His dad is his only family left and he needed to be with him, to surround Z with people who he trusts. I just wish I could join them.

Grabbing my bag and the worksheets I need to grade over

the weekend, I shut down the classroom and make my way to my car. I wave over at Brooks sitting on his bike, two rows down. Nix still hasn't eased up on the guys watching over me, especially with him being away. Brooks waves back and I get in the car. I honestly have no idea how I used to do this every weekend before I met Nix. When you're so used to having someone around breathing in your presence, you forget how lonely you were before.

My phone rings in my hand and I can't stop the thrill of thinking it might be Nix. *Seriously, Kadence?*

"Hello," I answer without even looking at the screen.

"Hey, baby girl," my dad's voice booms down the phone. Even though I wanted to speak to Nix, my dad is my other favorite guy in my life, so my disappointment is short lived.

"Hey, Dad," I smile into my cell.

"Don't *hey, Dad* me. Where the hell you been? You haven't come to see us in over four weeks, girl." He sounds concerned, but I don't get a chance to respond when my mom takes the phone off him.

"Ignore him, honey. He's just upset you haven't brought any of your famous apple pie," my mom's soft voice calls down the phone.

"Hey, Mom." I smile when I hear her swatting my father away as he yells he wants pie.

"How are you?" she asks. I can detect the small amount of concern in her voice.

"I'm good, Mom. I met someone," I admit straight away. No point in hiding anymore, and I would hate for them to worry. When I was going through all the shit with Zane, I pushed everyone out, including my parents. I hated what I put them through.

"I knew it," she whispers. I can hear the happiness in her voice.

"I'm sorry I haven't been out to see you."

"Kadence, when I was your age, the last thing I wanted to be doing was coming home to see my parents when I had your father waiting for me." She giggles and I smile at my mom. She's not like your usual mom. Growing up an only child, she was like my best friend. We have a great relationship and there isn't anything I wouldn't tell her.

"His name is Nix. He's annoying, bossy, and gets on my nerves, but I think he might be the one," I admit quietly, knowing that he is the one.

"Sounds just like your father." We both laugh.

"I'll bring him out in a few weeks. Think you can hold off, Papa Bear?" I cringe, picturing their first meet. Do I have to be there for that one?

"I'll keep him at bay, just maybe bring backup. Holly might do," she laughs. My dad and Holly are the funniest pair to be around. Holly's crazy attitude and my bossy dad clash something fierce. I know he loves her and she loves him, but if you're looking for a showdown with sarcastic jabs, put those two in a room.

"Sounds like a good idea. I gotta go, Mom. Speaking of Holly, we have a movie date. I'll call you next week."

Okay, baby girl. I love you."

"Love you too. Tell Dad I love him," I say before hanging up.

Well shit. I didn't think I would be ready to admit that Nix was the one, especially to my parents. Apparently, shit just got real.

★★★

"Holly, let's haul ass, or we'll be late," I call out, coming out of my room.

"Cool your jets," she yells back with attitude. I don't know what has been up with her lately. Maybe I've been so caught up in my own drama that I've missed a vital piece of evidence, but something is going on with her. I just have no idea what. She walks out wearing lounge pants and a baggy sweatshirt, her messy blonde hair piled on top of her head. For the amount of years I've known Holly, not once have I ever seen her leave the house looking the way she is.

"Are you feeling okay, Holly?" I hold back the laugh as I look down at her chosen outfit. "You don't seem like yourself?" I push a little.

"I'm fine, Kadence," she bites back. I cock my eyebrow and look her straight in the eye. Fine my ass.

"Right, okay, let's go then," I say, walking past her to grab my coat. If she doesn't want to talk right now, I'm not going to push her.

"Kadence?" Holly's voice softly calls after me.

"Yeah?" I say, turning back around to her. Looking at my best friend, I know she is hiding something that is tearing her up. I don't know why she won't share. We've been through everything together.

"I'm sorry. I just can't, okay?" she softly explains. Her eyes are showing a sadness that I've never seen from her.

"It's okay. I'll be here if you need me. Just don't push me out."

I don't know how to help her through this if she doesn't let me in, but I do know I sat in darkness for three years pushing people away, and she stood by me every step of the way. If that's what I have to do, I'll do it.

Her eyes shine with unshed tears. Her head nods slowly. I'm worried about her, but I understand pushing her will not get me anywhere.

"Okay let's go on then."

Grabbing the keys, we head out. The stress and the worry of what might be happening with her weigh heavy on my shoulders.

"Oh, God, can you believe that ending?" I say to Holly, walking out of the movie theater. Sometimes movies just don't do it for me anymore. Give me a book with all the details.

"I know, right? Complete bullshit." She smiles back at me, a little glimpse of her happy, crazy self.

"Where's Brooks?" I ask, looking out to where he was sitting before we went in.

"I don't know, but I need the bathroom," she says, leaving me there. Something doesn't feel right. Brooks and all the boys have been taking this 'looking out for me' seriously. Brooks not being there is putting me on edge. The people walk out around me as I try to call his cell.

"You ready to go?" Holly asks, coming back from the restroom.

"I tried to call Brooks but he didn't pick up," I tell her, starting to freak out.

"He might have had an emergency," she says uncon-cerned. "Let's go see if he's outside," she says, pulling us out the doors. Most people have left; the parking lot is almost empty. Turning the corner, I notice Brooks' bike sitting unattended next to my car. What the hell?

"Hello, Kadence." Zane's voice startles me. I look up to see him resting against the building. I scan our surroundings looking for Brooks, but I come up empty.

"Holly." He turns to her with a little smile on his face. Holly's grip on my arm tightens as I see her grab her phone.

"What do you want, Zane?" I ask him, getting the attention off her.

Zane's right hand comes out fast, and at first I think he's about to strike me. My hands come up to protect my face, but his hand goes to my throat. The hold on me is so intense I can barely make out Holly's screaming. For a brief second, I notice her struggling with another man.

"Shut the fuck up, Holly," he yells over at her, "or I'll kill her." Her screams stop abruptly.

He smiles, looking back at me. His grip still tight around the soft flesh of my neck, black spots dance in front of my vision. My heart and lungs are working overtime from the lack of oxygen, desperately trying to gulp down air, but it eludes my grasp. My fingers claw at his hold. Trying to pry his death grip, my nails cut his skin. Kicking my legs out, I try to fight with everything I have.

"You need to stop fighting me, Kadence, or I'm going to put a bullet in Holly." He laughs an evil laugh as he drags me around to the back of the building. The darkness that slowly starts to creep in fades as he loosens his grip. I don't know if he will follow through with his threat, but something screams inside of me to keep fighting, and not give up. A wave of adrenaline washes over me, giving me strength to fight. Why is this asshole trying to kill me? What the hell did I ever do to him?

Clawing at his hand again, I use all my strength to try to

pry his grip away from my throat. My knee comes back to build momentum, before I push forward, delivering a hard and fast blow between his legs. The connection is brutal as the attack takes him unaware. His grip loosens enough for me to drag in a large breath down my aching throat. I spin to my left, my surroundings flashing past me as I twist my way out of his hold and step out of his reach.

He's too fast, stepping forward and pulling hard on my hair. I feel the sting of the sharp tug all over, the sensation prickling my skin. My heel goes back into his groin, and my elbow connects with his nose simultaneously. I don't know where my movements are coming from, but the thought of dying at the hands of this man replaces my fear and leaves me with an all-consuming rage. It bursts from me, taking me somewhere I've never known. Anger like this doesn't come from nowhere. It comes from deep-down hatred for a person who has tried to take everything from you. Spinning around, my fingers go to his dark hair. Latching on, I rip back with all my strength. He has already taken too much from me, and now here he stands in front of me, back for more.

I don't think so, asshole.

"You bitch," he spits outs, his hands coming out in front of him, trying to gain the upper hand. Holly's whimpers echo out in to the night, but I can't get my body to turn fast enough to see if she's okay.

"I'm going to kill you like I should have done three years ago," he spits, his face contorted in rage

Hot blood surges through my body, burning furiously in my veins. I release the hand from his hair, closing in for his eye, my thumb gouging out with all the strength I can muster. A painful force pushes me back, his knee coming to my stomach. My diaphragm contracts under the force and my knees buckle under the pressure, connecting with the rough surface of the asphalt. A kick to my side and a loud snap has me gasping for air, each inhale screaming for me to stop.

"You think you can overpower me, Kadence?"

A fistful of my hair brings me up to my grazed knees; bile rises up, as the pain is too much to bear. He grins, standing in front of my kneeling body. "Fuck, you're pathetic," he laughs as the upper side of his free hand connects with my face with a backhand. I hold back the urge to cry out as the force splits the side of my mouth. The metallic coppery taste of blood invades my taste buds as he leans forward, closing the distance. The smell of stale cigarettes fills my nostrils, and the familiar black stars dance deliriously behind my eyes. Holding on, I fight the darkness, not ready to go down.

"Fuck you, Zane," I force out past the intense pain at my side and my chest, my voice scratchy from the strong force his hands had around my neck. His hand reaches the waist of his pants, pulling out a gun.

"With pleasure," he sneers before bring the butt of his gun across the side of my face.

Everything goes black.

I wake to the soft cries of Holly across from me. It's dark but I can see the bright glow of the moon coming through a small window.

"Holly?" I croak out, my voice not my own.

"Kadence, thank God, you're awake," she cries harder. I try to sit up from the hard concrete floor, but my chest hurts too much. I take stock of my injuries. My face is throbbing, but not as bad as the soreness of my throat. My hands and knees sting, but it's my chest that I'm feeling the worst pain.

"Something is wrong with my chest," I croak out the words and try to still my erratic breathing.

"It's okay, Kadence. Sy's on his way."

"Where are we?" I try to focus my eyes, but I can only make out shadows, my head throbbing.

"I don't know, but Sy is gonna find us." She sounds so sure, so I don't question her with my doubts of him finding us.

"Are you hurt?" Shit, the last thing I ever want is Holly getting hurt because of me.

"I'm fine. I'm tied up, but I put up a good fight." The proudness in her voice makes me smile on this totally messed up night.

"How long have we been here?"

"We've been here for an hour, but it's been two hours since they put us in the van," she tells me. Two hours. Oh God, there is no way anyone is going to find us.

The door on the far wall creaks open. My breathing stills as I wait for what, I'm not sure, but this can't be good. The room is suddenly bathed in bright light, blinding me for a moment as Zane walks into the room.

"Oh, good, you're awake." He walks up to where I'm lying on the hard cold floor. I look around; we must be in a shed.

"What the fuck do you want, Zane?" I ask, the wheeze of my chest burns after each word spoken. Even though he has the upper hand, I'm not going down without a fight.

Zane's rough fingers clutch my chin, forcing me to look up at him. "Oh, Kadence, see what happens when you hang with biker scum? You start speaking like biker scum." He shakes his head like a father disappointed in his daughter.

I shake my head out of his grasp, the movement sending an excruciating pain down the left side of my body. His hand reaches out, fisting my loose hair, bringing me up in one forceful jerk. I scream at the sting of my head and the shooting pain through my chest, my lungs struggling to seize some air. Bile surges up my throat at the sheer pain. Forcing it down, I tell myself not to break. How could he be doing this? You think you know someone, think you love them... I shared my bed for three years with this man, shared my dreams, my body, my life, but I don't know him at all.

"I want your boyfriend out of the picture, baby."

"Don't call me that."

"Why? You used to love it. Loved it when I was fucking you hard. Maybe we could go another round, for old time's sake."

I whimper at the thought, knowing he probably will, but I would rather die than have him inside of me.

"Don't fucking touch her, asshole," Holly yells out.

"Don't worry, Holly. You can watch, then you'll be next."

"Don't," I plead with him. "You can have me, but please don't touch her," I say, giving myself to him. I couldn't bear to know he touched her. Fuck, this situation is just getting worse. I don't know how we are going to get out of it.

"Don't sound so disgusted by it, Kadence. I'll make sure you enjoy it."

"You're a piece of shit, asshole," I say, trying to calm my panic. I know I shouldn't be goading him, but disgust courses through me, and I can't hold my tongue. I won't allow him to break me.

"You're right, babe," he agrees, a smile now replacing his

disappointed scowl. He looks over to where Holly sits up against the wall. The same guy she fought with earlier stands above her, a gun pointed at her head.

"Zane, this has nothing to do with Holly." I try to hide the fear in my voice, but think I fail when he looks back at me.

"Oh, I know." He smiles his evil smile. "This is all about you and that asshole you've been seeing. He needs to be gone and what better way to make him listen."

"This won't change anything, Zane. He'll still fight you every step of the way," I try to get him to see. "Hurting me or killing me won't get him to step down."

"See, that's where you're wrong. I set it up. Make it look like that the Mayhems did this and all I'll have to do is sit back and watch the fucking show." He laughs like he has completely lost his mind.

"You're crazy," I tell him, knowing there is no way we are getting out of this; the man has gone nuts.

"I'll tell you what's crazy. Gunner can't fucking get his trade in this shit town 'cause your fucking boyfriend has some sort of truce. Fuck that. Fuck the truce. We've been trying for years to get a foot up on him, and our luck changed when your fucking dumbass started sucking his cock," he sneers. "Tell me, Kadence. Do you like the way he fucks you?"

I don't answer his question, afraid of the outcome, afraid of his reaction.

"ANSWER ME, YOU WHORE!" he screams, striking me across the face with his gun again. The black stars are back, and I fight desperately to push them away. I can't pass out again. I can't leave Holly alone.

"Yes, Zane," I answer, looking him straight in the eye. He nods, turning his body toward Holly's direction. The loud bang rings in my ears, my eyes glued to Holly's form in front of me, red blood seeping from the bullet hole in her stomach. Her dazed stare looks back at me.

"Holly!" I scream, trying to stand. *Oh, God, Holly.* I try to move to her, to break free. Oh, God, no, no, no.

"Don't, Kadence, or she gets one in the head." Zane forces me back to my knees.

I try to fight the internal battle of wanting to fight, but his grip is painfully tight in my hair.

"I hate you," I spit out past the tears falling, knowing Holly is so close to me, yet I can't get to her. He just shot her. What's going to happen to me?

"Oh, Kadence, I hate you too. Didn't you know? That's why I left you in the house to burn," he confesses, smiling down at me. I cry harder as the sounds of Holly's gasps come from the side.

"Which is why I can't wait to end this bullshit once and for all." I don't see the movement in Zane's hand until a small black barrel stares at me two inches from my face. I briefly see the outline of his finger, lightly touching the trigger. The darkness of that small black hole drags my eyes away. I want to fight him, reach up, and push it out of his hands so I can go to Holly.

"Don't even think about it, Kadence," he warns like he can see my thoughts.

Everything in the small space around me fades; my best friend lying shot next to me, the pain in my chest gone. Everything stops for a moment. My eyes sting, begging me to blink, but for the life of me, I'm stuck, fascinated by the hollow shape staring back at me.

Memories of my mom and dad flash before me like a

playback on an old movie reel. Holly and I on our first day of college, the day Zane got down on one knee and asked me to be his wife, the fire that changed my life. Each significant moment plays like a movie before my eyes, then fades fast when Nix's voice breaks through. His gravelly voice, telling me to get on his damn bike. Z's smiling face is staring at me as I hold on to his dad's hand.

The small black hole moves forward, the coldness of the metal meeting my forehead. I close my eyes, willing to see Nix and Z again, my mind knowing that they are the last people I want to see. I don't hear the words coming from Zane. They bleed into each other. I focus solely on remembering the touch of Nix's hands, the taste of his lips.

I'm going to die, and I'm never going to see him again.

My breathing comes back, dragging and forcing air into my lungs, the encompassing pain pulling me from the haze. A bone-chilling roar, followed by a loud thud has me twisting away. A force like no other pushes me down, and a heaviness falls over me. Before my back hits the solid ground, the darkness takes me.

26

Nix

"TELL ME YOU GOT A FUCKIN' HIT ON HIM," I ROAR down my cell. The pain in my chest feels akin to someone slamming into me, reaching in and tearing me apart. I don't know what will kill me first: the blinding rage that's searing through my heart or the paralyzing fear that she's been hurt. The fury that's building inside of me shows no signs of calming anytime soon.

I got a call an hour ago. The last thing I ever expected to hear was that Gunner and his men took Kadence and Holly. I'm seething, and I'm trying to remind myself to stay levelheaded, but the unknown is worse than the truth. He could be doing who knows what to her and I'm still fucking an hour away helpless. Sy got the call from Holly's cell, the muffled sound of a struggle, and then Holly trying to relay what was happening in the back of the van. He lost contact with her five minutes ago, and every second that's ticked by is the second that I'm left wondering in the dark.

Nothing can happen to her. Nothing. It will kill me.

"Mayhems are on board and putting a recon team together as we speak. We've narrowed it down to an old farmhouse an hour away. Jesse and I are on our way now." Sy sounds calm and collected, but I detect the controlled anger he's keeping at bay. Brooks was taken off guard when he was knocked over the head waiting for Kadence and Holly, and now Zane has her. I shouldn't have thought for a second leaving her was smart. My head messed up with Z and Addison's shit, I left Kadence vulnerable and open to an attack. I fucking knew Zane would pull this shit. He's so far up Gunner's ass I'm not surprised when he found out Kadence was dating the enemy, he moved in and took his play. Only now he's gone too far. I don't give a fuck about what side of the law the MC lives on; the motherfucker is dead.

"Keep me posted, and Sy?"

"Yeah, boss, you don't have to tell me." He cuts me off before I say it. I know he's feelin' me. I know I'm not gonna get back in time. It's on Sy, Jesse and the Warriors of Mayhem. I just pray the fuckers pull through for us. I want the asshole fucking dead. I survived losing my mom. I'm not sure if I'll survive losing Kadence.

I watch the fluorescent light flicker above me, the buzzing sounds replacing the bright light, before switching back into the full light only to repeat all over again. I look around at my family and my friends, all gathered in the waiting room by my side. My mind won't still, racing through thought after thought.

How much fucking longer?

Sy stands near the double doors, his back against the wall. Blood matter covers the front of his shirt and cut. He hasn't spoken a word to me since going over the details when I first made it to the hospital. He's fighting some serious rage behind his eyes. I didn't push him; the tension rolling off him is telling me he's about to snap.

Brooks and Jesse sit watching the muted TV. After only just leaving the emergency room himself with ten stiches at the back of the head, I told Brooks to go home, but he still refuses. He won't leave until he knows they are okay.

Jesse's leg bounces up and down, impatient to hear the news. He filled me in on what Sy couldn't say. After receiving the call that the Warriors of Mayhem had found where the girls were being held, they floored it to meet them. After T and his boys took out the two assholes guarding the perimeter, Sy took Zane, while Jesse took out the other fuckhead holding Holly. I know he is dealing with some serious shit over there, probably replaying the fact he just killed another person, but I don't doubt he doesn't regret it. The asshole had it coming, and knowing that Holly is fighting for her life, we all know those assholes deserve more.

I look over to where Beau sits on the one side of Z, with my pops on the other.

"Will Kadence be okay?" Z asks when my eyes go to him. I don't miss the stagger in his question, my strong boy trying to hold it together. I told Pops to stay behind, but the old bastard didn't listen. I'm glad he's here. After spending the last three nights with him, he's come to know Kadence through me constantly talking about her. I know our relationship was strained after losing Mom, but after he turned his patch in and allowed the club repair, we were able to build it back. I don't get to see him as often as I like now that he lives out at the lake house still mourning my mom. Z and I were on our last night away, both impatient to get home to Kadence. The hilarious yet smart-ass shit she pulls with me has become the highlight of my day. The way she's shown nothing but compassion to my son, nurturing him through the fallout with his mom, only makes me fall in love with her more.

While having Kadence around us has been healing for Z, I needed to be able to make sure he wasn't just okay because of her, because of us. I wanted to be right with him. In order to do that, I had to do it away from Kadence. She consumes me and takes all my attention. It's like my body is drawn to hers. Getting away for a few nights helped me separate myself from that and focus solely on Z. We talked through everything that was concerning me; where his head was at and where we are going from here. I wanted to make sure Z was okay with being with me full time, and see how he was handling the thought of not having his mom in his life. He seems to be accepting it for what it is, knowing it's not his fault. I can only hope that Addison doesn't fight me on custody.

A large bang pulls me from my thoughts. Looking up I see an older man slam his fist down on the nurses' station. A small petite woman tries to calm him, her dark hair pulled back from her face. Her features are strikingly similar to Kadence's. Shit, these are her parents.

It's not how I expected to meet them, especially here

tonight. The small woman ushers the larger man to the waiting chairs, when the nurse just shakes her head no. I'm not sure what to do in this situation. Should I go over there? Introduce myself to them? I'm not even sure she's told them about me. Hell, I only told Pops about her this week. My decision is made for me when the doctor walks out through the doors. Sy pushes off the wall coming forward to meet the older man. "Kadence Turner's family?" he calls out. I look to the older couple as we both walk to the waiting doctor.

"Who are you?" the old man questions, looking around us as all the brothers move in. His eyes zero in on me.

"Nix," I tell him, holding my hand out to him. He looks at it, not sure if he should trust me.

"You with my daughter when her asshole ex hurt her?"

"No sir, but we sure as hell made sure the asshole paid." The burning rage builds back up again, thoughts of what Sy told me he witnessed fill my head. If Sy hadn't been there, I don't want to think about what would have happened to her. The old man holds my gaze, nodding slightly before taking my hand and shaking it tightly.

"How is she, Doc?" He turns his attention back to the Doctor.

"Well, Miss Turner suffered a broken rib which caused a traumatic pneumothorax."

"What the hell does that mean?" I bark out, interrupting him and thinking the worst. I feel one of my brothers grab my shoulder, trying to calm me. I don't want to be calm. I wanna fucking see her.

"In layman's terms, a collapsed lung. We've had to drain some of the excess air and now we are just monitoring to make sure that she doesn't need surgery.

"Surgery?" I snap again, fear now replacing my anger.

"Will she be okay?" her mom softly asks beside me, while reaching out for my hand. I don't know what to do, so I just hold it in mine. The move nearly floors me, but at the same time comforts me.

"She will be, but she will need to stay in for a few nights for observation, just to make sure that lung doesn't collapse again."

"Okay," Mr. Turner nods, taking in the news while I quietly shake in rage.

"She also suffered an injury with her larynx. It will cause some trouble swallowing for the next day or two and her voice will be hoarse, but I must warn you, the marks on her neck are somewhat confronting. She was very lucky. Things could have been a lot worse," he adds, noting something down on his clipboard as his pager beeps from his pocket.

"Can we see her?" I ask, my body humming in need to see her with my own eyes, to touch her with my hands.

"She's still in recovery, but will be up in her room shortly. A nurse will come down to get you," he informs us before walking back through the same doors he came out of. Kadence's mother squeezes my hand once, and then lets go, visibly relaxing next to her husband

Her father nods at me and directs his wife over to the waiting chairs.

"Pops, I'm gonna need you to take Z home," I say, coming to sit next to him.

"Dad, I wanna see Kadence," Z interrupts.

"I know you do, bud, but she is gonna be real tired. We can come back in the morning to see her." He looks like he wants to argue, but he doesn't. "I'll let her know you wanted to see her, okay?" He nods, satisfied for now.

"Nix?" Mrs. Turner comes to sit next to me.

"Yeah?" I reply. I honestly don't know what to do in these sorts of situations. The last time I did a 'meet the parents,' I was eighteen and didn't give a fuck if they liked me or not.

"Kadence was only telling me about you this afternoon," she smiles a sad smile. "I'm sorry we had to meet like this."

"Me too," I agree, wishing Kadence was here for the first meet. I feel like this is some important shit and I'm gonna mess it up.

"Nix?" a nurse calls from the double doors.

"Here." I stand at my name being called.

"Kadence is asking for you." The small blonde holds the door open, waiting for me to follow her. I smile back at Kadence's mom. I feel like I should let them go in before me, let them see their daughter, but the urge isn't strong enough. I just need to see her.

"I'll let her know you're here," I tell them as Mr. Turner comes to stand by his wife's side.

"Fuck that, I'm goin' in boy." Mr. Turner booms, shaking his head.

"Frank," his wife scolds him, slapping his arm. Jesus, you can see where Kadence gets her quirks.

"Oh, please, Jolene. If he's any type of man, he'd understand my need to see my girl." I nod, knowing he's right. No fucking way would I not want to see my daughter after someone attacked her.

"Of course," I agree, not wanting to piss her father off, but if the nurse says one at a time, I'm not gonna fucking stay back. Telling the guys I'll be back, we walk through the doors, passing room after room. My fingers itch to touch her soft skin, to see for myself that she is okay.

The nurse stops us at the door, letting us walk past her into the darkened room.

"Oh, baby girl." Frank's rough voice echoes around the room.

My eyes find hers as I walk through the door. A low guttural sound erupts from deep within, building each second my eyes run over her messed-up face.

"I wish I got to fuckin' kill him," I say, coming to stand on the opposite side to where her parents stand. Her eyes haven't left mine since they locked on to me.

"He's dead?" she asks. Her voice doesn't sound like hers. I nod and watch her body relax. I can't speak. I can't even touch her. I'm stuck, my body vibrating with an untapped rage.

"Oh, honey," her mom leans down closer and lightly brushes some hair off her forehead. Her black eye is now fully visible. My pulse quickens in response.

"I'm okay, Mom," she rasps. The tiny movement sends pain across her face. I follow my natural instinct to reach out and grasp her small hand in mine. Her hand responds, squeezing me back.

Standing closer to her, I can see the busted lip held together by a small stitch. Her delicate neck bruised from the asshole's hands. Seeing her lying in bed with her beautiful face battered and the thumbprint shaped bruises covering her neck, I realize I could have just as easily lost her.

"How's Holly?" she asks.

"Still in surgery," I answer. It doesn't look good for Holly, but I don't want to tell her that. She looks so lost, lying there, not the strong woman, I know.

"Whatever you got goin' on in your head, get it out." I squeeze her hand. I can see the guilt she holds playing out all over her face.

"It's my fault, Nix," she cries softly, a tear falling. I knew she would take it on her shoulders, knew she would feel guilty.

"It's not your fault." I pull the chair up beside the bed. "It was that asshole's, so quit your bullshit blame game, or I'm gonna have to take you over my knee, woman," I finish quietly.

"Oh, I like him," her mom giggles.

Her dad growls

Obviously, I wasn't so quiet.

"Geez, Nix, my parents are in the same room," she states the obvious, shaking her head, wincing at the movement.

"I don't give a shit. I'm not sittin' here watchin' you go inside your head over some seriously fucked-up shit your ex pulled. The fucker is lucky Sy put the bullet in him 'cause I would have to kill him with my bare hands for layin' a finger on you," I tell her.

"Calm down, Nix," she says.

"Kadence, I don't think you get just how crazy I have been waitin' to see you. Knowin' that asshole had you for two hours, doing who knows what, who knows where... Jesus, Kadence, I can't even comprehend the heaviness in my heart right now."

"Well then, I'm glad he's dead. You wouldn't be any good to me if you were in jail," she states, staring back at me. Even in a hospital bed, the woman wants to argue with me, test me. I hold her gaze, our eyes locked in a stare off, but she breaks it, looking over at her mom.

"You didn't have to come, guys."

"Like hell we didn't," her dad barks out beside her mom. I smile. I'm beginning to like the guy. He speaks my language.

"Of course we did, Kadence. Your father was racing to the car before I even hung up the call from the hospital. Can we get you anything while we're here?" She begins fussing over her. My heart aches watching it, remembering my mom being the same.

"I'm good, Mom, but you should get some rest. It's the middle of the night."

"I know, honey. We just wanted to see you. Make sure you're all right. We'll be back first thing. If you want to do up a list, we can go pick up your stuff and take it back to our house, for when you're ready to come home."

"That won't be necessary," I tell them straight up. They all look over to me,

"Nix," Kadence begins before I cut her off.

"No, Kadence, this one thing I'm not budgin' on. You're stayin' with me. Respect to your mom and dad, babe, but you're with me; that makes you my responsibility. I look after what's mine."

"Nix, I'm not a possession to claim. I can get Mom and Dad to look after me. You have Z."

"Like hell, you're not. You're my woman, one of the most important people in my life. You're mine and it's killin' me seein' you in this bed. I promise you, Kadence, this won't happen again. I'm not lettin' you out of my sight." She rolls her eyes and tries to hide her pleasure at me claiming her in front of her parents.

"Quit sassin' your man, darlin'. If he's a good man, he'll look after his woman," her dad orders, looking over at me.

"He is a good man, Daddy," Kadence quietly replies,

looking up at me.

"I know, baby girl. I can already tell," he agrees, leaning down to kiss her forehead.

"I'm sorry, but your time is up." The young nurse from earlier comes in checking Kadence's chart.

"We'll be back tomorrow morning." Her mom leans down kissing her, while her dad comes around to where I sit. I stand when he stops in front of me.

"Good to meet you, Nix." Offering me his hand, I take it in mine. He moves forward into my space, his voice lowered, "I don't have to remind you that she's my only girl, and we've already been through a world of pain. You mess with her, you're messing with me."

"I wouldn't expect anything less," I tell him, looking him in the eye. I have no intention of messing with Kadence. This week has proven to me just how much I want her in my life. He nods, letting my hand go and stepping back.

Mrs. Turner steps forward. Her small arms come around me. She stands at the same height as Kadence. "Look after her," I hear her say quietly before she pulls back. It's not a question, more a request, one I very much plan on doing. With a final goodbye, they leave us alone, following the nurse out.

Leaning down, I gently kiss her over her eye. She holds on strong, the pain and anguish kept at bay until her parents leave the room. Her body slightly shakes the moment the door latches, unraveling in front of me.

"I swear, Kadence, I'm nearly comin' out of my skin seeing his marks on you and watchin' you break."

"I'm sorry," she cries harder, tying to wipe at her swollen face.

"Hey, it's okay. It's gonna be fine," I tell her, wiping at her tears with a tissue.

"Will you find out about Holly for me?" She looks up, concerned for her friend.

"I will," I promise, still holding onto her hand tightly. I want to climb into the bed with her, crawl inside of her, and take the pain she's feeling away, but I know that I can't. I can barely touch her without the fear of hurting her.

"Z, Pops and the boys are in the waitin' room," I let her know. I want her to know Z is here for her; that all the boys are worried about her.

"Z's out there?" she says shocked while trying to sit up. "How was your time away? Is Z okay?" she fires off, and her response warms me. This woman owns my heart. Lying in a hospital bed, surviving what she just did, and she's worrying about my son. Fuck, I love her.

"He missed you," I tell her the truth. "And quit tryin' to move. You have a broken rib."

"He did?" she ignores my concern.

I nod, smiling down at her. "Wanted to come home early so he could have you make him the lasagna dish you served him last week."

"I missed him too. I missed you both like crazy," she whispers, looking unsure. She's only saying what I'm thinking. As much as I needed to be away with Z, I still missed her, wished every night I could hold her in my arms.

I reach out and run my finger along her busted lip. "I missed you, too. Missed you so fuckin' bad."

She nods. A tear slips from her eye and I wipe it away with my thumb.

"I need to say goodbye to Z and let Pops know I'm gonna

stay. I'll be back," I tell her.

She protests, telling me there is no point because they won't let me stay.

"Don't care. I'll sleep outside your door," I state. "I'm not lettin' you out of my sight, Kadence." I won't. It's my promise. With Zane dead, who knows what Gunner will retaliate with. I don't trust the fucker or anyone else for that matter.

"Sir?" The young nurse interrupts, cutting Kadence off from arguing with me anymore. "You need to leave," she insists.

"Goin' now and not 'cause you told me to. Fair warnin', I will be back shortly. I'm not leavin' her side. You need to find whoever is responsible for that process and let them know." Her eyes bug out, like she's frightened by my voice or the tone of it. My deep rumble always helps to get my point across with fewer arguments.

"Quit your bossiness, Nix. You're scaring the poor girl," Kadence calls over my shoulder.

"Just givin' the woman some warnin'. I'm coming back and I'm gonna be in this room," I warn them, looking back and forth. The nurse nods, probably not sure she wants to argue with me. Kadence rolls her eyes; the action makes me smile and thankful she's still here.

Tonight could have gone a lot worse. The truth of that lays in the fate of Holly, right now still in surgery fighting for her life. In my opinion, Zane fucking Edwards got off way too easy. I'm not sure a bullet in the head will ever make up for beating my woman, but Kadence is right; sitting in jail wouldn't help her or Z. I know I made that vow five years ago to stay clean and keep on the correct side of the law, but if anyone so much as tries anything again, that promise will be broken.

27

Kadence

THE DULL ACHE IN MY SIDE STIRS ME. THE DISTINCT
smell of antiseptic burns my nostrils. The annoying beep of
the machines beside me breaks through, bringing me out of
sleep and back to my hospital room. The door pushes open
and the same nurse who was here the night before last walks
in.

"Do you ever leave this hospital?" I ask, smiling at her. My
voice is starting to feel slightly better, but still croaks on
certain words. She shakes her head at me. Her blonde, short
hair is tucked behind one ear showing off her cute face. The
blues of her eyes shine brightly when they meet with mine.

"Just started my third shift of a five-day roster," she

groans, and I feel her pain. I'm not sure who has it worse, me with a broken rib, or her dealing with patients and long shifts.

"I don't envy you," I say as she comes to the end of the bed and picks up my chart.

"How's the pain?" she asks, taking notes down on the folder.

"I feel a lot better today," I tell her, trying to sit up with as little pain as possible.

"Did Nix come back last night?" I ask, wondering where he is.

"If you mean the sexy-as-sin man who has been demanding and overbearing since you got here? Then yes, he's out in the waiting room."

"Oh, God, he doesn't know when to stop," I cry out. The insufferable man makes my heart stop, my mind go crazy and still manages to make me smile.

"Going by that smile, I'd say you're not bothered if he never stopped?"

If she only knew.

"I wouldn't either," she continues before I can answer her. "I just ran into him and a whole lot of male hotness. They nearly gave Jan, at the nurses' station, a heart attack. All that leather is dangerous."

I smile at her description of the Knights Rebels. Dangerous is an understatement.

"Have you heard any news about my friend?" I ask, hoping she has something more to tell me. No one is saying much. I know Holly just came out of her second surgery last night, but I can't get a solid answer if she is going to survive. The thought that she might not live is tearing me up. I don't think I will ever cope if she doesn't pull through.

"She's going to be okay. She woke up in the middle of the night." She delivers the news I've been so desperate to hear.

Holly has had two surgeries in the last twenty-four hours. One to take out the bullet Zane put in her and the second to relieve a second bleed. She was rushed down last night for emergency surgery. If Sy and Jesse hadn't come to save us when they did, I don't think we would have survived.

The crack and thud of the bullet going through Zane and his body landing on me were the last things I remember. It took me a few minutes to come to with Jesse kneeling over me. I tried to get to Holly, but the pain in my chest was too unbearable. I felt like I was drawing in razor blades. I just remember Holly's body lying in a pool of her own blood across from me, Sy working her chest trying to make it start again.

"Don't you fucking die." His words still ring in my ears as he yelled them repeatedly. The light and sounds of emergency services drowned out by those four words replaying over and over. "Don't you fucking die."

I know Nix doesn't want me to blame myself with what happened, but I can't help but feel responsible. Zane was my crazy ex. I forced her out that night and it all comes back to me.

"You're awake." Nix's voice coming from the door pulls me from my thoughts.

"Hey," I say, watching as he nods to the shy nurse as she leaves us alone.

"I brought some people who wanted to see you," Nix announces, moving aside to let Z, Jesse, Sy, Brooks, Beau and an older-looking man past. Oh, God, just seeing their faces, sends a runaway tear down my face.

"Hey, sweetheart." Jesse comes to me first, leaning down for a soft kiss to my cheek, wiping my tear with his thumb.

"Don't cry," he shakes his head.

I nod, trying so hard not to break down in front of them all. I know they have wanted to see me, but with the club on lockdown and all Nix's attention on me, they've had to keep things running smoothly. In the short time that I've known these men, they've come to mean so much to me. Jesse helping me through my darkest hours after the fire. Brooks being the big brother I've always wanted. Sy, my savior, and Beau, well, Beau is still pissed about me sneaking out, but still.

"Hey, Jesse," my voice croaks from the tears stuck in the back of my throat, causing Jesse to flinch.

He moves back, allowing Brooks to approach next, his hand coming to mine squeezing it lightly.

"Hey, doll, you doing okay?"

"I'm good. How's your head?"

"It's fine," he dismisses my concern. "I'm so sorry," he leans in and whispers.

"Don't," I say, knowing he will be feeling bad for what happened. He holds my stare, his eyes fighting with wanting to argue, but doesn't.

Beau pulls up a chair next to me. He smiles slightly, his dark hair pulled back into a messy ponytail. "Still the prettiest thing I've seen," he mutters, reaching out to grab my hand. Even though Beau and I started off on the wrong foot, I've come to see what a great guy he is. He's loyal and fiercely protective of his club, but most of all, he's Nix's best friend. They have been through everything together.

"Thanks, Beau." He nods, his eyes no longer holding that calculating stare he likes to give me. "Am I forgiven?" I ask hopeful. I don't think I can handle him acting indifferent to me, when I'm becoming so close to the rest of the guys.

"Yeah, we're cool, but if you pull that shit again, I will have to spank your ass." I gulp down my gasp. He wouldn't?

"Watch it, brother," Nix rumbles from the end of the bed, as Beau starts laughing, I don't know where to look. I feel the heat of my blush break out over my cheeks, the men all looking at me. Shit. I focus my eyes on Z, who stands awkwardly at the end of the bed next to his dad.

"Hey, Z," I smile at him, reaching my hand out for his. He looks so unsure. His father nudges him forward, telling him he won't hurt me. He steps closer, slowly making his way to me. This little man has worked his way into my heart, and seeing him affected by what happened to me breaks me. He finally comes forward, close enough for me to touch. "It's okay, Z. You can't hurt me," I tell him. He takes my hand, coming to stand next to me. "How was the lake house?" I ask, trying to keep everything normal.

"It was good. Dad, Pops and I did some fishing on the lake."

"Cool. You catch anything?" I continue asking questions, wanting him to be comfortable.

"No," he shakes his head. "Just Pops did. Are you okay?" He softly questions, his eyes filled with concern. His big heart is more worried about me than talking about his time away.

This boy melts me.

"I am now that you're here," I tell him and watch as the smile spreads across his face. "I missed you this week," I confess, hoping he gets that I feel the same way as he does.

His smile brightens more, filling me with light. "We missed you too. We were coming home early to see you. It didn't take too much to persuade Dad." I laugh, the sound getting caught in my swollen throat. Beau reaches for my water, handing it to me to help soothe the burn. Z shows concern again. His smile now gone, worry lines currently replace it. All the guys' faces are filled with anxiety, anger and even rage.

"Hey, I promise I'm okay," I tell them all, looking into each of their eyes. They don't look convinced, their tight nods telling me they won't push. My eyes connect with the older man who I now recognize as Nix's dad. He smiles then comes forward.

"Hello, beautiful girl, hate seein' you in this bed, but I'm glad I finally get to meet you. Between my son talking my ear off and Z telling me all about your baking, I was feeling a little left out."

I smile at his attempt to make me feel comfortable. "Thank you for looking after them, Mr. Knight."

"Call me Red, or Pops, but either way, please don't call me Mr. Knight." I laugh and nod my head. He pulls back to stand next to Sy against the wall.

"Hey, Sy," I awkwardly wave. He nods, and then looks over at Nix, a silent request that has him moving everyone out of the room. Before I get to say goodbye to them all, the nurse comes back in, topping up my drip. Jesse notices the nurse first and his cheeky persona comes out to play.

"Can you escort me out, nurse?" He looks down at her chest, slowly moving his eyes to the rectangle nametag, "Nurse Belle?" He smiles his panty-dropping smile. I can see the shade of crimson that flashes down her face from the bed. The poor girl doesn't know what's hit her with the massive flirt. She shakes her head, letting him know she won't before hightailing it out of there so fast, I wonder if she was even in here in the first place.

"Play nice, Jesse," I warn, as he follows closely behind her. He waves me off, nowhere near ready to play nice.

Brooks and Beau go next, telling Nix they'll meet him later at the clubhouse. Z leans in and kisses my cheek, telling me to hurry up and come home. I promise I'll try my hardest to get better and watch him leave with his Pops.

"How was your sleep?" Nix takes Beau's vacated seat next to me, holding my hand.

"As good as one can with a broken rib," I tell him. Looking across the room, I see Sy still standing to the side, quietly taking everything in.

"How are you doing, Sy?"

"Been better. Not as bad as you." He winces like he just said the wrong thing.

"Thank you," I tell him, knowing it's nowhere near enough.

"I'm sorry that I didn't get there sooner," he says, a hard gaze coming over his face.

"You saved my life," I choke out. "Saved Holly's life." At the mention of Holly's name, he slumps back.

"I wasn't fast enough."

"Sy, you saved us. You need to understand that. This isn't on you. Words won't ever be enough, Sy," I tell him, watching as he nods, not needing to say anything. He pushes off the wall and walks to the bed.

"I wish I got there sooner. Wish I could take it all back." He leans in kissing my temple. Before I can reply, he promptly turns and leaves Nix and me alone. Turning back to face Nix, I see his concern for his friend written all over his face.

"Will he be okay?"

"I'll keep an eye on him."

I nod, knowing that I trust that he will. He won't let anything happen to his brothers. "Have you come to take me home?" I ask, hoping to get out of here. If I have to stay in any longer, I'm going to scream.

"Not yet, babe, you got one more night. Then you'll be free." I pout at the thought of another night here. I can't even scream; my lungs, chest, and sides hurt too much.

"Well, can you at least take me to Holly?" I ask hopeful.

Nix clears his throat, an uncertainty crosses his face.

"Umm, Holly's not takin' visitors," he informs me, shifting in his chair.

"What do you mean she's not taking visitors?"

"Her brother's guardin' the door. No one's allowed in."

"Well, he has to let me in," I argue back, certain he will be fine with me seeing her.

"Babe."

"Don't babe me, Nix. She is my best friend. I'm not leaving her alone in this. Take me to her room," I demand. Panic starts to rise. I know Holly. I know she won't want me turned away.

"Okay, Kadence, just calm down." He moves forward, pushing the button to call for the nurse.

I need to see her, need to know she doesn't blame me for what happened, even though I blame myself.

Five minutes later, Nix is wheeling me down to Holly's room, my drip still attached to the pole extending from my wheelchair. Belle came when Nix pressed the nurse call button, and after seeing me in my crying mess, agreed to organize a wheelchair. Holly's parents stand outside in the hall with their eldest son, Sam.

"Oh, Kadence." Holly's mom comes rushing forward to me. The tears come harder, knowing it's not just my life affected; they too hurt because of me, because of Zane.

"Hey, Mrs. McAdams." She barely contains the gasp when she hears my voice and sees my injuries up close. I haven't looked in the mirror, but the look on her face shows me it's not great. Geez, the boys didn't even flinch. Much.

"How is she?"

"Not good, dear," she tells me, worry etched in her brow.

"Can I see her?"

"No!" Holly's older brother yells out, stepping away from the door.

"Sam," his mother scolds him.

"No, Mom, if it wasn't for Kadence, this never would have happened." I drag in a sharp breath at his words, while Nix steps up beside the wheelchair.

"Watch yourself." The threat is louder than his voice. "I know you mean somethin' to my girl, so I'm gonna give you the benefit of the doubt here, that you're just messed up with your sister in that room. You're not thinkin' straight, but you don't get to put this shit on her," Nix tells him.

"Like fuck I don't," Sam argues back, stepping forward into Nix's space. Sam is tall like Nix, but lacks the build. However, the fire burning behind his eyes suggests he wouldn't care if he was up against the Hulk; he just wants to protect Holly. "Her ex shot her. She lost the baby," he chokes out.

My breath stops for a moment. The thumping sound in my ears rings loudly, blocking everything around me. My heart feels like someone just twisted it out of my chest.

"What?" the word barely comes out as I push it past the bile rising in my throat.

"The baby," he repeats. "You didn't know?" He asks incredulously.

Is this why she has been acting strange the last three weeks? I knew something was up, but this?

"Baby?" I choke the word foreign to my lips.

"She was seven weeks along," Holly's mom cries softly beside me. "She only just found out. I only just found out," she adds.

I can't believe Holly didn't tell me; that she kept it from me. I know Holly likes to date, but I also know she is very careful. Who is the father? Does she know? Is that why she didn't tell me?

"Let me in, Sam," I demand, the urge to see her growing with every question my head keeps throwing out.

"No, she doesn't want to see you."

"Bullshit," I say, not believing the lie.

"Kadence, she won't see anyone," he sighs, his features drained. "You need to give her time."

"No, I'm not leaving. She was with me every step of the way when I needed her. You know she's not thinking straight. She needs me, Sam. Don't make me let her down," I plead. If anyone knows just how much Holly means to me, it's Sam. He lived through the nightmares of me pushing everyone away. Holly is my person. There is no way in this world I'm going without letting her know I'm here. I won't leave her alone. He must see through my plea, the agony on my face. My best friend is mourning the loss of a child alone and only twenty feet away from me

"Don't say I didn't warn you." He steps aside, letting Nix push me forward.

"Go away," Holly's voice calls out as soon as Nix opens the door, and pushes me into the darkened room.

"No," I simply say. I've been in this situation before; the realness of it so raw, only this time we're on opposite sides.

"Kadence, I don't want to talk," she snaps as Nix pushes me closer to her bed. Leaning down, he brushes his lips to my temple. "I'll just be outside the door." I nod, letting him know I'll be fine.

"Fuck off, Kadence," Holly sneers.

"I'm not going anywhere, Holly," I calmly tell her, even though I can feel her pull away.

"Holly," I begin, ready to apologize, wanting her to see that if I could take it away, I would.

"Kadence, I don't want to talk about it," she warns; her cool and angry state slowly starts to slip.

"That's okay, Holly. We don't have to talk, but I'm not leaving you, babe, so shut up and let me be here for you." She looks over at me, her eyes empty. It stings my eyes and burns my throat that she looks broken, so defeated. A runaway tear rolls down her face, the slow descent followed by another.

"I didn't know how to tell you." Her voice breaks as the first, raw sob breaks free.

"It's okay, Holly." I reach out and take her hand, squeezing it. I hold back the urge to cry out at the injustice of it, the ugliness that I've brought into her life. I need to be strong, for her, for me.

"No, it's not. Everything is fucked, Kadence." Her tears become uncontrollable as her sobs take over her body. The pain and devastation of what she's lost, sinks in all around us in the darkness of her hospital room.

"Do you remember when I was laying in the hospital after that last surgery?" I ask. "I was broken and feeling sorry for myself. I didn't want to deal with anyone looking at me?" She nods, remembering that dark time, her eyes looking heavier and heavier.

"You climbed into my bed, and you held me and didn't let go, and then you said something to me that I would never forget. You told me, 'Kadence, everything is going to be okay, just not today.'" She shakes her head no, squeezing her eyes tightly shut, like it will stop the words from coming. "You were right, Holly." I hold back the lump building in my throat, watching her deny my words.

"You're going to be okay, Holly. Just not today." A sob escapes her, and I can't help but follow her into a state of distress. The nurse comes in, trying to calm her as she breaks down. I want to climb into bed with her, hold her, and take away the devastation she is living, but I can't. Instead, I sit here helpless and watch them as they administer something into her drip.

I hold my best friend's hand, the only comfort I can give her as I watch her body fight the pull of the darkness. I don't let go. I don't leave her alone, knowing she would do it for me, has done it for me. And I do it knowing those words she once told me hold more truth than I've ever known: she's going to be okay. We both are.

28

Nix

"I WANT HIM FUCKIN' FOUND AND I WANT HIM DEAD," I calmly tell the table of my closest brothers and my dad. Beau sits to my left and Jesse to my right.

"You sure about this, Prez?" Jesse asks.

"About as sure as I fuckin' know Kadence is in that hospital for another night. Her best friend shot," I shout. I know Jesse is only looking out for me, but Gunner Jamieson is dead, preferably by my hands. I don't give a fuck what I have to do. The fucker is mine.

After learning about Holly and the baby, something broke in me. I thought Kadence was gonna come back okay, but knowing what I know, I don't think that's gonna happen.

"Might have a problem with T," Beau speaks up. "He's got his markers on him. He might get him first."

"Well, make sure he doesn't," I spit. The fucker deserves to die. I don't tell the boys Holly's situation. Kadence made me promise to keep it quiet, but I know if they knew, they wouldn't be sitting here trying to get me to calm down.

"Fuck," Beau curses under his breath, knowing I won't stop until he's found.

"Think about this, Nix," Brooks says, trying to reason with me. The problem is I've lost all reasoning. I lost it all when I watched my girl mourn with her best friend.

"Think about the situation," he continues.

"Brooks," I warn, cutting him off. "How would you feel if some asshole put his hands on Kelly and nearly strangled her to death?"

"I get you, brother. I do, but we have to be smart. All that hard work getting us clean will be for nothing. Think about Z," he pushes.

"I am fuckin' thinkin' about Z," I shout out across the room.

"I've got no problem doing it," Sy says, sitting next to Beau. We all look to him.

"No," I tell him

"Why the fuck not? You got Kadence and Z to worry about. I've got no one."

"I want him."

"It's not about that, Nix," Brooks tries again. "Leave it to T."

"Fuck T," Sy's deep voice booms. "Look where that got us."

"I don't like this," Jesse pipes up.

"Me either," Brooks adds.

I can see this going around in circles. Jesse and Sy start arguing, Brooks shaking his head.

"Fuck, everyone, calm down." My pops finally speaks up and the room falls silent as the old Prez's voice echoes around the clubhouse. "Nix. You're not thinking straight. Your head is fucked up with seeing Kadence. I get it. I've lived it, but if this were about one of the guys, you would be looking at it differently. You've got this shit with Addison and Z. You can't be getting yourself into a situation that will come back on you. Kadence is coming home tomorrow. You need to be here for her. Don't make the same mistakes as I did." He speaks directly to me, his tone telling me to get my head out of my ass. I know what he is saying is true, but this untapped rage is spurring me on. The last time I felt like this was when my mother was killed.

"I'll fucking do it," Sy says again.

"No one is fucking doing anything," Brooks barks. "This club has seen too much shit. I'm not gonna sit down and watch you walk down a path that you fuckin' worked so hard to get away from. Think about it, Nix. Give T time to sort this out."

I know what they are saying is true; this isn't who we are, what I am, but if we don't get a handle on Gunner, he will only try again.

"Fuck." I run my hands over my face, frustrated. "Fine, I'll give T a week, and then I'm goin' after him," I agree, and mean it. If T doesn't handle it, I will make it my mission to fucking kill him.

29

Kadence

THE SMELL OF ZANE'S BREATH OVER ME, THE coolness of the gun meeting my forehead, wakes me in a screaming cold sweat.

"Fuck," Nix sighs next to me. "You okay, babe?" He pulls me closer to him, his strong arms protecting me.

"Yeah, I'm good," I lie, the reminder of what we went through still fresh in my memory. Some nights I sleep peacefully knowing that Nix will keep me safe, and other nights, I wake myself screaming, trying to escape the darkness. Those nights are the worst, Nix having to hold me down as I lash out at an empty threat. I know it's going to take time to move past it all. It's only been eight weeks since I left the hospital.

"I hate this so fuckin' much." His lips come to my hair, kissing and breathing me in. I hate that he has to see it too, but I can't stop the ugly memories from visiting me in the middle of the night.

"Imagine how Holly feels?" I know it's not my fault, and saying those words to Nix is the wrong thing to say, but the guilt I'm feeling just won't leave. That night did more than just mess with her. Losing the baby she was carrying and getting shot broke something in her that I don't think anyone can fix. The first four weeks after leaving the hospital, she wouldn't talk to anyone, pushed everyone away. I tried my best to break through. That one moment in the hospital room was the only time I ever felt close to her. When Nix came in and took me back to my room was the moment I lost her again. She built her walls so far up, even I couldn't scale them. It's been hard not knowing if she blames me for that night.

"Holly is dealin' with her shit the best way she can, Kadence, but if you don't stop blamin' yourself, you won't get better." Nix turns me to face him. The light of the moon sends a soft glow through the window, outlining his face by the shadows. I know he's right, but what Zane took from her, I can't ever give back.

"Didn't she just start a new job?" he asks, sitting up and flicking the bedside lamp on. This has become our new norm. On the nights I wake up, we end up spending the next half-an-hour talking about anything and everything. It's Nix's way of trying to get me to forget the nightmare I just woke up to.

"Not yet. Next month, she starts back at a new salon, new clients." I sit up against the headboard, resting my head on his shoulder.

"That's good, babe. Just give her some more time. She's comin' to the clubhouse for your birthday party, so that's progress." I nod, agreeing with him. I wouldn't be having a damn party if Nix didn't insist.

"My parents said they would take Z for the night," I tell him as his fingers wrap around mine.

"Good, 'cause I have plans for you next weekend." He grins his sexy grin.

"Can't you have plans for me tonight?" I whine. Yes, whine. I am seriously over my Nix rations. I've been on bed rest and light duties. *Apparently, sex is not classified as light duties.*

"Kadence, how many times do I have to tell you? Not until the doctor clears you."

"Nix, you won't hurt me," I try to convince him. I know it won't get me anywhere; the man is too strong to break. I've begged, cried and even tried to seduce him. Nothing.

"You want my mouth?" he asks, rolling me over to my back and covering me.

"No, I want your cock."

"You can have my cock in your mouth," he offers

"I want your cock in my pussy." I lift my hips off the bed, trying to find some friction.

"Fuck, Kadence, don't be a tease. You know I won't cave." He pushes my hips down with his body weight. I pout like a child. *Asshole.*

The doctors put me on strict restrictions for the first month and then limiting physical activity for another 4 weeks. I know I will be fine, but Nix is just too damn stubborn, and as much as the dirty teenager acts help fill the void, there is nothing better than feeling him sink himself deep inside of me.

"Nix, it's been sixty days. Sixty longs days since I've felt you in me, pounding into me, destroying me. I need you." I try for the begging this time. I'm not lying. I do need him. I need him more than my next breath. I crave that connection. I want the intimacy of what only he can give me.

"And I need you, so fuckin' bad, but it's only one more week. You can last," he smiles, leaning in to kiss me. I let out a sigh of defeat.

"Fine," I snap, annoyed that he just rejected me again. "Get off me then." I try not to get upset, but seriously.

Rolling back off me, he reaches over and flicks the light off.

"When I do take you, Kadence, it will be well worth the wait," he promises, dragging me back in his embrace, his front to my back. "Sleep," he demands, and I roll my eyes and force myself not to be a smartass. He doesn't see my struggle, yet I feel the strength of his body as he holds me protectively close. Curling into his side, I hear a faint whisper, words I can't make out. The sound of his voice is a simple, sweet caress and fills me with warmth, helping to lull me to sleep.

"Hey, Kadence, will you be my mom?" Z asks the next morning when sitting next to me on the sofa. These past four weeks, Z has been on summer break, no longer my student and now my healing buddy.

"You have a mom, Z," I say, sitting up to grab the remote to pause the TV. We've been watching a marathon of the *Walking Dead*, something that I'm never going to un-see. That shit is crazy whacked.

"I know things are bad at the moment, Z, but I can't take

that role away from her." I watch his face fall, devastated I just pretty much told him no. I don't know how to handle this one. *Think, Kadence.*

"My mom doesn't even love me." His voice cracks a little at the admission.

"Hey, that's not true. She loves you, Z." I reach out and take his hand.

"She hasn't spoken to me since." He looks down at our joined hands. I can't help but want to hold him, tell him she doesn't deserve him and I would love to be his mom, but I can't. Could I?

"I know, honey, and as much as the thought of being your mom sounds amazing, it just doesn't work like that. But I can be your friend," I add. "One of your bestest friends. I promise to look after you, drive you when you need to go somewhere, feed you all the food you love and always be here for you to talk to." I smile down at him.

"So pretty much do all the things a mom should do?"

"Yeah, I guess," I admit.

"It's not fair. Why can't you be my mom?" he questions and I can see his frustrations. "I love you more than my mom," he softly admits.

I draw in a deep breath through my nose to stop the sting of tears. "I love you as much as a mom should love their son, Z," I tell him.

"So can we just pretend you're my mom?" he smiles, hopeful.

I nod letting him know that I'm okay with that. He moves closer, and nestles gently next to me. I feel more love for this little man than his mom has ever shown. If that makes me his pretend mom, so be it.

"I love you, Kadence," he declares, settling in for the next installment of the zombie madness.

"I love you, Z," I softly reply, kissing his head. A tingling sensation crawls over my skin. Feeling Nix's eyes on me, I try to keep calm. I know he just witnessed me telling his son that I loved him. I don't turn and acknowledge him, afraid of what I may see. Instead, I hold on to Z's hand and cherish the moment we just had, knowing that the man I love stands behind us, giving us the space we need. And I love him even more for it.

30

Nix

"HE'S GONE."

"Gone for now or gone for good?" I ask down the phone. I've been waiting on this call for weeks, waiting for the moment I can either put Gunner Jamieson behind me or for the chance to fucking kill him with my own hands. I know I said I'd let T handle it, but deep down if I had to, I would. I would kill him.

"Gone for good," he answers.

"Right," I say, understanding T's meaning of good. I don't ask questions. I know how it works.

"He might be gone, but someone else will replace him," he continues, telling me what I already know.

"Don't see it being a problem if we don't have problems, T," I lay it out for him. The clubs might have the truce, but T never shook on that. He might get a wild hair and pull back on it one day.

"We're good, Nix. The last few years have been smooth. Got myself a woman and baby on the way. Don't need more fucking drama."

"Fuck, I hear ya there," I agree. "That all?" I ask, ready to go let the boys know about the asshole. They've been on some strict lockdown preparing for retaliation.

"Yep, speak again in another few years," he suggests, enjoying our relationship just as much as I do.

"Make it longer," I tell him truthfully. I'm grateful for their help, but the less we have to do with them, the better.

"Gotcha," he says before hanging up. I pocket my phone and head down to the clubhouse. One major shit storm cleared up, now I just have to deal with Addison.

★★★

"No. Fucking. Way," Beau nudges me to look up as we walk through the doors of Bare Assets the next day. I knew coming here would be hell. The last thing I wanted to do was see this shit, but looking up at the lit up stage, no more than five meters in front of me and seeing my ex-wife climb a pole like there is gold at the top is worse than fucking hell. I had no fucking idea she was doing this.

"Can I get you guys anything special?" A blonde dancer walks up to us as we approach a table wearing nothing more than a thong and a smile.

"Yeah, you can fuckin' tell Addison, when she's done shakin' her ass, I wanna to speak to her," I tell her, pointing up at the stage as Addison bends over, playing fucking peek-a-boo between her legs. How the fuck she got a job here confuses me. Sure, she looks the part, fake tits, bleach-blonde hair, but she's pushing forty. Times must be tough for the owner.

The last time I saw Addison was the afternoon I read Z's statement. Even after I ripped her a new one, and warned her that she would have a huge fight on her hands, she said she would fight me. Yet she never fucking showed.

"What are you gonna do?" Sy asks beside me.

"What can I do? It's not my fuckin' problem now. She wants to ride the pole over being a mother, nothin' I can do." He nods agreeing.

I can't make her be a good mother, but I need to know what the fuck her plans are. Z doesn't need the uncertainty of when or if he sees her again. This week has been hell. Addison not showing up to the hearing only proved to Z how much she didn't care. Her shmuck of an attorney tried to reschedule, but the judge denied that request. Said the testimony of Z's statement and her lack of responsibility goes to show she's unfit, and full custody was awarded to me. It didn't feel as good as I thought it would when I saw the look on Z's face. I know he wants to be with me, but seeing his mom not show, not even try to fight, just broke his heart more.

"What do you want, Nix?" Addison comes up to the table when she finishes up on stage. The only reason I knew she was here was because one of the boys came in last night, saw her shaking hers ass and called me straight away.

"So this is more important than showin' up for Z? To show your son that you want to be a part of his life?" I accuse.

"Don't fucking patronize me, Nix. We both know that you

would have won custody." She rolls her eyes, which just pisses me off.

"Fuck, you're a piece of work. You don't deserve him. I know that, but he's fuckin' eleven years old; he fuckin' needs his mom."

"Well, it's good that your little teacher slut is all moved in, ready to go," she hisses.

"Don't even go there, Addison. Kadence has shown more love to my son in the last two months than you ever have. He even asked her to be his mom. How does that feel? Your own son knows how fuckin' pathetic you've been?" I hit her low. She might not want to hear it, but she needs to. Kadence has been more of a mom to Z than his own mother. That day, when I walked in and heard her and Z's conversation about being his mom, I nearly got down on my knee right there. I was close to demanding that she tell me she loved me and then make her promise to be my wife and Z's mom. But I didn't. I stood there trying to keep my shit together, listening to her tell him how much she loved him. That's all I want for my son, to experience that love only a mother can give a child.

"I'm glad for Z then, as I'll be leaving at the end of the month."

"You've got to be shittin' me? Fuck I can't believe I even thought about givin' you a second chance." I stand, done with this fucked-up woman.

"Yeah, I'm sure you were gonna give me a second chance, Nix," she calls out as Sy and I walk away from her.

"I would have for Z," I tell her, turning back to her. I didn't want to, not after everything that she has done, but visitations, lunch meet ups, shit like that, I would have tagged along for Z. But she can get fucked now.

"He doesn't want to see me," she mumbles, her head dropped, looking at the floor.

"Well, you'll never know now. I'm done." Without another word, I turn and walk out. I don't want to deal with her ever again. The sooner she moves out of town, the better.

"Come on, Kadence. Let's get fuckin goin'," I yell out from the kitchen.

"Hold your horses, you big lump," she yells back. It's been nine weeks since Kadence left hospital, nine weeks of pure hell. Having her in my bed, in my home, and not been able to have her, I feel like my balls are about to explode.

With her broken ribs, there was no way I was getting anywhere near her. Not with the way we fuck: hard, fast and fucking explosive. Don't get me wrong, I can do slow, but the thought of hurting her even in the slightest had my balls crawling up into themselves. That's not to say we haven't done other things, but there's nothing quite like the feeling of sinking yourself into the woman you love. And I do I love her. I've loved her since she kneed me in the balls in the bathroom in the bar. I just need her to admit it.

"How do I look?" Kadence steps off the bottom step, pulling me from my thoughts.

"No way you're fuckin' wearin' that. Go change." I drag my eyes down the low dip in the front of the dress, her sexy tits sit perky, showing the world her delicious cleavage.

"Shut up, Nix. What's wrong with this?" she asks, looking down at the sexy-as-fuck dress she's got on.

"Christ, woman, are you trying to kill me? Please go put some fuckin' clothes on." I adjust myself, trying not to get hard right now.

"I have clothes on, perfectly fine clothes. Stop being a caveman and let's go. You were only bitching about leaving two minutes ago," she smirks, walking by me. My gaze follows her as she passes, and I almost come apart when I get a look at her back.

"Kadence," I try to control my voice.

"Yes, dear?" she smiles over at me. She knows what she's doing. The damn dress has no fucking back.

"We're gonna be late," I tell her, stalking over to where she stands, I don't give a fuck if the first time I have her is against the kitchen wall.

"Nix," she warns, backing herself up into the wall

"It's your own fault, Kadence. You shouldn't have poked a sleepin' bear." My hands come to either side of her head, caging her in. "You got two options here. One, go change, or two, I'm gonna fuck you up against this wall, after I shred this dress off you.

"You wouldn't." Her eyes narrow to mine.

"Try me," I challenge her. No way is she leaving this house with that dress on.

"You forgot about the third option, Nix." She smiles up at me.

"There is no third option, babe."

"You see, that's where you're wrong, honey." She drops to her knees and starts unbuckling my belt.

"Kadence," I warn. The fucking minx and her mouth think she's gonna outsmart me. No way.

"Nix, there is no way you're getting this dress off," she explains, taking my cock in her hands. "For one, you'll ruin the surprise I got going on underneath, and two, there are fifty people waiting for us at the clubhouse." She leans forward, licking the tip of my glistening head. I don't care how many people are waiting for us, but I know this night is important to her.

I groan when her hot mouth envelopes my throbbing cock. With my arms still firmly planted on the wall, I drop my head forward and enjoy the warmth of her mouth. The doorbell rings, breaking her suction as she pulls back.

"Don't fuckin' stop," I plead.

"We gotta go, Nix. Jesse's here," she replies, coming up from her knees. What the fuck? Why is Jesse here?

"Fuck, Jesse, he can wait. Get back on your knees."

"Nix, that's rude. I'm not going to suck your cock while Jesse waits for us at the front door." She adjusts her dress, smirking at me.

"Why the fuck not? He'd probably do the same," I say, knowing full well the fucker would.

"Come on, honey," she smiles sweetly at me. I'm left standing there. My cock hanging, neglected out of my pants as Kadence sashays her ass to the front door.

Fuck, I just got played.

I sit back in my chair and look out around my clubhouse as my brothers, my family, and our friends come together to celebrate my woman's birthday.

The whole club is here tonight. My pops, Z, even Kadence's parents. Z's staying with Frank and Jolene this weekend, to give us a night free. Since Kadence came home from the hospital, Z has become close with them, especially Jolene.

Looking over, I watch Z as he stands with Frank, no doubt talking about the fish that he and Pops caught earlier today. He's been doing a lot better the last couple days, taking all of my girl's attention too.

Jesse has already picked up for the night; the blonde who's been sitting on his lap is a teacher at Kadence's school. Kadence's mom and Kelly are fussing about in the kitchen while Beau and Brooks sit talking with my pops over by the bar, and Sy is sulking in the corner. Ever since the night the girls were attacked, Sy has been holding on to some serious fucking anger. Holly won't talk about it to Kadence, but my bet is there's something going on between them.

The situation is fucked.

The last eight weeks have been about healing and coming to terms with what happened. Holly pushing everyone out was her way of dealing with her shit. I can't say I blame her. It didn't stop me from being pissed with her though for pushing my girl away. But I gave her that play, let her go with it for a month, and then it had to stop. The nightmares that plague Kadence, and the guilt she is feeling is enough. She needs her best friend. So I paid Holly a visit, told her she needed to pull her head out of her ass and start letting someone in. Kadence might put up with her being a bitch to her, but I wouldn't. I wasn't an asshole about it. I communicated that to her nicely or as nicely as you can when you tell someone to pull their head out of their ass. I think that's all she needed, someone to get her out of her head. The last four weeks have been a huge difference with Kadence and Holly even having a few girls' nights in. Holly is slowly coming back to herself and my girl couldn't be happier.

"Have you seen Holly yet?" Kadence comes up to me, her

short dress still pissing me off.

"Not yet, just relax, babe. She's comin'.." Her top teeth bite at her bottom lip in concern, worrying about something that is out of her control. I reach forward and pinch her ass. "Quit worryin' about it. She'll be here," I tell her just as Holly walks into the club. Her long blonde hair is gone, replaced with a shorter hairstyle. Holy shit.

I turn and look for Sy and see him regard her, before stalking forward in a slow but deliberate way. He grabs a hold of her wrist as everyone looks on, watching her struggle.

"Sy, what the hell do you think you're doing?" Kadence races over to where they stand. I follow behind, knowing shit is about to go down.

"Stay out of it, Kadence. This is between Holly and me." Sy's eyes drill into Holly, not releasing his grip.

"Like hell, Sy, let her go," she snaps back, moving in to break the connection he has on her friend.

My arms come around her waist, pulling her to me.

"Nix, let me go. Tell Sy to let her go." She fights my hold.

"Cool it, woman. Let them work it out." I pull her back a step

"Nix, she's frightened."

"She's fine. She's just playin' hard to get," I explain close to her ear. Her fight slows as she watches their exchange. Sy pulls Holly into him; his head lowers to speak something in her ear. Her eyes narrow, but you can see something moving behind them before they soften. Understanding and acceptance wash over her as her rigid body softens in his embrace.

Kadence relaxes her body as she notices what I see. Taking her hand, I walk her back to our now empty table, giving

Holly and Sy some time. Most of the guests continue back as they were, or make their way outside.

"What was that about?"

"That was Sy puttin' his foot down. The woman has been pushin' his buttons for the last three months. Seems like Sy has had enough."

"I don't blame him, with the way she looks tonight," Kadence smiles. Looking over at the new Holly, I have to agree. Her dress is just as revealing as Kadence's. "She looks amazing," she continues. "I can't believe she cut all her hair off. She looks hot."

"Not as hot as you," I say, watching her. She rolls her eyes, but I can see the light behind them. "Except when we get home, this dress will be ripped off. Don't think I've forgotten about your little game earlier." I lean into her. "That little stunt cost you a spankin', and fair warnin', it's not gonna be gentle. My balls are feelin' neglected, and if I have to sit here and watch you creatin' hard-on's in your wake, I'm gonna get my payback."

"Oh, please, Jesse had to pick up the cake. I didn't play you. Besides, you love it. You love them knowing that I'm yours," she tells me, looking out at everyone around us. She's right, but I'm not going to tell her that.

"I love you, and I can sure as fuck tell you I do not like seein' other men rake their eyes over you." I hold her gaze. Done with waiting, done with holding it back, I lay it out for her in the middle of my club. I can see the struggle play out over her face. The fight her head is having with her heart. It's been the same way from the start of the relationship, her body wanting one thing, her head telling her another. The woman is a pain in my ass, and as much as I love that she pushes me to work harder and to be better, right about now, it's starting to piss me off. Wanting to get through to her, I do what I've always done to get a response. I challenge her.

"You still falling in lust, Kadence? Or are you willing to admit you already fell?

31

Kadence

"...ARE YOU WILLING TO ADMIT YOU ALREADY FELL?"

I roll the question around my head, trying to stall. Of
course, I love the man, who wouldn't? However, saying the
words have been harder than I first thought. I've guarded my
heart for such a long time I didn't want to give it away again
so freely, but Nix being Nix, not only stole it, he possesses it.
I don't know what my reservations are; there have been plenty
of opportunities to tell him how I felt over the last few weeks.
Every night while he's held me and helped me heal, I've
wanted to blurt it out. However, every time I've felt the words
begin to roll off my tongue, I held back, feeling awkward and
out of my element. I know he's wanted to say it, holding on to

thinking I don't want to hear it, but that's not the case. It's not that I don't want to feel loved. I do. I crave his love as much as I crave him, so what's holding me back?

Nothing, my head declares, my heart agreeing. My feelings for Nix are more than love. He's more than words. It's a fierce and consuming power that demands everything I have to give. I've fought him and he's won. I've played him and he's won. I've surrendered to him, shed my shields, bared my soul, and he took it, owned me. Completely peeled me open, left me stripped, and not once did he leave me alone. I love this man devastatingly, irrevocably, incandescently and absolutely more than I've ever loved anyone.

The three words on the tip of my tongue spill out, holding back no reservations.

"I love you, Nix."

"You love me?" he asks, shocked I just admitted to him what he already knew. Love is not words. Love is feeling and love is doing. He just needed the words. Nix's knowing smirk pushes me to answer what he's known all along. I nod, affirming what he needs.

"Words, babe, I need the words."

"Yes, Nix, I. Love. You." I roll my eyes at another thing he has bossed out of me.

"Woman, don't sass me right before I'm about to ask you to be my wife."

The words don't register, or the fact that he stands from his chair, takes my hand and pulls me up. He kisses me deeply and passionately before going down on one knee in front of me, in front of everyone. The small box he pulls out of his back pocket frightens me; the platinum diamond ring sparkling in front of me renders me speechless.

He wouldn't?

Nothing registers.

Nothing breaks through

Until he speaks.

"I feel like I need to stitch those words into my heart with a needle and thread, Kadence," he exhales, his emerald eyes anchoring me to my spot. "Kadence, you set me on fire, woman. You walked into my life all attitude and spunk and I thought I had to have you just once. Then you kneed me in the balls and I fell. I fell hard." Everyone around us laughs at hearing how he came to fall for me, but my eyes stay firmly on him. "I've been everythin' I want to be in this life, but one thing... your husband. Marry me."

The music around us has stopped. Looking around, I notice our friends and family have gathered looking on, waiting for my reply. It's like I'm stuck on pause, watching a show. My heart is beating out of rhythm as I take in his proposal.

"I only just told you I loved you, Nix. Don't you think this is moving too fast?" I try to ask quietly.

"Babe."

"What? It's true!"

"Jesus Christ," he curses under his breath.

Shit, now I feel bad.

He looks up at me still down on one knee. "You love me. Why wait? I'm not givin' you a chance to change your mind."

My body is screaming at me to accept, my mind telling my mouth to speak the word 'yes,' but I don't know how to process, with everyone waiting.

"Come on, Kadence. Don't leave me hangin' here. The only time I've ever gotten down on my knee and you're makin' me beg? Do I need to fuck you into a yes again?"

There it is, his cocky attitude, his Nix-way of getting anything he wants, by pushing me. He doesn't even care he just used fuck in his marriage proposal in front of both our parents. I'm mortified, but only a little.

"Yes. Yes, I will marry you," I laugh, smacking him when he stands from his kneeling position. He takes my mouth in a desperate kiss, his hands cupping my face. Pulling back, he whispers soft kisses over my face, telling me how desperately he loves me. Reaching for my hand, he places the most amazing ring I've ever seen down my finger. I admire the platinum gold, cushion cut, halo diamond ring, before he abruptly pulls me behind him as our family and friends cheer on.

"Where are we going?" I ask panicked, trying to hold him back from our descent out of the club.

"To get married," he responds as if he just told me we're going to the bar.

"What? Nix, wait," I yell, confused. Flash backs of our first date come to mind, making me giggle.

"No waitin'. That shit took longer than I thought. I need that piece of paper sayin' you're my wife, now!"

"Nix!"

"What?" He stops pulling me along,

"I love you, Nix, but this is crazy."

"Nothin' crazy about it."

"Nix, we are not getting married tonight!"

"Why the hell not?"

"Because, because..." I can't seem to find the words why this would be a bad idea. Maybe this is crazy and it would be amazing, but I want to be able to celebrate with my family and our friends

"You want to," he accuses. "You want nothin' more than for me to take you to Vegas right now and claim you as my wife." I can't help but agree. I do, but I also want the whole thing, the dress, my mom and dad. I want what I deserve, what we both deserve.

"I do, Nix, but as much as the madness of all that thrills me, I want my mom and dad there, and Z. I need Z there. I want to do it right." I watch as understanding falls over him, accepting my need for my family to be there.

"I am crazy for you. Do you feel that?" His hand engulfs mine, moving it over his heart.

"Yeah, I feel it," I say, laughing. "I felt it when you asked me to marry you just because I told you that I loved you," I joke, knowing just how crazy he is.

"I've had that ring in my pocket for the last nine weeks, the day you came home from the hospital."

"You lie."

"Never."

"Why? Why would you do that?" I ask confused.

"'Cause, Kadence, the moment I realized I couldn't live without you, I also realized I never wanted anyone to have that feelin', knowin' how much Kadence Turner made their lives pure. I bought the ring, so the moment you finally realized you loved me, I could make you mine, on the spot. You have been the one for me since the moment you opened that mouth and gave me attitude, and I'm not ever lettin' that go."

"I love you too, Nix. I love you more than I thought I could love somebody." The words fall easily off my tongue.

"Kadence, nobody will ever love you the way I do."

He's right. No one has and no one will. I believe it with all my heart, and all my soul.

"Come, let's go see our parents. I'm sure your dad might feel the need to have a few words with me." He pulls me back to our family and friends

"Did you ask for permission?" I ask, hoping that he did. I know my dad would have like that.

"Babe."

"Don't babe me."

"Babe," he repeats.

"What kind of babe is that anyway? Like 'Babe, I'm Nix Knight. I don't have to ask for anybody's permission, or 'Babe, of course I did,'" I ask, more annoyed that any babe works.

"Neither, it was a 'Babe, give me your sexy, smartass lips, kiss your fiancé and let our parents congratulate us.'"

I don't argue. It won't get me anywhere, so I do as I'm told, like a good girl; 'cause there is a time and place to be a bad girl, and the day you get engaged is not one of those days.

★★★

"Hold on to the headboard and don't let go."

"Nix," I begin before his hand comes down on my ass again.

"Don't argue either, or this ends now." I crawl up the bed and hold onto the headboard.

"I've been waitin' nine weeks to sink myself back in here," he purrs as he runs his finger through my wetness. "I'm not gonna be gentle," he promises, and the thought alone has me shaking.

It's a few hours after my party. After Nix proposed to me,

we stayed late celebrating with our family and friends. My mom and dad couldn't be happier. The boys were excited that they get a bachelor party, and Z, he can't wait to officially call himself my stepson. Holly was happy but I could tell she was uncomfortable being in back at the clubhouse with Sy not letting her out of his sight.

"Kadence, are you listenin' to me?" Nix growls from behind me. I know his face is between my legs as I can feel his hot, breath on my most sensitive flesh.

"Yes, Nix, I'm listening."

"What did I say then?"

"That it's not going to be gentle."

"After that?" he continues to hum directly into my pussy.

"Umm."

"So you weren't listenin'?" he pushes, still teasing me.

"Well, it's hard to concentrate when I'm on all fours and your face is only inches from my pussy." My ass gets another slap in response, this time harder.

"Pay attention," he scolds while rubbing my ass to soothe the sting. I can't help the moan that escapes my lips as his fingers glide through my wetness. His hand comes down again, harder, more forceful. My grip on the headboard tightens. I feel like I could explode just knowing his cock is so close.

"Tonight, I'm gonna redden this ass until it's glowin' and you are not to let go, not for anything. Do you understand me?" I nod, my breath caught as his tongue swipes at my center.

"Words," he growls, his lips now touching. "Give me words, Kadence."

"Goddamn it, Nix. Just spank me, fuck me, or lick me out.

I don't care. Just do something," I snap, my patience wearing thin.

"What's the matter, Kadence? It's all fun and games when you tease me, but not when I do the same?" His palm comes down fast this time. I yell, the sound vibrating around the room. Nix's tongue comes out lashing hard at my clit. I sink back against his face, trying to get more friction. The struggle is real, the buildup so amazing. My hips move in time as his tongue brings me to the crest.

"Fuck. Fuck. Fuck. Nix!" I scream out as the orgasm takes me, my insides explode.

"Nothin' better than making you scream with my mouth. You taste delicious." He kisses my ass, the wetness of his lips left behind after each peck.

"Can I let go of the headboard?" I ask, not even attempting to release it. The asshole will punish me more.

"No. I'm nowhere near done with you." I roll my eyes. If he thinks this is punishment, I'll make sure I tease him more often.

"Now that you're gonna be my wife, Kadence, we have a few things we need to sort out."

"Like?"

"Like if you ever put my cock in your mouth, you better hope you finish what you start. Do you understand me?

"Yes, Dad."

"Kadence," he warns again.

"What are you going to do, Nix? Spank me?" I smile. Fuck I love teasing this man. Strong fingers come to my hips digging in as he enters me in one forceful movement.

"Fuck,' I scream as the intrusion I wasn't prepared for fills me.

"Jesus," he grasps as he draws out and slowly enters me again, this time slowly. "Tell me again," Nix demands as he leans forward, his front close to my back.

"I love your cock, Nix." I hold back the laugh as he growls behind me.

"No." He thrusts forward.

"I love you spanking me?" I try again, holding in the moan.

"Kadence." His fingers come to my hair, fisting and pulling it back.

"I love you," I pant and his movements become frenzied.

"Again."

"I love you, you bossy annoying asshole. Now shut up and fuck me hard," I demand, over talking about it. I need Nix and his cock.

"I swear, woman, I love you enough to know I'm not spanking you hard enough." He swats my ass again as he continues pounding into me.

And he's right. It wasn't hard enough; another spanking wouldn't hurt anyone, would it?

★★★

"Addison is leaving town," he says as we lay in bed recovering from our first time of being together in nine weeks.

"What. Why?" I ask, instantly on alert.

"Don't know why. Didn't ask. But know by the end of the month, she's out."

"Shit," I sigh, knowing that Z will be heartbroken.

"It's okay. He doesn't need her," he assures me, reading my thoughts.

"He does, Nix. He needs his mother," I argue, even if their relationship is strained.

"He has you and that's all he needs." He gathers me further into him, knowing I'm about to turn to face him. He keeps me tucked in, nowhere to move.

"Don't even bother arguing. He loves you. You are all he needs." His breath is at my ear.

"I don't know how to be a mom, Nix."

"Well, start knowin' it. We are havin' kids as soon as I can get you knocked up."

"Ummm, no, Nix."

"Umm, yes, Kadence."

"Oh, my gosh, you are a pain in my ass," I huff out, annoyed that I can't argue with him.

"No, Kadence, the pain is from my hand comin' down on it earlier." He laughs at his stupid joke.

"Agh," I continue to pout. The damn man makes me crazy.

His hand comes to my stomach, his fingers lightly grazing the skin. "Can't wait to see this belly, so beautiful, so big." He rolls me back on to my back. "Nothing would make me happier to know that we created a child together, Kadence. I want that. I want that for Z. Don't deny that for us," he whispers, and this time I cave. *Why does he have to be so sweet?*

"I'll have to make an appointment with the specialist; the scarring might be an issue," I tell him. I don't know how much of an issue, but the skin might not be able to stretch. His finger comes down and traces the scar, his face morphing into anger.

"I hate they did this. That he did this." He moves down my body to kiss the ugliness. I hate when he does this, but there is no stopping him. "Gunner's dead," he continues, ignoring my discomfort at him kissing me there. "Nothing will make up for what they did and I can't ever take that back, but know that they won't ever hurt you again," he promises. And I know he's telling me the truth.

"I know, Nix, and I don't hold that anger anymore." I look down at him. "It's over. Zane is dead. Gunner is dead. T and his boys helped save me, and you still have the truce." I tell him everything he already knows. "Let's be happy," I say, for once at peace with my life.

"I am happy, and I'll never stop making sure you're happy, baby," he tells me, and I know he will. He's Nix Knight: the man does what he says he's going to do.

Epilogue

Nix

I ROLL UP ON MY BIKE FEELING A NERVOUS ENERGY STIR THROUGH me.

"You ready for this?" Beau asks beside me. The fucker looks ridiculous in his nut-hugging slacks, wearing his cut and riding his bike.

"How the fuck we end up here?" I ask, laughing as the rest of the boys pull up next to us. The whole crew's wearing suits, their cuts replacing the jacket.

"You're the fucker who fell in love, asshole," Sy grumbles beside me.

"Yeah, well, the suit wasn't my fuckin' idea," I tell them, but they just shake their head knowing I'd do anything for her.

"You right, boss man?" Jesse asks, watching me quietly.

"Yep. Wanted this fucking months ago," I tell them, knowing it's true. I didn't care how I got here or how long it took me, I wanted this day.

"You might have wanted this day, but you look like you're about to puke," Beau laughs beside me.

He's right. I don't know what the fuck is wrong with me. I'm Nix Knight. I don't get nervous. But fuck. I am. Today is one of the most important days of my life. Today, I make Kadence my wife.

"Keep still or I won't be able to get it right." Holly swats my hand away, while still holding the curling iron close to my scalp.

"Don't burn me, Holly," I complain.

"I won't if you stop moving," she argues back.

"I can't help it. I'm nervous. I feel like I could spend the day on the toilet." Her insane laughter fills the room, and the sound heals a little of the pain I hold for her in losing her child. It's been four months since that night, and even though the same funny, crazy Holly is standing in front of me, doing my hair for my wedding day, I feel like she's still missing a little piece. I've searched and searched for that small piece, but no matter how far I travel, how deep I dig, I can't find it. I've come to realize it's not something I can give her. It's something she can only find herself. It's just coming to terms with that.

A knock at the door has me jumping in my chair.

"Keep it together, Kadence." Holly laughs at how nervous I am. My dad walks in looking handsome in his suit. He wasn't impressed when mom and I picked it out for him, but I could see behind his eyes that he would be secretly proud to wear it for his daughter's wedding day.

"You're late," he croaks, quickly turning away from me.

"Are you crying, Mr. Turner?" Holly calls out.

I smile at her jab, but I feel slightly sorry for my dad. I've never seen him cry. "Are you okay, Dad?"

"Yeah, I'm fine. Just got something in my eye," he explains as Holly snorts behind me.

"We are almost ready, Daddy," I tell him, using the name I know that he loves to hear.

"Done," Holly declares, moving away from me. I stand from the chair and walk to look into the full-length mirror. Shit. I draw in a breath. The floor-length ivory gown sits snug against my body, a small band of crystals cinching my waist in. The sweetheart neckline is covered in a sheen of beaded lace, cut off in a capped sleeve. My dark hair is woven up into a low updo, leaving soft curls falling around my face. The ivory-netted headpiece that Holly just secured in covers half my face, the crisscross pattern sitting two inches over my left eye.

"I love it, Holly." I turn to look at her and catch the last look of pain cross her face. "Are you okay?" I ask, walking to her.

"I'm okay, Kadence." She wipes the lone tear away. "You look breathtaking." She pulls me in for a short hug and then steps back smiling at me. I know she's happy for me.

"I love you, Holly."

"I love you, too. Okay, let me just grab your bouquet and mine, and let's get this shindig started." She leaves through the connecting door, giving Dad and me some privacy.

"Are you okay, Daddy?" I look over at him, still trying to keep his tears at bay.

"Fuck no! My baby girl's getting married, and by God, you're the most beautiful bride I've ever seen." He walks up to me, engulfing me in his strong embrace.

"Dad, don't make me cry. I'll mess up my makeup."

"Don't even care. You'll still be beautiful." I fight the urge to tell him he's just like Nix. I'm sure he's already aware of that. "Jesus, Kadence, you're breakin' my heart here. I feel like I'm losing a piece of me." A sneaky tear escapes, but this time I don't even care.

"You're not, Dad. You'll still be my dad. You will always have a special place in my life," I promise.

"Good, just make sure you tell that to your husband when he tries to take all your time," he sniffs back his emotion.

"Daddy, I promise. I will always have time for you." He leans down and kisses my cheek, squeezing my hand. I never thought of it like that. Here I am freaking out about giving my life to another, while my parents feel like they're losing a part of theirs.

"Oh, God, I leave you for two minutes, Mr. Turner, and you made her cry?" Holly comes back carrying my bouquet made up of purple roses. "Come here. We're already late." She fusses about, fixing the damage my dad did in two sentences. God, I'm not going to last with Nix's vows.

"Okay, let's do this," she says after finishing up the touches.

My dad takes my hand and leads me out the door to the chapel. The chapel was Nix's idea, to marry in the same one as his parents did. I loved the idea so much; I agreed instantly, a special part of them both with us on our day.

I love his dad. Since meeting in the hospital, he's been coming back into town every other weekend and staying with us. Nix and Z love it, but I know Red loves it more. The boys have even had a few weekends out at the lake house. I know when Nix lost his mom things were tough between the two of them, but looking at them now, you would never know. You can tell how much Nix loves having his dad in town and has even hinted at wanting him to move back, to be closer to Z. I can't blame him. Now that I have moved in with Nix and Z, my parents have been coming over more often. I'd love to say it's because they miss me so much, but it's all to do with Z. They've fallen in love with him just as much as I have. Their grandson, they tell everyone. Z loves them just as much as they do him, even choosing to go stay with them while Nix and I are away on our honeymoon.

"I just want you to know, Kadence, your mom and I couldn't be more proud of you," my dad whispers, close to my ear. "Be happy. You deserve it." He kisses my cheek.

"I am," the truth rolls off my tongue. I have never been happier in my life.

We step over the threshold of the aisle, and I watch Holly, in her pale lavender floor-length dress, walk down the aisle. Sy's eyes follow her as she walks slowly to the front. I don't know how much longer she's going to hide her feelings for him. We all see it, but for some reason they both live in their own delusional world, thinking we don't. I worry about them when he finds out the truth, but until then I have to just be there for her.

The soft music ends when Holly reaches her spot, the sounds of an acoustic guitar now coming to life, filling the small chapel. Our family and friends come to their feet, but I only have eyes for Nix.

Standing in a white dress shirt, black pants and his cuts, he holds the hand of Z, both smiling over at me. It didn't take much to convince him to wear a suit. He agreed, but the cuts stayed. Jesse, Brooks, Sy, and Beau also followed his lead, wearing matching attire. There isn't much the boys wouldn't do for me. I know they only do it for Nix—keeping me happy keeps him happy—but I like to think they love me enough to grant me one small wish, even if they do try to push me for a reaction. Having them standing there on our special day, on their best behavior, was my only wish.

After the bachelor and bachelorette party, I wouldn't put it past them to try something. Canceling the male stripper Holly ordered for me, and replacing him with a female was the start of a very eventful night. Waking up to the messages that Nix was in jail the next day was the last thing I wanted to hear hung-over. Nix was more pissed at his shaved eyebrows and shaved balls than him ending up in jail. I was beyond mad, telling them all if they pulled any funny business at the wedding, there would be hell to pay. Nix made them promise no shit during the ceremony, but I know the party is a free-for-all. I'll be cleaning up the clubhouse for days. My new role as old lady is already a daunting task, but one I'll take on with an open mind.

I quickly glance up, my eyes locking onto Nix's. He's watching me, taking every inch of me in. All my nerves and worries are gone by just one look. No words spoken, no smile given, the only encouragement I need is staring back at me with his emerald green eyes. I draw in an exhilarating breath; these men are my life, my family and my world.

I take my first step to them, knowing I'm walking toward my ultimate happiness, unwavering love and the most beautiful thing of all, my amazing family.

COMING NOVEMBER 2014

Sy's Story

Acknowledgments

I can't believe I'm even writing an acknowledgement page. So in saying that, there are many people I need to thank.

Alissa Evanson-Smith: Lovely, there are no words. I feel like I found this friend at this amazing time in my life. You have become part of my daily life and I honestly feel lost if I don't talk to you at least once a day. You have been there for me from day one, and I can't thank you enough. I love you hard woman.

My C.O.W.s - Alissa, Ash, Jess and Bel:

You ladies seriously are the best. Thousands and thousands of messages, laughter, tears, miles, you name it. You all have been so supportive of me and there is no way I would even be sitting here writing my final words of Nix and Kadence's story. This one is for you guys.

P.S Seriously, if ANYONE ever read our private MSG threads, I would die. Fall over and die. You girls are crazy, funny, smart, and beautiful. Oh, and downright dirty. I don't know what I would do without all. I DUCKING love you all… **Quack!**

Thank you to my lovely beta readers, Jodie, Gil, Stephanie, Bella, and Angela. Your enthusiasm for Nix and Kadence pushed me to be better. Get ready for Sy and Holly; things are only just getting started.

Kylie, from Give Me Books: Do you get sick of all the acknowledgments you're in? No? Good. Thank you for the hard work you do. I appreciate it more than you know. You are the blogger to end all bloggers.

C.P. Smith: You really went above and beyond and really helped me more than I can thank you. You are a gem and I can't thank you enough for all the hard work you have done for me.

Nina Levine: Dude, I think you must cringe every time my name comes up on FB messenger. Ha-ha. You, my friend, have shown me the true meaning of helping out your fellow author. You, lady, have class and I will be forever grateful.

Louisa from LM Creations: Girl, I feel like I should dedicate Nix and Kadence to you. You, my friend, rock my world. I can't believe you still like me after the many changes, and the many mess-arounds we have endured. I promise *Sy's* book will be less painful. If not, then I'll dedicate that book to you also.

Thank you to the many people who saw me through this book; to all those who provided support, talked things over, read, wrote, offered comments, allowed me to bug you with questions. Thank you.

To my Rebels: You ladies truly are amazing. From the hot naked men, to the outrageous things we get up to. You all rock my world. I love you hard. (Even if you spam my news feed with cock.)

To the Bloggers: Thank you for your support. I wouldn't have been able to get my name out without you guys pimping my book, sharing my teasers and just supporting me through.

And finally:

My husband, who cheered me on, kept me fed, looked after the children and didn't complain once. You married a crazy person, do you know that? This year, hell, our life, has always been crazy. Without you none of this would even be possible. I could never have accomplished half the things I have without you by my side. You get me. You love me. And most importantly, you've never left me. I love you.

About the Author

An avid reader of romance and erotic novels, River's love for books and reading fueled her passion for writing. Reading no longer sated her addiction, so she started writing in secret. She never imagined that her dream of publishing a novel would ever be achievable. With a soft spot for an alpha male and a snarky sassy woman, Kadence and Nix were born.

River would love to hear from you. You can contact and/or follow her via...

Email: riversavageauthor@gmail.com
Facebook: https://www.facebook.com/riversavageauthor
Follow River on Twitter: @RiverS_Author

WANT TO KEEP UP TO DATE WITH ALL THE NEWEST NEWS?

Come hang out with River's Rebels

https://www.facebook.com/groups/1513339432229460/